Idle
Sin

I0660479

Judson Bayer

National Library of Australia Cataloguing-in-Publication entry (pbk)

Author:	Bayer, Judson, author.
Title:	Idle Sin / Judson Bayer.
ISBN:	9780994184504 (paperback)
Subjects:	Escort services – Fiction Sex-oriented business - Fiction
Dewey Number:	A823.4

Published by Judson Bayer and InHouse Publishing
www.inhousepublishing.com.au

Prologue

It's difficult to imagine she was once male. Since having the snip seven years ago, this tall, leggy, wavy-haired blonde has been one of the Gold Coast's most desirable escorts.

Arriving late for some booze-up in aid of a children's charity nobody other than sick kids and their parents give a shit about, she swings her convertible into an over-sized gammy spot beside the club's main entrance, and we climb out. Inside, up for grabs to the highest bidder, a dress supposedly worn by Judy Garland in a Hollywood musical I've never heard of.

The building's glass front doors slide open and a young guy wearing a hospitality uniform steps out.

"You can't park there!" he spits. "That's for handicapped people."

The dolled-up tranny scans the full carpark and rushes toward him.

Conjuring a deep, manly voice from times past, she says, "I'm an amputee," pats his cheek with a manicured hand, then continues quickly through the doors.

He stands frigid, open-mouthed.

I smile despondently skyward. "Really? I've got to put up with this crap *every* day?"

1

When guys find out I drive for a brothel, knowing grins tug mouths sideways as naïve visions of *Pretty Woman*, news items of attractive prostitutes caught with politicians, or images of limitless free sex with uninhibited women cloud normally lucid brains. They may have read 'tell all' books by ex-prostitutes putting themselves through university or striking a mighty blow for female empowerment. Happy hookers? Ecstatic hookers.

Reality's a little different. To paraphrase Malcolm Muggeridge, most are merely lazy women who like to sleep late.

I don't care what they're like. I make shitloads. A week's pay most nights. Tax free.

It's been a long shift. Sex workers can be a tad wearing. As I step through the tall Colorbond side gate to our carpark, Billie, the receptionist, runs after me.

"Can you take Sean to a job?" Smiling hopefully, she holds up a piece of paper with a john's address scribbled in blue biro.

"Telly's dropping four girls home," I say. "Can't one of them do it?"

"The client wants toys. No girl in Telly's car has any on them." Her eyebrows lift, head tilts like a hopeful puppy.

Toys? Stop at a corner shop, for Christ's sake. Buy a carrot.

Young, good looking, dressed in a red mini and tight white top, Sean struts out of the brothel kitchen holding a glossy, string-handled black shopping bag and stands beside Billie.

"What about the day driver?" I ask. "Isn't he on his way?"

"Yes, but he picked up a girl and I sent him straight to a job."

Sean jerks the bag handles about, checking out God knows what inside. A lowlife sitting behind the wheel of an unregistered twenty-year-old Ford watches our exchange. He's the charmer who drops his wife off to fuck other men all night so he can park his work-shy arse on a stool in the local bar, get drunk, feed poker machines, bet on losing nags, and generally be The Man. Fortune's yob whom other arseholes look up to. An occupied baby capsule sits unanchored on the back seat.

Awaiting his dearly beloved to skip out and hand over the night's hard-earned, he sucks in marijuana smoke and turns away to avoid eye contact. Even with his windows up the scent is unmistakable. Interior smoke is so thick it permeates the car's *exterior.* Might as well give the suffering six-week-old in the back its own wacky to enjoy first hand. Or maybe a cigarette for starters. Low tar for good health.

The lowlife turns back and smiles. Genial. Shameless. Blameless. I have to work with his wife, so offer a cosy grin and knowing nod. One clued-up guy to another.

"C'mon, Myers," Billie continues. "Half hour. Sixty dollar drive."

Sixty dollars is well above the odds for a drive fee. If Billie got the john that high, he must be desperate. I concede, pluck the address from Billie's hand and turn to my car, Sean skipping along behind.

We join speeding morning traffic on the old Pacific Highway, windows down, music on. It's already stinking hot, and my air-con isn't due to be fixed for a few days. Sean's long, straight dark hair blows about. Her current one month crash diet to bring the belt in that last half notch, ridding herself of tiny love handles, isn't working.

A month ago she was the new girl, working name Tiana. Other hookers mistakenly called her Tania. Telly, another driver, and I referred to her as Tinea. Unhappy with this, the following day her name was Fleur. A poor choice. Not only is Fleur a brand of condom, and tampon, it's French for flower. So not to be outdone, and sticking with the flower theme, Telly and I persisted with Ragwort, Stinkwood, or Poison Ivy all night. It's been Sean ever since.

She pulls a penis-shaped fluorescent-blue vibrator from her bag of tricks and turns it on to check battery levels. She then rubs the piece down with her hands, confirming my first thought that it doesn't get cleaned properly too often. She notices me looking.

"Nice cock, isn't it?"

"Wonderful. But it's a tad unrealistic. Is it soft or hard?"

"Unrealistic's gooood." She holds it up so any passing motorist can spot the piece. "It's soft. Feel."

"Pass."

Understanding my reluctance, she flicks it end over end, catching the tip. "Touch the bit near the base. That hasn't been inside me."

A Lexus-driving yuppie keeping pace beside us toots. Sean turns and encourages him with a demure, flirty wave. She then flashes her tits. He smiles, his day made. He has a water-cooler story to break office drudgery, maybe swap high-5s with the boys.

"Don't do that again," I say.

"It was just a bit of fun. And he was good-looking."

"It's peak hour morning traffic. It only takes one person to complain, then my car's on the cops' radar."

Sean, with her unsterilized bag of tricks, is duly dropped at the client's address. While she's inside stretching tenderness and caring to the max, I complete the morning paper's crossword. Thirty minutes later she returns and hands over the cash. Easy job. Neither participant injured.

Once again the vibrator receives a manual once-over, her freshly licked index finger rubbing a couple of dubious spots until they disappear. Seemingly pleased with the cat-wash, she gives a little sigh and drops it back in the bag, ready for its next outing.

She adjusts the seat, leans back and lifts her top to expose a silver stud dangling from a recently pierced navel. Placing thumbs either side, a small drop of clear goo is squeezed out and transferred to her short skirt via a swipe of the fingers.

Back in the brothel kitchen, without wasting water or troubling the soap dispenser, Sean goes straight to the communal refrigerator, removes individually wrapped slices of cheese and a few pieces of white bread. A toastie-maker is lifted off a shelf and plugged in. When the green light comes on, bread and cheese are positioned in place, lid clamped shut.

"Want some, Myers?"

A short time later I'm sitting amongst riff-raff in a government building in Tweed Heads, waiting for my name to be called. I'm lucky. After scanning queues and seats I've not spotted any hookers. Although they also scam the system, it doesn't stop wink-wink nod-nod teasing for a week or two once they've actually seen you in the dole queue. Also, after there's some kind of falling out, one informs the authorities on the other.

People are called for scheduled interviews. If nobody answers, names are futilely repeated. Not many seem to turn up. They are elsewhere, attending more pressing matters. Because a cyclone sits a hundred kilometres or so off the coast, surf's up!

A bespectacled, disinterested thirty-something walks to the front desk ten minutes after my appointed time and hollers my name. Looking repentant, I rise and follow her through a labyrinth of semi-private, make-do cubicles to her little corner.

The woman's personal space is a joke. Childish territorial markers clutter the place. A half dozen photos of her and four or five female friends partying are thumbtacked to the wall. Small white teddy bear clips hug either side of a thin computer screen, one with 'Jane' dangling on a chain around its neck. A little, cheaply jewelled wooden box sits at the end of her keyboard. It's all adolescent girlie stuff that should have been discarded ten years earlier and replaced with professional things.

Following a laid-out plan, the interview begins. My information fills her computer screen, which she nods at thoughtfully. I sit and wait for the formulaic questions to commence.

Finally, once the all-important last key is tapped, she looks my way showing no emotion. I'm informed, again, of the numerous facilities here, totally at my disposal. Phones, computers, photocopiers, daily newspapers. Extra money is also at the ready for transport, courses, clothing, training, etcetera. At thirty-four years of age there is really no valid reason I shouldn't be employed.

I listen attentively to everything she says. When her hands clasp together and rest on the desk, conveying completion, I give her my sorry, well-rehearsed tale.

I live in an area with no public transport — which is true. It's a two and a half hour walk to the nearest bus stop — also true, if I snail's pace it. In the last month I have written away, as directed by the government, for no less than twelve advertised jobs — again true, but my letters were atrociously drafted, and I know absolutely nothing about glass-blowing, nuclear physics, paediatrics, tree doctoring, editing a national magazine, aiding and abetting in the management of a merchant bank, nor of golf course maintenance. But I have a sneaking suspicion the real reason I never hear back from these prospective employers is because every application letter I sign 'Love, Myers.'

Unemployment is secured for another few months, and I did it all without telling a single lie. My bounteous fortnightly payment covers petrol costs and most food. Sometimes there's enough left for a couple cartons of imported beer. As long as career politicians make generous decisions best for their careers, not the nation, you won't hear any complaints from me.

Now absolutely famished, home stretch in sight, just before my turn-off I stop at a local burger joint. I enter and shudder at their greasy menu. The health department should have blown up the place years ago.

Purveyors to the undiscerning.

After watching Sean put together her toasted sandwich, I contemplate the seven-dollar chicken job. Under this, the menu offers a thirteen-fifty toasted turkey sandwich. Expensive, but it sounds promising. I glance down at the grey-haired, black-clad Italian granny leaning idly on the worn Formica counter waiting impatiently for my order, tapping pen in one hand, small yellow post-it pad in the other.

She looks at me like I've interrupted her morning soap, which blares on a television out back. That, or there's been a chip on her shoulder since the age of twenty-six after realizing she's this planet's only small-breasted Italian grandmother.

"I'll have a turkey sandwich, thanks."

She adds an exasperating sigh to her indignant look. "Out of turkey."

"Make it chicken then."

She's seen me many times. I spend lots of money here. Her family and Ronald McDonald come close to keeping me alive.

"If we had chicken," she says condescendingly, "you'd've got your *turkey* sandwich."

I screw up my nose at the money-grubbing cow. "Yeah, silly me." I smile cheekily. "Heard a great joke yesterday. You'll laugh your tits off. Oh, I see you've already heard it."

"You fuck off and don't come back."

"How bout a burger?"

I stop at the gate to shoo away a dozen cows before driving fifty metres up the fenceline and parking beside my rent free accommodation. I hook up a single electric wire to protect my car, then walk around to the front.

Fifteen minutes from the Queensland border, Casa del Myers is a poorly maintained one-bedroom kitset shack perched among trees on top of a hill in the middle of a cow paddock. Thick chains anchor the small dwelling to a concrete slab, preventing it joining Dorothy in Oz. Resilient wall-squatting ants endure a weekly can of bug spray, then, high on fumes, scamper out looking for snacks. Thieves have no reason to sniff around here. It appears I'm trailer trash.

Friends who visit remark on spectacular golden sugarcane plantations stretching into the distance, but unless those fields are being burned before harvesting, I barely notice them any more. The view is merely what I look at through my windows every day.

I slide open the unlocked glass door and step in. Nothing has moved. I pull out the small, little-used oven from its custom built wall-surround and reach behind for the hidden biscuit tin. From my wallet I remove a thousand, in hundreds, and add it to the one hundred and thirty-seven thousand already in the tin. I drop it back, replace the stove.

A disconnected land line phone sits on the sideboard. Out of habit I check its blue answer machine light. I grab an imported beer from my ancient fridge and pop its top in the mouth an ugly big-nosed Polynesian god figure with string hair kneeling on a tall stereo speaker. From the fridge's freezer compartment I retrieve my last nutritionless TV dinner, peel back the lid's corner and toss it in the microwave, setting the timer for nine minutes. The freezer needs thawing. Stalactite ice almost kisses stalagmites inching from the bottom.

I spark up my little bedroom air-conditioner and close the door. When sliding into bed in an hour or so, a couple of blankets will be needed to keep chills at bay.

I change into football shorts and sunglasses, turn on the stereo, then sit out front on a canvas director's chair, eating and drinking, early sun's rays refreshing my bare skin.

Once food lines my stomach, I retrieve another beer and sit reading Dostoyevsky's *The House of the Dead* while listening to George Michael's *Songs From the Last Century*. Lounge music. Soothing before bed.

Five pages in, I hear a car getting close. Brendan's driving his wife's red Range Rover slowly up the fenceline. He spots me but doesn't bother waving. A minute later he steps onto the concrete carrying a dated plastic suitcase I vaguely remember from our schooldays. It's seen a bit of action. Corners are badly scuffed. Worn, faded stickers cover ninety percent of its exterior. He drops it flat beside me, goes inside, returns with a beer and another spring-loaded chair. He snaps the chair open and sits. Cows finally spot him and run up to the knee-high wire in front of us like love-starved pets patiently awaiting a pat or kind word. I mark my place with an out of circulation Australian one-dollar note and drop the book on the concrete before looking over my sunglasses at Brendan.

"Shouldn't enter a man's house without his leave."

He sips beer before giving his cattle a stupid grin and silly finger wave. "What the fuck you on about?"

"My leave. You didn't have my leave to enter the house. A man's leave is important. That beer you're drinking is now stolen."

"No shit." He takes a longer drink, spins the case around with his foot, pops its latches and leans back without opening the lid. "Friend of mine had a stroke yesterday. Only thirty-nine, poor prick. Got me thinking. I had this buried under a tractor on the farm. If something happened to me, it would stay buried. Do I have your *leave* to bury it here?"

I shrug, happy he's here for a reason, not a drinking session. "It's your twenty-five acres. Bury it where you like."

"I'm serious, mate. If something happened to me you're the only one I trust to see it goes to my wife and kids."

I finish my beer, liberate two more, resume my seat. "You don't have any kids. And why not leave it where it was and tell your wife? Isn't that what married couples do?"

"Jesus, Myers. You know what she's like. She'll tell a close friend" — he makes air-parentheses — "*in confidence*, and it's out." He flicks the suitcase open. It's chocka full of hundreds in neat, affable ten thousand dollar bundles wrapped in rubber bands. "Almost two mill, buddy."

I figured there'd be a lot more. From the brothel he siphons a minimum ten grand per week. Outstanding weeks, twenty or twenty-five. From his restaurant and other interests, God knows. Must be stashed elsewhere. Or maybe he's been buying other pieces of land like this one.

"I never liked you. Soon as you leave I'm going to dig it up and disappear."

"Look, I'm not supposed to tell anyone, because, as you know, Janet's had two miscarriages already. But she's pregnant again. And it looks like it's going to take this time."

"Take. Don't think I've heard it phrased quite that way before. It might *take*. Do you mean like glue, or perming solution, or—?"

"You mind or not?"

"For a second there I thought you were going to say *we* are pregnant. You know I'd have to shoot you if you got that bad."

"Mate, if I ever become that pathetic, I'll load the fucking gun for you. Now, yes or no?"

I shoot him a look implying he needn't have asked.

"Thanks, buddy. Owe ya."

We drink our beers. I grab two more, put three different CDs in the automatic changer and return outside. Brendan's making improper faces at his cows. I hand over his bottle and sit.

"Y'know, I'm not implying anything here, but I've seen a video of a guy standing on a stool fucking a cow."

"Yeah?" he says, finishing his facial gestures. "Wasn't an ugly cow was it? Hate it when they make bestiality movies using ugly animals. It's just not believable."

"The guy was the ugly one."

"Bastards."

"Heard the world's shortest joke?"

He shrugs, waits.

"A baby seal walked into a club."

"You mean he walked into a bar."

"If I meant a bar, I would have said a bar."

He looks at me funny. At that moment I figured something was not quite right. Being slow on the uptake is uncharacteristic. Something else is on his mind. Something major. Maybe related to that bullshit story about the stroke victim.

Finally he gets that familiar understanding grin and nods at his beer.

"I can use that when I go to Canada on business in a few months. Fucking tree-huggers up there will hate it."

2

Hookers talk. I hear it all. Mostly shit, such as money troubles, boyfriends, husbands and clients. But occasionally a juicy titbit wafts above the din.

A recent recruit used to work at an illegal Tweed Heads brothel. Conditions sound primitive. No client showers, one overworked communal toilet catering hookers *and* clients, plus loosely slung curtains between beds. Furnishings, hygiene and scruples play second fiddle to keeping the till ticking over. Another used to work for a skodie boss who deducted fifteen dollars per job from his girls for 'tax purposes'. But come financial year's end, try asking for some kind of tax form and you'll be laughed at, or if he thinks you're serious, told to fuck off.

Brendan's house of ill repute is classier than most. Legal, modern, private spas in five of nine bedrooms, complimentary bar, tasteful porn playing on large screens in every room and in the lounge, appropriate paintings and titillating Greek statues of semi-naked women spread throughout. If you have to pay for it, this is where you want to be.

* *

I'm sitting in the kitchen doing a crossword. Babs comes through from the girls' room to make coffee. At 26, her amazing natural beauty on a slender 175cm frame makes her one of the best looking women I've ever seen. Even at the end of a shift, having serviced seven or eight clients, makeup removed, casual clothes, she still has it. But her antics can be a little over the top. It's like an idiot frat boy resides in her head promoting inane, childish pranks. If somehow she managed a Pygmalion transplant, even I might be tempted to throw a few dollars her way.

After I hit her she didn't talk to me for two weeks. My head buried in a crossword, she snuck up and thrust her slobbering tongue into my ear. Kind of feeling something was coming, I feigned surprise and sprung a firm but friendly backhander, knocking her on that lovely tight toosh. God knows where that tongue had been.

Telly strolls in with four night shift pick-ups. A long weekend in Queensland, over the border, where we illegally deliver most of the outcalls, means plenty of extra punters.

A busy night anticipated.

Three of the four pick-ups — hookers with no personal transport — are generic prostitutes. Bottle-blonde, slim, generous tits. Personalities differ. Gina: quiet, makes good money. Bobby: up herself, fat ankles. Skye: airhead, holds herself well for forty, referred to as The Alien because she drives everybody crazy with weird ideas about UFOs, government conspiracies and shit. X-Files junkie. No intelligent conversation there.

Fourth is Nikki. Pride of the fleet. Head like a racing tadpole, but copiously applied makeup does its best. Having very little chin doesn't help. Covered with milky white skin, it appears sunlight has never kissed her body. Loud hair tints change weekly. But to be fair, on first impression she isn't chronically unattractive — in an odd, inexplicable kind of way.

Dropping his newspaper on the table, Telly liberates a can of Coke from the fridge and pops the top. I'm looking at the back of his freshly shaved head when Sammy, tonight's receptionist, spots it from the office.

"Holy hell!" she says.

He closes the fridge door, smiles at her, then me. His pale scalp gives his face and neck a fake tan aura.

I shake my head disbelievingly. "Some people don't have the right shaped head for shaving. Ever heard of Ferengi?"

Telly leans back to admire himself in one of two mirrors hanging beside the door to the clients' lounge. He runs a palm suavely over his temple, smoothing down hair no longer there.

Watching this piece of theatre, Sammy laughs. "What the hell were you thinking?"

The front door bell rings in the office. Sammy checks outside monitors before pushing a button, releasing the front door. She stands, straightens her clothes and moves to the foyer to admit the guest. On her return she buzzes the girls' room. "Client."

Seven hookers, ready for intros, enter the kitchen before meeting him individually. Two of them I've never seen.

Babs introduces these new recruits to Telly and me before taking her turn in the lounge. Neither of us digests new names. By end of shift their handles may be different. Or unimpressed with fellow workers, or conditions, tomorrow they may have even moved on, never to be seen again.

The first new girl's prettiness is overshadowed somewhat by an apathetic demeanour. Doesn't want to be here. Doesn't want to be anywhere. Even being a kept woman would soon bore her. At school, she probably snuck into the cheerleading line-up one year, but was forced out the following season because of a slack attitude. Gets my vote for most likely to suicide. The second tidies herself in a mirror, colourful dragon and tiger tattoos on her shoulder blades, smaller, matching cubs on her ankles. Confident, she flicks black-rooted blonde hair about as if she has something extra. They smile our way and say hi without much warmth.

When all girls meeting the john have plied their pitch, Sammy returns to answer any questions he may have about the prostitutes, or payment. Awaiting the outcome, girls hang around the kitchen, smoking and asking if any have serviced him before, what his particular quirks may be, and hoping, or not, they get picked. Unless he's loaded, or adventurous, there will be only one winner. And some of the time I don't think it's the bloke who wins.

This time Heidi and Tattoos get the nod. Looking from Tattoos to Heidi, a young, busty blonde, I come to the conclusion this guy's confused and doesn't know what the hell he wants. Leftovers mince back to their room. The office phone rings. Sammy puts it on speaker so Telly and I can listen.

"Hello," she says, innocent school-girlish. "Can I help you?"

"Yeah," — the guy's drunk — "how mush ya charge?"

"That depends on where you are and what you want, sweetie. What area are you in?"

"Umm . . . town. What can I get for fifty bucks?"

"A couple of large pizzas and a Pepsi." She hangs up.

Next call comes almost immediately. I recognize his voice. A tentative holidaying husband who booked a girl for half an hour the previous night for himself and his wife. Apparently they enjoyed themselves. Now the ever-sweet apple has been plucked from its tree, primeval urges and desires override any morals and possible embarrassment that had, until last night, kept their curiosity in check. Yessiree, the bottle has been well and truly uncorked. Tonight they require *two* girls, for *four* hours.

Sammy quotes the hourly rate, and they don't haggle. Telly and I smile. That's a forty-dollar driver's fee per hour, per girl, ticking over while we do other deliveries. Had they negotiated, after the first hour their discount comes out of the driver's fee. We're always getting shafted.

Pressing the intercom, Sammy informs Babs and Gina they're going out with me for a four-hour job. She tells Nikki to go along.

"Nikki!" I spit.

"No point going out without a spare," Sammy says.

"Yeah, but Nikki!"

"What's wrong with Nikki?"

"Yeah," Telly smirks, "what's wrong with Nikki?"

"I'm worried I'll take her to a job," I say to Sammy, "and the bloke will come out and bash me for bringing her."

Carrying bags of makeup, condoms, lube, the three girls and I hit the road. Immediately Nikki rummages through music discs in my glovebox as if she has a say in what's played. She's wasting her time. Nothing is labelled.

"How d'ya know what's on them?" she bitches. "I thought you said you were going to put labels on them."

"What do you want to hear?"

"Not that weird shit you played last time. Got any Pearl Jam, or Xzibit?"

Xzibit. Gangsta rap. Surely ye jest. I retrieve a disc from inside the armrest between my front seats and ease it into the slot.

"Try some George Michael."

"He's okay. I spose. The first song comes on and she turns to me. "This ain't him. I've heard all his stuff and this ain't him."

Having no idea we speak of her derogatorily, I keep it polite. "Yeah, it is. It's a track off a single only released in England."

The entire disc consists of bits and pieces not on his albums. When the second song begins, I can tell she's miffed.

She points at the disc player. "He's gay, y'know."

"No shit. Well I liked him before he turned, so I'm still allowed to listen."

Sammy rings with an hour job for Nikki. I pull over to write the address on a piece of scrap paper. Nikki is now first drop.

After a slight detour, I pull up beside the Legends Hotel front doors. A huge multi-storey job, anybody passing can look through massive glass frontage into the foyer and reception. I give Nikki the room number and price, then watch her clomp on long blacks heels into the hotel. Her short black dress offers a reasonable front view, but at the back, gaps of lily-white skin show above elastic-topped stockings.

Once she's in, and paid, I receive the call that everything is go. We carry on to the Marriott for Babs and Gina's four-hour romp.

It's forty minutes back to the brothel. Too far for me to drive while Nikki is in a job. Telly will have to hit the road and drop me another girl or two if more outcalls come in. So I purchase an out-of-state newspaper from a nearby twenty-four hour shop and park opposite Legends doing the crossword.

When Nikki's exiting call comes, I fold the paper so its puzzle is visible and move slowly into the covered driveway. Within minutes she's coming through the huge glass doors, a half dozen guests and two receptionists following her every step.

Spot the hooker.

Aware critical eyes are on her, she climbs into the car and slams the door. "What the fuck are they looking at?"

On our way back she gets a half hour job from one of her regulars. The fact there are men out there wanting to see her regularly baffles me.

She must do something these guys crave. Babs insists the only way to hang on to a man is to keep his stomach full, his testicles empty. Nikki must have a creative knack of draining them completely.

When the half hour is up, back in the car she informs me he only required her to watch him jerk off. Easy money. Why she feels compelled to share this I have no idea. I wonder what a shrink would class that guy's activity as. Humiliation? The guy tried for a discount for doing everything himself. Sorry, the price is pre-arranged. Consider it part of your humiliation.

Closer to home, another half hour is called through. With no land line to confirm the client's identity through directories, it leaves me the option of not doing it or escorting Nikki into the complex to make sure all is in order. It's early, and quiet. I choose the latter.

I push a driveway buzzer and we're admitted into a fenced, cheap-housing Legoland. One of a thousand on the Gold Coast. Fifty-odd single-storey units separated by small garages housing ten-year-old cars. Nesting grounds for solo mothers and nosy neighbours. In no particular pattern, each tiny front lawn sprouts poxy native flora resembling common flax.

We walk up to the door, where a short, chubby, fiftyish Greek opens up. Nikki licks her chops, introduces herself, steps in and closes the door. The odd-shaped brick recess where I'm left standing has an acoustic anomaly of which the owner is obviously unaware. Sound from his open laundry window beside the door drifts out as clear as if I were standing inside beside them. Sound quality is so clear I can even tell she's trying to keep her voice subdued to stop it seeping through the door. Her sales pitch begins with silence.

"What do you do?" he eventually asks.

"Absolutely anything you can do with a condom on," she replies. "And a lot of things without."

A shiver runs down my spine.

We're back at the house before ten, where I hand Sammy all collected money. Nikki's is placed in a locked box every hooker has for her shift. House money goes in numbered envelopes and dropped through a slot in the top of the safe. Mine is put in an envelope in a drawer. Lest one of us gets stuck in the boonies doing bugger all, when working together Telly and I split our money.

Already on his sixth job, he departed with three girls shortly after I left. A couple of girls showed up late, giving the house an adequate crew. This is a tad surprising. Last night being financially beneficial to all, there should be more sickies. Some aren't seen for three or four days. On their deathbeds, or kids need rushing to hospital. Full pockets mysteriously equates to prostitutes' kids being more prone to sickness and accidents than non-hookers' kids. Childless prostitutes get sick mothers. If mother is dead, mother still somehow manages to get the flu. Excuses, every night, lame and unimaginative. Offering these weak pretexts to a Woolworths or K Mart supervisor every other day would see them sacked. None of these women could hold down a regular job for any sustained length of time.

Not one.

Sammy takes a call and speaks through the intercom to the girls' room. Immediately Madison comes crashing into the kitchen and leaps across to the open office door.

"That's my record producer," she states, as if claiming ownership, or an album is in the pipeline. "He's cool. And he's always good for a three hour extension."

Sammy sits back and looks at her. "You just told me your period was here and you were going home. He asked for you, but I told him you had the night off."

"I'll scrounge a sponge." Madison runs back for her gear before Sammy can refuse.

"Okay," Sammy says to me, "He lives—"

"I know." He lives in the penthouse — as all la-de-da record producers should — of a 20-storey tower just over the border, fifteen minutes away.

Madison returns resembling a music video lingerie vixen. White lacy bra, white lacy knickers, white garter belt supporting white stockings, white stilettos. A very short white nurse's smock hangs open.

"You can't wear that," I tell her. "Nurses wear scrubs these days."

She rolls her eyes and zips up. "You're not funny, Myers. Nobody has a spare sponge. We'll have to stop at an all-night pharmacy on the way."

The all-night pharmacy is, of course, closed. Her next suggestion is a twenty-four hour supermarket on the border. Doubting any supermarket sells specialty sponges that fit up the cervix to soak up blood, or on occasion double as contraception, we continue on and roll into a half full supermarket carpark.

Looking idiotic wearing a short coat in oppressive night heat, Madison jumps out and disappears through the main doors. She returns without the required item, but made do. From her pocket she pulls a four-pack of rectangular kitchen sponges and tears off the plastic wrapper. She removes a blue one, then rips a third into a few decent sized chunks. Next, perched on my passenger seat's edge, knickers are pulled down and the dry scraps of sponge get unceremoniously inserted and pushed as far as possible into her vagina.

I don't profess to be an expert on female anatomy, but if she's on the rag, shouldn't something come out of there before all the other stuff is rammed in?

Still, I have to smile. Other people make twenty-four fifty an hour sitting in stuffy offices all damn day looking at boring computer screens. I get . . . this.

The record producer's dick better not be too long. He may wonder what the hell Mr Happy is nudging.

The result is a three-hour job. Within twelve minutes I'm back in the office drinking coffee with Sammy. Replacing one of a dozen mobile phones to its upright charger, she leans back, sips coffee from a mug and swings around in her seat.

"You and Brendan are going to see Springsteen in a couple of nights."

I nod.

"That boy band you like is coming here to do a concert. Going?"

I'm stumped who the group could be. No boy bands are even close to the top of my list. "I'm in my thirties," I say. "Can't do those anymore and be the oldest one there."

"Some of those boy bands are now older than you," she states. "I'm forty-six and went to a Willie Nelson concert a few years back."

Imagining a pall of dope smoke hanging over any stadium Willie Nelson played, I give her a look. "That'd be like going to a Stones concert. Everyone in the crowd are old laid-back potheads, balding — including the men, and need coke-bottle bifocals to see the action."

"You know there's a radio station running a nighttime competition to see George Michael in Hawaii? He's filming an unplugged type performance at a small venue in Waikiki. They're giving away a couple of tickets, with airfares. I think you get to meet him, too."

I sit up. "You're shitting me."

"I shit you not."

I jump up, flick off a small TV perched on top of the fridge and switch on the radio beside an electric jug on the bench. "What station?"

"The one it's on."

I give it more volume, resume my seat in the office and wait for details of my trip to the islands. "How do I win?"

She doesn't know for sure. "I think you answer questions on his career."

While she answers phones and ensures girls meet incoming clients, I listen intently to the radio, wondering why the hell I haven't heard about this competition before now. Three songs later, a trendy but ageing voice announces that when we hear a George Michael song this hour, he will take the fifth caller.

Okay, there are two of us in the office, and more than a dozen bat-phones in the girls' room. I walk up the hall, past washing machines and dryers, tap on their door and announce myself. When a voice tells me to enter, I step in. Skye's sitting topless at a table, tweaking makeup. Eight more slouch in armchairs and sofas, watching an old sci-fi movie on the box. Handbags, shoes, clothes and glossy magazines litter the floor. All look at me.

"You guys know there's a George Michael competition on the radio?"

Three or four say yeah. A couple shrug.

"A gorilla to whoever who gets through for me."

They look at each other for a few seconds, taking it in, suspicious, a little what-the-fuck's-he-on-about-now.

"What?" Skye says. "You'll give the person that gets through a thousand dollars?"

Her forty-year-old tits defy gravity a little too well to be real. Plastic is sometimes good.

"Yip."

Money. The magic word. All spring to attention. A digital clock radio sitting on another table is immediately turned on. Phone batteries and credit status are checked. I return to the office to wait for the song.

Never having heard a tough radio competition in my life, I figure this will be no different. Dummies for contestants, therefore straightforward and undemanding questions are factored into the equation. Advanced Alzheimer morons could dribble out a correct answer. If not, DJs always have the right to nudge them in the right direction.

When the song finally comes on, Sammy and I dial, push buttons to disconnect, then hit redial, over and over.

We get nowhere. When the announcer comes back on with lucky caller five, no prostitutes appear in the kitchen holding out their phone.

Rules are explained. Caller five, plus last hour's rollover contestant, if there is one, each get a question. If one cannot answer correctly, they're done, and it goes to the other person, assuming that contestant answers their own question correctly. Anyone with ten right questions goes into a play-off in a few weeks, so there isn't much time left. If no one gets ten points, whoever has the highest tally wins.

Starting with last hour's winner, the announcer goes into competition mode.

Sooo, Daveyboy, you've got two right, so you can go first. What was the name of George's partner in Wham?

Andrew Ridgley?

Correct-a-mundo, Daveyboy. Don't sound so unconfident. Now, Mandy, you were the lucky fifth caller. Are you ready for your question?

Jeez, I hope so, Rick.

Okie-dokie, Mandy. What was the name of George's song in nineteen-eighty-seven that the accompanying video clip was banned in a lot of countries? I Want Your. . . what?

There's a pause while she thinks. The answer is Sex. *I Want Your Sex.* Only an idiot or a blind and deaf eight-year-old who has never watched MTV wouldn't know this.

Jeez, Rick, it's a bit tough.

I need an answer, Mandy.

Um, money?

Money? MONEY! Unbelievable! I'll ring and offer the stupid bimbo a job. The brainless bint should fit in well around here.

With this pathetic quality of opposition, *Aloha-oi.*

3

There's something funny going on with the radio competition. Not funny haha. Funny peculiar. Despite numerous people trying for five hours last night, not one of our calls was answered — even as an early number before the correct caller got through. If it was during a peak morning show, when every man and his dog were trying, I'm positive at least one of us would have gotten through, even as an *un*lucky caller. Should the same thing happen tonight, I'll know something's dodgy.

It's my night to do pick-ups, but Mistress Jacqui's 7 p.m. booking lives further out this way, so it falls to me to collect him. Telly's not happy. He must now drive all over the coast collecting girls. Tough titty.

Mistress Jacqui. The real deal. Bondage and Discipline at a thousand an hour. And there's no shortage of takers. I'd like to say it's because of her upbeat personality, no sob stories, dramas or whining. But I know it's safety pins through the foreskin, electric shocks and other tailored pain and humiliation. Things the wife can't be asked to administer, let alone understand. My sphincter clamps tight at the thought.

* *

5.30 p.m.. Breakfast consists of mixed nuts and sliced bananas over Cornflakes drowned in milk. On the way home this morning I stopped at a CD shop and purchased two George Michael DVDs to refresh myself with his music clips in case they come up in the competition.

While eating at my little breakfast bar, I flick one on. Of the first half dozen clips, four reveal a parade of shapely supermodels combining provocative dance and sexual innuendo to such an extent it leaves me shaking my head. George could virtually have his pick, but opts for a Y chromosome. I don't get it.

I concentrate on details that may be asked as part of the competition. After an hour I shower, check there's three or four hundred in smaller notes in my wallet the girls can use for change, and head out.

Mistress Jacqui's client is a timid little bastard. He says hi and smiles, but I get the impression he's a smidgeon embarrassed. For our twenty-minute trip he sits in the front seat saying bugger-all.

I drop him at the brothel's front door, park, then enter through the side entrance. Telly's sitting at the kitchen table drinking decaf, grinning to himself for God knows why. I make a regular coffee and park myself at the table to enjoy quiet we both know won't last.

Sally, the manager, returning from greeting Mistress's client, sits in the office. She is what PC idiots refer to as 'big boned.' A two week Caribbean vacation, obviously not spent on a treadmill, has tanned her golden brown, but fifty-five years' sun worship has morphed her skin to old leather. It also appears recent sun lightened her short hair. But there's every possibility that came from a bottle.

"Come have a look at this," she says to us.

We pick up our cups and join her in the office. Her dog, Jewboy, sleeps in a corner on a bathmat. The size of an overgrown rat, the stumpy-legged, flat-faced little bugger has a nasty disposition that far outstrips his size. Named after Kinky Friedman's band, The Texas Jewboys, I wouldn't hazard a guess as to the mongrel's pedigree. Its mother had a few callers.

Sally taps an impossibly long fingernail painted with palm tree, surf and setting sun, on a screen. A man sits naked, blindfolded, gagged and handcuffed to a wheelchair in the girls' room. She turns up monitor volume and we hear girls taunt and call him degrading names. I lean closer.

"Look at the size of the guy's hard-on."

"Fucking sicko," Sally says. She flicks the picture back to outside.

Telly and I chuckle and return to the kitchen.

"You've gotta love Mistress Jacqui," he says. "Could be an interesting night."

With any luck we won't be here to see it. A couple of long hotel bookings means hitting the road reasonably early.

Sally stubs out a cigarette and informs us a couple of hookers' cars are pulling into the carpark. Telly looks at me. I look at Telly. Sally looks at both of us. Unfortunately I'm closest to the side door.

"Well," I say. "I'll go and let them in, shall I?" I open the gate to three regulars and a new one dressed in skimpy mini-skirt and stockings. Good body. Nice head.

They express greetings and tote bags to the fast overcrowding girls' room. When I sit back at the table to imbibe more caffeine and consider who I'll take to Hawaii after winning the competition, the clients' lounge door bursts open. Startled, Telly and I quickly turn to see what's going on.

Trouble. Quasi-laughable, but trouble nonetheless. Smiling devilishly my way, Mistress Jacqui stands in all her B&D magnificence.

Shoulder length mousy blonde hair frames sharp covergirl features. Tonight's outfit: thigh-high black leather boots on six-inch stiletto heels, black leather corset, black leather panties with polished chrome zipper running up the front. A black leather bra pushes large breasts up and out. Chrome-studded collar, studded leather wrist straps and jockey's whip top it off incredibly. Unfortunately, an overweight, balding, lily-white male wearing a big nappy with large safety pins, studded dog collar and lead, kneels sheepishly beside her. Eeeeh.

Sporting that slick smile while wielding her whip, she slaps the poor guy's butt to start him crawling on all fours.

"Can't we stay in the room, Mistress?" he whimpers, timidly turning his bowed head up to plead his case.

Knowing exactly his wants, how far to push things, she whacks his arse harder. And why not. Nobody likes a mouthy bastard.

"I didn't give you permission to talk!" she says sharply. "You've upset security." She whips his nappy repeatedly, steering him toward me. Finally cowering at my feet, he looks up to her mournfully, for which he receives another stroke.

"Mistress didn't say you could look at her," she says. *Whack!* "Security here thinks you're a low weasel. And he didn't like the way you looked at me!" *Whack!* "Kiss his feet and hope he forgives you, you worthless *baby*!" *Whack!*

Bitch. Telly and I have told her not to pull this shit, but she doesn't seem to know when to curb it. Thinks it's funny. We understand it's deadly serious to her client, but the way it's sprung on us we've guffawed on more than one occasion. Telly and I would catch sight of each other, and away we'd go.

Now virtually immune, we *try* to make each other laugh. He blows me silent kisses. I gesture he's a wanker.

Jacqui's nappy-clad schmuck kisses my scuffed Reeboks' toes for a good thirty seconds. I can't help but feel sorry for him and his ilk. He may also be one of the idiots Mistress Jacqui sees twice a week. For two grand I'd rather whip *myself,* pay off a mortgage ten years quicker.

She stands over him, dominant, business-like. A few times I've tried estimating how much money she earns. Knowing little of her outside clients makes it difficult. She's here two days a week, and sees many private clients in their homes or offices. She often flies to Sydney or Melbourne with her bags of gear. There's a fortnightly regular in Byron Bay, for which she pays me two hundred to drive her. Even with so little information on which to base calculations, it must be a minimum half million.

Easy come, easy go. The penthouse she leases wouldn't be cheap. No driver's licence necessitates cabs everywhere. When smokes are needed, a taxi is rung to fetch them, tripling the price. Hungry? — taxi. Booze? — taxi. Her idea of financial planning is pondering which Lotto numbers to play.

Sally says 'Mistress' and flicks her head toward the carpark. Someone's driving in. Mistress Jacqui whips him one last time before forcefully ordering him to crawl back to the dungeon and await her return. Once he slithers away, she closes the door, spins a wooden chair around and straddles it in front of me. Her hair looks good teased back, dangling. More often than not it's tied tightly in a bun or ponytail, with darker eye makeup to present illusions of severity and sternness.

"Word has it," she says, "you're offering a gorilla for getting through to the radio competition. If you want to go, I'll pay and go with you."

"Where's the guy *I* brought in?" I ask.

She gives me a creepy smirk. "Honey, you don't want to know where he is."

A paid trip to Honolulu would be nice, but I'm sure there are no concert tickets for sale. However, she probably knows as many influential people as Brendan. Maybe more.

"I'm fairly sure the public can't buy tickets," I tell her. "Have to win them or be invited. Know anyone in Hawaii?"

A long, elegant finger taps the top of the chair while she stares at the wall, trying to conjure a name. The nail is manicured, red and highly polished, matching her lips.

"I'll give it some thought. But if I get through to the competition, can I go with you instead of taking the grand?"

As if comparing invisible weights, Telly's open hands begin alternating up and down in front of him. "A grand," he says. "Hawaii with Jacqui. A grand. Hawaii with Jacqui. That's a fucking tough one."

I, too, could think of worse things. So sportingly I give her the once-over, head to toe then back again, stopping at the odd well-defined curve or crease.

"Okay. As long as you don't tell the others. I don't want them thinking they can do the same."

Telly rises to make another coffee. He leans back against the bench, folds his arms and looks at Mistress.

"A fucking nappy," he says. "You think in forty or fifty years when he's an incontinent old pervert and *forced* to wear one it'll still arouse him?"

Nobody answers. Large sub-tropic raindrops begin thumping the roof as Mistress stands to leave. Spinning the chair around, she says she'll get on to someone in Hawaii soon. Those heels send her to over six feet. I check out her butt while noisily drawing a breath through pursed lips.

"Know why men like women who wear leather?" I ask her.

She stops at the lounge door, turns and lets go a cheeky, titillating smile. I'm about to be toyed with as only she knows how. It starts with an eye-to-eye stare so intense I can't help but feel a little stirred. This well-rehearsed gaze creates an instantly deep sensual connection that sends nerve ends joyfully tingling.

"No," she says slowly. "Why?"

I smile broadly to break the spell. "Cause they smell like a new car."

Unable to leave me the last word, acutely trained feminine instincts take over, and I'm given the ultimate riposte. Legs part slightly, torso leans forward, lips pout tantalizingly while those magnificent breasts are cupped and pushed together at me. The *pièce de résistance* is lightly hooded eyes accompanied with an imaginary kiss that would send most men crazy. As an exclamation mark, she spins, opens the door and cracks the whip playfully against her thigh-high boot before leaving.

Telly ruins the moment with his usual dry wit.

"I get through to the competition," he says, "I want the gorilla."

Outcalls come in. Four girls grab their gear, climb into my Nissan and we head townward. Vicious rain pounds the car and road as we reach the first job. Within thirty minutes I'm down to one girl. Babs. We park by the beach in Surfers Paradise and wait for the phone to ring. She fidgets as nicotine deprivation kicks in, but is unwilling to brave rain outside to light up. Her feet move about to avoid water running through a weathered windscreen seal, dripping slowly on her side. When the storm eventually peters out in ten minutes or so, water will drip another thirty. I grin to myself.

It's muggy. The radio is on. We're waiting for the competition to start. Girls at the house will still try getting through, because Sally's a gadget freak and can patch their phone through to mine.

Babs' foot taps the mushy mat while she looks around the car interior for faults. I'm in here daily, so am aware of a lot more than she will ever see. But she does her best to prove me wrong.

I'm told the upholstery is dirty, but apparently holding together well. The often wet passenger carpet mat is falling apart, but that's to be expected when my windscreen obviously needs resealing. She lifts the moulded carpet strip atop the vinyl dash, exposing three long chasms caused by relentless Gold Coast sun. Without mentioning many lesser flaws, her verdict is we sit in a heap of shit. And what's with the odd steering wheel and airbag? This model piece of crap had a different wheel altogether.

The rain stops as suddenly as it started, and we open windows. I look around the interior. Maybe it is time for a later model work vehicle. However it's difficult giving up a car that doesn't want to die, or even fall ill.

It's busy. Most of the night my girls are working. I'm picking them up one at a time and dashing to the next job. Finally, at 3.45 a.m., with one girl in tow, Telly and I meet at a Surfers Paradise outdoor café to compare notes. We sip cappuccinos at a table on the footpath, inches from crawling traffic.

"Don't know why we can't go to the casino for a drink," the girl bitches.

I put down my cup. "We've had this conversation before. You'll get a job, then I'll spend forty minutes trying to find you."

"No you wouldn't."

"And then the house will call and ask why you haven't been dropped off."

"I'll stay close."

"And then they'll want to know why the girls who've rung out haven't been picked up."

"I'll pay for your coffee at the casino."

"And because Sally's left bullshitting the client about why you're late, she'll be on my case — not yours — for the rest of the night."

"So that's a no?"

Telly shakes his head. "Jeez, Myers, you're a bastard."

The girl says she needs a bathroom, and trots off. Telly looks at his night's tally and grins.

"Love this job."

"Better than Sydney?"

"Fuck Sydney. It's cutthroat down there. Flat ten dollar drive fee per job, no matter how far out you drive. Fill up the car with whores and go flat out all night for bugger all. Even here on the coast most places pay a flat twenty dollars per. If the receptionist negotiates a bigger amount, it goes to the house. Mate, we've got it damn good."

An unhealthily large woman waddles past and stops to admire sugarcoated goodies in a glass cabinet making up half the café's counter. I don't think I've ever seen an arse that big — on any animal. Telly also notices. His eyes follow like it possesses magic powers.

"Fuck," he says. "Skin's a marvellous organ. Not much else could stand up to that kind of punishment. If that were fabric, the slightest nick and it'd split rapidly right around the body, letting everything spill out. Not skin. Sew it up and carry on our fat, merry way."

"You've given it some thought, then."

Passers-by stare and nudge each other as the behemoth opens a fridge door for a family-sized bottle of high octane coke.

"Hey!" Telly calls. "Put that back!"

She turns but doesn't recognize either of us. A frown creases her fat forehead while wondering if it was she being addressed.

"Yeah, you," Telly says. "Look at the size of you. Put that back and take a *diet* coke. A *small* one. Why don't you take a little pride in your appearance. Whadda you weigh? Twenty stone? Twenty-two? Am I even close?"

His derisive comments mean nothing. She places a two litre coke on the counter, then orders a half dozen donuts and cakes. Loaded up, she moves across to stand in front of him.

"You're not my father, you're not my brother, you're not my husband and you're not my boyfriend. So go fuck yourself." When chins stop wobbling, she continues her awkward waddle down the street.

As if the exchange hadn't taken place, Telly sips his cappuccino. "No Hawaii competition on tonight?"

This job wouldn't be the same without him.

"It is," I say. "But I'm forever missing the damn thing because of calls or looking up addresses." He does the silent mime-weighing thing with his hands and we both smile.

The girl returns from the bathroom as Telly's phone rings. He pulls a notepad and pen from his shirt pocket before answering. One of his girls is having difficulty. Nothing serious, but the client is high on something. She's finding it difficult to leave. Telly says the address, and we hop in our cars and race the short distance.

The girl stands on the grass verge awaiting rescue. A shirtless john drunkenly leans in, arm around her shoulder, can of pre-mixed bourbon and coke in hand. Although the street is poorly lit, I can make out tattoos on his left pec and biceps. Bare feet. There's only just enough arse on him to prevent beltless jeans dropping. He slobbers in the hooker's ear, crowding her space. Her nose crunches at his breath and she turns her head away in disgust.

I glide to a halt opposite, yank the phoney airbag cover from the steering wheel and grab my illegal taser hidden beneath. Forty thousand volts. Nightie-night time.

Taser in my back pocket, I cross the road. Telly's car rounds the corner and momentarily lights us. I still haven't seen the john's other hand, hidden, curiously, behind his back.

"You okay?" I ask the girl.

She nods. His arm holding the can falls off her shoulder and he turns to me a little jelly-legged, reeking of bourbon. Eyes pinholed, he begins aggressively spouting shit about the dominance of an Alpha male. Surely he doesn't mean himself.

I lunge and juice him, mid sentence. I ram that thing up under his tattooed pec, giving him the lot. The arsehole almost lights up, stiffly quivering and shaking as electricity surges his body. The can drops and suddenly both hands are in front. His other hand drops a sharp kitchen knife. I turn off the juice and he drops unconscious to the grass.

Telly leaps to the sidewalk, late as usual. "Another Alpha?"

"There must have been a documentary on TV recently. *Everybody* thinks they're an Alpha."

"I know. Now, where'd you get the zapper and how do I get one?

"What zapper?" I ask, taser still in hand. "Zappers are illegal. I don't know what you're taking about."

I crouch to check Alpha's pulse. I'm no doctor, but a weak throbbing in a neck vein tells me he'll be fine in a few hours.

I look about at houses showing inside lights but see no heads watching us, or moving curtains. I lift Alpha under the armpits and drag him into a dark part of the garden, behind a bush, where he can sleep it off undisturbed. With any luck a Funnelweb or Redback spider might bite him and we won't have to worry about the dickhead ringing for another takeaway.

"Thanks for helping move him," I say sarcastically to Telly. He merely nods. It was no trouble at all.

"He's got a bundle," the girl says, moving toward the shrubs, possibly to lift Alpha's wallet. "Holiday pay or something."

Telly grabs her arm. "You've been paid for the job. Leave it at that."

She isn't happy, but that's the way things are left. Telly drives her straight to another job, then picks up one of mine for a double with a hooker from a different escort agency. A short time later, passing the street where I used the taser, Telly's car rolls slowly toward the intersection's Give Way sign. That sly bastard's been back to empty the arsehole's wallet. I toot, pointing at him accusingly to let him know he's been sprung.

He waves.

Sixty minutes on, filling our cars at a service station, Telly relates a convoluted version of what he did in that street.

"Mate, I genuinely did the guy a favour."

"And how do you come to that conclusion?"

"He's not going to remember anything when he wakes up. I left him a couple of hundred so he'll not think it's robbery. He'll imagine he's just pissed away the money somehow, like it's probably happened before. The guy's a binge-drinking, pill-popping dickhead. Relieving him of his cash was regrettable but necessary. I'm hoping it'll force him to see the error of his ways, realize what a mistake it is to carry on like a sauced-up idiot. I'm hopeful he'll turn a corner for the better. Y'know, weigh all the negatives in his life and amend it for himself *and* his friends' benefit."

"You're shitting me."

"I'm serious. This is my roundabout way of doing an intervention. The guy needs it." He holds up a handful of folded notes. "Your half. Eleven-fifty."

Would there be a cut for me had I not seen him exiting the street? Doubtful.

"On reflection, Telly, you make a well-rounded and persuasive argument." I pocket my share. "I suppose somebody had to do something to try and help the poor guy. Mate, you're a credit to the human race."

"Yeah. I know."

4

I wake to an annoying hiss in my ears that I don't recall being there the night before. But there are a lot of things from last night I can't recall.

The Springsteen concert comes vividly back to me. Third row, dead centre. Three exhilarating hours jumping around like half drunk teens. I told Brendan we should have driven to Brisbane, but no, his wife was out of town so he insisted on hiring a well-stocked limo. We ended up somewhere between paralytic and poisoned. Spasticus Autisticus.

Asking the woman sleeping face down beside me might forward some answers. However her short, natural blonde hair is unknown to me, and I really don't want to speak to someone who brought a stranger back to their place as drunk as I must have been. It shows a distinct lack of good judgement. And who's to say she'd remember anyway.

Now successfully reasoned into stealth mode, it's time for a quiet, strategic withdrawal, dignity more or less intact.

I pull back the black satin sheet and find myself naked. There are no clothes on the floor and my phone is not on the side table. Ah, I purposely left it in my car. Another flashback hits. Brendan was refused service at a nightclub. After telling a tribally tattooed Caucasian bouncer thug it was a damn shame he had no tribe to belong to, we were escorted out the door. Brendan then took the limo home while I straightened as best my drunkenness allowed and stumbled to a classier joint a few doors down. I know it was a classier joint because two guys on stage played a baby grand and double bass, and drink prices were criminally above the odds. For now, that's where it all stops.

I look at my watch but can't make out numbers through the Heineken haze. My stomach feels a tad queasy. Since hitting thirty my body occasionally fights back. Days of coming home legless, setting the alarm for a two-hour snooze before heading off to work, may be behind me.

My sleeping partner moves and eases out a comfortable little moan. Now half her face is visible, I'm impressed with myself. I pinch the sheet lightly and lift— Holy hell! That's my idea of a ride. But does it count if one doesn't remember getting The Prize? At this stage of the game no court in the land would convict me of Going the Grope. My small head tells me that staying for breakfast on the terrace would even be tolerable.

I resist both, settling to merely admire her petite back, buttocks and ample breast while reminding myself she brought home a totally drunk person. I gently lower the sheet, slip off the bed and exit the room.

Body moving, blood circulating, my eyes finally focus. 8.45 a.m.. Why is she not readying for work? Ungenerously I tell myself she's unemployed. An out of work drunk who brings strangers home. A pathetic analogy, but it reinforces my cowardly withdrawal.

I step through an unusually wide arch to an entertainment room. Shelves on the opposite wall house thousands of movie cases and CDs. An Academy Award stands centre. A photo of a smiling man holding it aloft on stage leaning into a microphone hangs above it. Wide tuxedo lapels suggest the eighties or early nineties. A huge screen faces a sofa and two large leather armchairs. Old, framed movie posters dot the walls.

Casablanca, North by Northwest, Dr. No, Mogambo. Eight tall speakers sit about the room, a large stereo beside the TV no doubt connected to at least a couple. A rumpled pillow and blanket on the sofa indicate someone slept here. Familiar clothes tossed on the glassed-topped coffee table in front suggest it was me.

I don jeans and shirt, but don't spot my runners. I move back through the arch to a large, tidy living room. My shoes aren't here either. A black leather handbag sits on a breakfast bar in the kitchen. Probably my best hope of finding a phone, I move quietly over to look inside. A pink flip-top phone nestles amongst makeup and other crap, so I pick it up and park my arse on a tall stool.

The top of a red plastic traffic cone in front of the sink catches my eye. I lean over the breakfast bar to see a second cone, a Gold Coast City Council Men At Work sign, my runners, a pair of high heels, two empty Dom Perignon bottles, plus four long-stemmed champagne flutes lying on bright blue tiles. Four glasses? Jesus, what the hell happened here? Maybe I should have eaten something before heading off to the concert last night. Looking at this aftermath brings no memories rushing back, but it explains my queasy stomach. Mister Perignon's bubbles never liked me.

I look inside her purse. She lives on credit cards. The gold and platinum kind. Six hundred and forty in cash nests neatly in a side compartment. I check my own wallet. It's four hundred light, but another seven hundred is intact. Without recalling my movements, it sounds reasonable.

I slide out her driver's licence. Vanessa Diana Rayford. 23. I dial a cab company and give the address on Vanessa's licence. Before dropping everything back in her bag, I study her impeccable facial features on the licence in case we bump into each other and she recognizes me.

Ten minutes later, a cab smelling of spew and stale beer runs me to a beachside high-rise carpark. Exposed to the elements all night, my trusty Nissan has a salt crystalline veneer thick enough to render the windscreen close to useless. A squirt from the reservoir under the bonnet spits a few drops at the screen before wipers turn it all into a smeary mess. Now my car is totally undrivable. A cop would red-sticker it, putting me off the road.

I squint through the murk, roll down to street level, pay the ransom and drive away.

Nearing home, my bat-phone hiding in the glovebox goes off. Instead of letting it ring, I foolishly grab it, check the displayed number and answer.

"How's the labour?" I ask.

"Labour?" Billie the receptionist says. "What are you talking about?"

"Collective noun for moles."

"Oh. Labour's okay. Got a job for you. Want it?"

"It's my day off."

"I know." She doesn't give a stuff. "But it's local, and you can pick up Phoebe from her house."

"What happened to the day driver?"

"He put the hard word on a girl this morning. Sally sacked him."

In fifteen minutes I can be comfortably seated in my director's chair in front of the shack, relaxing, recuperating, finishing Dostoyevsky while sun pleasantly warms my skin.

"Can't you get someone else?"

"He's on his way, but it'll take him fifty minutes to get here. This job's local, and it's a fifty dollar drive, otherwise we'll lose it."

"Just this one," I say reluctantly. "Tell Pheeb I'll pick her up in ten. She better be ready."

I really shouldn't be driving. Blowing into a breathalyser could prove disastrous. *Can I please keep my licence, Your Honour? Who will drive the prostitutes?*

When I pull to the curb, Phoebe flounces out her front door and plonks her arse in the passenger seat. She's a hottie. Young. Long blonde hair. Big tits. A tight, pink, low-cut stretch top accentuates her bumpy bits, while a little white pleated skirt hides the rest. Deep, even tan. Stupid. Boyfriend's doing time for breaking into a cop's house while the cop was having a barbecue in the back yard. She says it was just bad luck.

"Hey, Myers." She screws up her nose at my dirty windscreen. "Thought Kenny was driving today."

"So did I."

She flicks the sun-visor down to make use of the little mirror, pulls makeup from her bag and starts delicate touch-ups around her deep green eyes. "So where is he?"

"No idea," I lie. "You'll have to ask Billie."

In less than ten minutes we're parked by some guy's gate. Phoebe alights like a glistening beacon, adjusts her dress like an excited transvestite, then minces her way up the path.

The guy's nervous. From behind a curtain he checks the street, left and right. His front door opens before Phoebe can knock, and he gestures her to hurry inside. My phone goes. I'm informed all is well. Phoebe will be out in one hour.

I drive over a couple of streets to a garage, fill up, wash my windscreen and buy a paper for the daily crossword. Getting back, I park around the corner from the job and contemplate Vanessa, how wonderful she looked lying face down between sheets of black. But why would she possibly take a person in my state back to her house? It's perplexing. Maybe beneath the exterior she's your classic dumb blonde, with dumb blonde attributes. I do vaguely recall somebody last night asking my star sign.

Opening the paper to Classifieds, of eighty-odd two- or three-line escort ads under Personal Relaxation, a dozen or so would be ours. Busty Betty. California Beach Babe. Open-minded Greek girl. A few novelty shags have made today's selection. Old, fat, ugly. Broadminded granny. Guys ring thinking someone private will arrive on their doorstep, but nine times out of ten the likes of me rolls up with their takeaway. So he's paying the girl, the house, and *moi*.

Next page, the crossword. I fold the paper and find a pen in the glovebox. My phone rings. I don't want to answer. It'll be Billie, abusing the favour I'm currently doing her. She'll want a different girl transported to a job. Or take Phoebe to another when this hour is up. I should have refused the original job.

I answer. "What?"

"She's coming out," Billie says.

Something's up. I've never known Phoebe to be thrown out early, or knocked back. I start the car and move off, phone to my ear.

"What's the problem?"

"Nothing. She's finished."

Finished? As a matter of routine the client is required to shower before any intimacy can take place, and prostitutes always shower before leaving. In this case it hasn't left a hell of a lot of time for momentous, seismic lovemaking. A few minutes at best. But who am I to comment on a guy's sexual prowess, or lack thereof. Gives new meaning to the word 'quickie'. *This won't take long, did it.*

When I coast up level with the stud's front gate, Phoebe comes out, pours herself back into the car and hands me money.

"There's a twenty dollar tip in there for me," she says. "I didn't have change. Well, I did, but I said I'd have to go to the car to get it, and I knew he didn't want me running up and down his path." She grins.

Phineas T. Barnum was right. There's a sucker born every minute.

I count it. "Everything all right in there?"

"Fine. He couldn't have been more than thirteen or fourteen. He was worried about his parents coming home. Wasn't even keen on letting me shower, but I insisted." She leans forward and slips off pink high heels. "Any other jobs lined up? My shoes are wet. I'll have to go home and get a different pair first."

Knowing an inane answer would result, but unable to resist, I ask the obvious. "Okay. So how did you wet your shoes?"

"Had them on in the shower."

She says this like it's an every day occurrence. But it kind of begs a follow-up question. Did the kid have her so rattled about his olds coming home that she actually put her shoes on and then got in the shower, or did she fuck him with them on, then just jump in the shower without realizing?

From Springsteen to this. Wonderful.

I resist asking. I drop her back at her house, stop at the brothel, drop off the money, then head home. Thirty minutes after receiving the original call I'm at my paddock's gate. I shoo the dozen cows away, drive in, close the gate and drive up to the kitset garage/shed.

Showered, I look for something to eat. The old fridge's freezer offers nothing but snowy ice. Apart from five six-packs, the only other things in the fridge are four leftover pizza slices sitting on a dinner plate. I toss these in the microwave and crack a beer. With so much alcohol still in my system, I only need topping up. A few of these and it's back to bed for the day.

While pizza slices heat, I open up Casa Del Myers, drop a seat outside, then put on a George Michael CD to keep in touch with the competition I'm no closer to winning.

Finally, I take the pizza remains, my unfinished Dostoyevsky and two beers outside to sit and relax.

Then I spy a few cows trotting toward the gate. That can only mean one thing. Brendan is here. This day is about to take a turn for the worse.

He, too, will only need topping up.

5

Oblivious of its imminent demise, the black cat sits grooming itself atop a fence post.

"Useless fuckin animals," Brendan slurs. "Native bird killers. Y'know, if you died in your house, a dog would lay down and die with you, loyal to the bitter end. Cat'd nibble on you to stay alive."

"No cats on the farm to keep mice and rats at bay?"

"Snakes do that."

The stray enjoys its final afternoon sun, leisurely but meticulously cleaning head fur, licking a paw before rubbing its face.

"How far you reckon it is?" Brendan asks.

Applying alcohol-impaired judgment, I calculate an answer.

"Bout a four iron."

"That *your* four iron, or Greg Norman's? Width of a state national forest difference," he smirks. "But you knew that already." He stands, accidentally knocking over a half dozen empties by his foot. He urinates over the electric wire to the sloping grass in front. His hips circle while he pees, as one does when outdoors, pissed and pissing. The cat hears our empties clatter and gives us a cursory glimpse before continuing its preening.

"When I'm king I shall turn every golf course into a motocross track." After a quick shake, Brendan eyes the cat. "You get beers, I'll get the gun."

I fetch fresh drinks and change CDs. When I come out Brendan's seated, trying unsuccessfully to insert a single round into a .270 rifle he keeps in the shed roof. It refuses to cooperate, falling to the concrete twice before finally slotting into the chamber.

"You're too pissed to make that shot," I say.

"Got a lazy gorilla says I can."

I hand over his beer and watch him take a long pull. He's leaning back, smug, rifle butt resting on his thigh, muzzle straight up. My liquor tolerance is greater than his, yet I'd be pushed to manage a clean kill from here. So I hold out my palm, which he casually taps with the base of his bottle. Done deal.

Placing his beer on the concrete, he stands, feet slightly parted, nestles the rifle butt into his shoulder, steadies his breathing, then begins slowly lowering the barrel into position to take the thousand dollar shot.

"Hey hey hey!" I smile, patting his chair's armrest. "You weren't standing when you made the bet."

He mumbles something I'm sure is derogatory before resuming his seat. He drinks some more, fiddles with the telescopic sight, then flashes me a big cheesy J.R.-style grin, implying that it doesn't make the slightest difference from whence he does the deed.

A downhill shot, he makes himself comfortable, crouching forward a fraction, elbows on knees. Again fitting the butt into his shoulder, the barrel moves about slowly until he's satisfied. With his slight exhale and hold, I turn to the cat, now sitting lion-like atop the post, grandly surveying its territory. Talk about when you least expect it.

A sharp clap rings out. The cat immediately does a high, spastic leap in the air and drops out of sight behind a small clump of tussocky grass.

I spring up, trying to see it land. "You only winged it."

Brendan leans back, cocky, picks up his bottle by the neck and says he hit it dead centre. The less than useless creature lies deceased, other side of the fence.

"You saw it jump," I say. "Hit but not dead."

"I got another lazy gorilla says it's finished, where it fell."

He holds out his palm. I slap it.

We carry our drinks down to confirm the result. I lead, walking slowly on the off-chance the cat needs time to clamber a reasonable distance from the drop zone. For the money on offer, I'd crawl down on hands and knees. We get there and peer over the clump of grass.

I'm out two grand. Useless bastard's lying where it fell, gasping helplessly for breath like a beached guppy, blood pulsing from a hole in its neck. All but, as euchre players say when awaiting that last point to put them out and win the game.

Within a few seconds it stops doing anything. Life's struggle over. Happy there's one less native killer in town, we return to our seats, drinking as if nothing happened.

"There wiz a guy in the brothel the other day who saw Nikki," Brendan slurs, "He told her he came home drunk one night and fucked his cat. When he got up in the morning the cat was dead. Ripped."

I think about that. In my half drunken state, the best retort I can manage is, "Y'know, I bet if he wrapped the cat in tape, it wouldn't've split."

Brendan sneers, calls me a sick cunt. I remind him he started it. We laugh loud and hard.

While I get two more cold ones, he puts away the rifle, then moves his cows to the bottom paddock. We listen to music and the odd car speed past behind the shack. When one of those cars stops by my gate, Brendan looks over.

"Fucking cops." He loathes the constabulary. Almost every one he's had dealings with, he told me in the past, is corrupt, looking for a backhander or some kind of freebie.

I lean forward to see round him. Leaving their patrol car on the grass verge, a uniformed pair step through the gate and stroll cockily up the well-worn dirt tyre ruts. The older one carries a few extra pounds, straining uniform shirt buttons around his middle. The younger is leaner, greener, looking around, observant. In a year or two that naïve shit will wear off. He'll swagger like his partner, the law on his side, his word against yours. Puffed-up moral superiority.

For whatever reason, they don't step over the electric wire to the concrete slab. They stroll around to stand in front of us, the heavy one stopping where we've been urinating. Clocking our empties, the younger lets out a cheery ain't-this-heat-something breath and turns for another gander at my scenery.

Careful his shin doesn't touch the charged wire, senior guy lifts his shoe tip onto the concrete. He places a thick hand on his knee, exposing an armpit sweat mark. Their patrol car would be air-conditioned, so early damp patches means he's well out of shape. The young cop is probably with him to catch the bad man should it come down to a foot race.

"Fellahs," senior says, beads of sweat dotting his forehead below his police cap visor. "Hell of a view."

We say nothing.

"I'm Sergeant Goldsmith. This is Constable Peters. Got a call there's been—"

"Hey," Brendan says to me, "know why cops go round in pairs?"

Of course I do. Jokes don't come much older. But I shrug to play along.

"One can read and one can write," he says flatly.

"Nice one," I answer. "Know why sometimes they bring a police dog along?"

"Yeah. In case a really *big* decision needs to be made."

We don't laugh. We sit deadpan, as if it's a sad fact. Peters, new to the job, smiles. Goldsmith, street-weary veteran, ignores our jokes and carries on in his non-confrontational tone.

"People been ringing saying shots have been fired around here somewhere. You fellahs hear anything?"

Brendan, as quick as he is drunk, quips innocently, "*What* cat?"

The cops look at each other. Goldsmith continues, talking directly to Brendan. "You live here?"

Brendan says no. We drink.

"Know who does live here?"

Brendan flicks his head my way. "Gee. Maybe him."

Goldsmith turns his attention to me. Peters pulls a smoke from a packet he takes from his over-sized shirt pocket. Before he can light up, Brendan informs him this is a non-smoking paddock, and the hand holding the lighter drops.

"My cattle disapprove of second hand smoke," Brendan adds, "ve-her-mint, ver-ma-hant— with a passion. Look at the bottom paddock. See any of *them* smoking?"

Without thinking, Peters looks toward the bottom paddock. He grins, nods to himself, pushes the cigarette back in its packet.

Goldsmith looks to me. "Know your neighbours?"

"Soon as it's anyone's business," Brendan says, "we'll let you know."

"I live just down the road," Goldsmith says, not remotely rattled. "It's good to know the locals."

"He doesn't speak for me," I say. "Captain Goldsmith. Sir."

"So," Sergeant Goldsmith continues, "I'll tell my wife not to come here looking to borrow a cup of sugar?"

Good luck finding *anything* in my cupboards.

"Depends how big her tits are," Brendan says with a wide smile. He wipes a drop of sweat from his cheek using the front of his T-shirt, stands and moves toward the open sliding glass door. "You guys want a beer? Only one between you, mind. There's only so much hospitality one can extend to cops before your friends hear about it and start having nothing to do with you."

Sergeant Goldsmith takes his foot off the concrete and flicks his head at junior. "Thanks for your cooperation, fellahs. We'll see you round."

Brendan stumbles out with drinks. "Give my best to your wife," he calls.

"What was all that about?" I ask.

"I've heard stories bout that piece of crap. Don't want to get too friendly with the likes of him."

"Ah."

We settle back, slurring more quantum physics theory. We don't try solving the world's problems like most drunks. The world can look after itself. With another four dead marines in the collection, we don't notice music discs have stopped changing automatically. Suddenly, uncomfortable vibrations of distraught, stampeding cattle thud up through the ground.

Instinctively we stand to see what's happening. The dozen cows run frantically up hill, close to where the dead cat lies. On their heels, jumping about like jackals on a night out, a yapping six-pack of black and white farm dogs.

"Damn dogs from next door," I say. "They're always at it. I'll get my bat."

Brendan lets out a loud country whistle, stopping the surprised dogs in their tracks.

"I've told that bastard next door about his dogs," he says. "I'll go have another word with the prick." We pick up our beers and wander into the next paddock over, the yapping pack now running parallel, just out of reach. We cross two more paddocks, then a small strip of trees marking the edge of a large banana plantation.

My neighbours' double-storey brick house sits wide open, every window ajar. Rolled-up double garage doors reveal an open internal door leading upstairs. A wheel-less heap, the only visible car, sits on blocks under a freestanding carport to one side.

Now comfortable in their own space, all six young dogs become friendly, waging tails while moving about our legs. Six kennels line the house's north side, so we hook a dog to each chain. Except for one, they immediately go mental, frantically trying to break chains or jerk backward out of collars. Figuring the quiet dog to be the only one tied to its own bed, Brendan swaps it with another to achieve a complete chorus of yapping malcontents.

He yells at the house. There's no reply. At the garage entrance he calls toward the internal door a little louder. I figure anybody within earshot would have come to investigate the dog riot. We look down toward the street before doing a slow perimeter wander, checking for workers. Back at the start, we walk in under a cobweb covered rolled-up garage door.

What a mess. Parents neither enforce discipline nor encourage standards of any kind. Toys lie about everywhere. Four pushbikes and numerous parts sit rusting on the floor. A wide board above a greasy newspaper-covered workbench boasts silhouettes of at least seventy tools, none of which is present. Large, poorly stacked, half filled cardboard boxes randomly abut walls. Two guns lean against an old, deeply scratched ride-on mower. The double-barrelled shotgun appears battered, but the deerstalker job sports new sights and polished wood. Both pieces are visible from the street. Criminally careless.

Stumbling up the stairs, Brendan slurs greetings a few more times. We're here to talk about their dogs, he yells, which have considerably quietened. We fall drunkenly through another open door at the top of the stairs. Except for heavily stained carpet and a few broken children's toys, the hall is devoid of furnishings.

First room belongs to a young boy. Halle Berry wearing an orange bikini clings to a wall above the bed. A bald guy, possibly Vin Diesel on a Harley, hangs above a desk. Clothes droop from drawers as if frenzied amateurs recently rumbled the room. DVDs and CDs lie about anywhere except near the TV and stereo, which sit on wooden kitchen chairs. Dirty sneakers and dirtier socks remain where they were kicked off. One mud-caked Nike rests sideways atop cluttered girlie magazines on a low dresser. Three mobile phones, an old record player and older valve radio awaiting assembly, or binning, cover the student's desk.

"No maid service in the boondocks," I say. "Every feral for himself."

Next, another boy's room. But younger. Toys for maybe a five or six year-old litter the polished wood floor. We move to the living room. With larger windows, this space is brighter, but no cleaner. Newspapers and old pizza cartons lie about. A computer keyboard, wire leads wrapped around, leans lengthwise against a bulky old computer screen placed on the floor next to a threadbare armchair. Squeezed-in-the-middle cola and beer cans lie where dropped after emptying. An unplugged stereo and TV sit against a wall by the door, as if ready to be taken away or repaired.

"Jesus," Brendan says. "Looks like the place has been tossed. Nobody lives like this, do they?"

"We've lived worse."

"We were single, living like bachelors. A young family of four lives here. You ask me, something's wrong."

We finish our beers and move to the kitchen. It's tidy, but an underlying germs-hunker-down-here-happy feel fills the air. Appliances stacked by the back door only make Brendan a little more suspicious, with maybe those guns downstairs forcing a precautionary report to the cops.

While he makes the call on his bat-phone, I toss my empty in a lidless bin beside the fridge. Brendan shakes last drops into his mouth and lobs his bottle. It marks the white paint above the bin before dropping in.

"Fuck it."

He reports his suspicions while I open the magnet covered fridge. There's lots of domestic beer, but it's in cans. Not only does aluminium taint amber liquid, it's supposed to bring on Alzheimer's. However, it's a long hike back for a Heineken, and the cops could be a while. I'll risk it this once.

I grab a can with my name on it and flip one to Brendan, who's turning off his phone. The can hits his chest, drops to the floor, cracks a tile.

"Fuck it," he says again, with not the slightest hint of regret.

I open mine and take a sip. Yuk! He picks his up and cracks it. A huge beer plume sprays over bench tops and windows.

"Fuck it."

"Idiot."

"This could be a crime scene," Brendan says. "We shouldn't be drinking their beer."

"Past caring."

"Shouldn't be touching their shit, either."

I grab a tea towel draped over an oven handle to wipe my prints off the fridge handle.

"What the fuck you doing now?" he asks, noisily sucking foam still erupting from his can. "That's now the only thing in the house with no fingerprints. How strange you think that's gunna look?"

More alcohol impaired reasoning brings a solution. "Okay, let's say for argument's sake the mother's Obsessive Compulsive, and she has to wipe certain things." I then rub an oven handle, freezer handle, a few cupboard knobs.

"Knock it off," Brendan says. "I'm not spot cleaning this dump just cause you wiped a fridge handle, moron."

To piss him off I randomly rub a few more spots around the kitchen. He shrugs, takes a good-sized drink and screws up his face.

"Shit, Myers, once you're past the foam, it tastes like crap."

As the can goes to his lips a second time, I point to writing on the bottom. PROPERTY OF QANTAS. NOT FOR RESALE. He raises it to look.

"This guy's got a source," he says. "Thieving bastard."

"Maybe the Qantas Gestapo came and took him away and are torturing the entire family right now to find his supplier."

"Maybe he's that fuckwit who *borrowed* a Qantas plane's life raft to go fishing a while ago, and when he opened it emergency services mobilized cause it had an automatic beacon that goes off when it self-inflates."

We laugh drunkenly at the homeowner's possible misfortune. Then I notice a cross with a nailed-on Jesus hanging above the hall doorway.

"Godbotherers. Fuckwits who think Sunday's the first day of the week."

"Isn't it?"

"On the seventh day He rested," I quote the Good Storybook. "The Sabbath. Sunday. Didn't God kill someone for working on the Sabbath?"

"Prob'ly smite or begat them in those days."

"You miss the point, Brendan. Can't have it both ways. You can't rest on the seventh day *and* have it the first day of the fucking week."

"Never thought of it that way. Which reminds me, what you doing for Christmas?"

"They're not still flogging that virgin birth story are they?"

"Hey," he says, "there's money in it. And will be for a while yet."

We hear a car pulling up the pebbled drive. Now used to the taste of cheaper suds, we leave a twenty dollar note in the fridge, grab a spare can each and walk back through the garage to meet our local cops.

Goldsmith and Peters. They look at us, then each other as they exit their air-conditioned cruiser. Dogs go berserk again as we move toward each other.

Sergeant Goldsmith notices our beers. "You boys having a long day? So what we got here?"

As best he can, Brendan explains the situation. Eventually he points a can toward the guns. The fat sergeant looks toward them.

"And you boys went inside? Anything could've happened in there."

"In our present condition," Brendan says, "we wouldn't have felt a thing, let alone seen it comin."

Peters leans his butt on the patrol car bonnet while Goldsmith disappears inside. He returns a few minutes later shaking his head, mumbling something about it not looking good. Moving to the cruiser's passenger seat to use the radio, he requests information on residents at this address. Almost immediately he's informed no one living here is a licensed firearm owner.

"Okay," he says into the radio. "Because of those shots reported earlier, we'll have to try and track down the owner's car."

Brendan and I smile. The shot fired before was us, but we're not going to mention that now.

"Phone the local school and see if their children are attending today. If not . . . hang on, someone's coming up the drive."

A dirty green four-wheel-drive rolls up and stops beside the patrol car. Sitting in front, mother and father take in the scene. Father's obviously not liking what he's seeing. Two sons, about five and eleven, stare fixedly at the cops from their back seat.

Father climbs out dressed in best country hick. Bare feet, baggy shorts, loose, holed singlet, three-day growth. All six dogs turn suspiciously quiet. He probably beats them.

"Fuck's goin on?"

Goldsmith asks if he lives here. The guy says he does.

"Looks like you might have been burgled."

"Shit!" The guy runs inside.

Brendan and I place our now empty cans on a tree stump, open the spares and take a sip. We all seem to be waiting for the father's return. The cops eye both guns leaning against the ride-on mower. Eventually, looking perplexed, the father returns.

"No we haven't," he says. Brendan and I roll our eyes, which he catches. "What the fuck are those two nosy bastards doin here?" He spots his cans. "They've been inside. I want them prosecuted for stealing."

Brendan holds up his stolen can as if toasting, writing on the bottom clearly visible. "Yip, you better bag this as evidence. Came straight from his fridge. I'll go quietly, officer."

Goldsmith eyes the father standing akimbo, fists clenched, angry but wise enough not to follow through with his complaint.

Goldsmith points with his head. "So whose guns are they?"

"Mine," the idiot says. "Why?"

"Because you don't have a permit for them. Even if you did, look where they are. Anyone driving past could see them, walk right in and pick them up. Then we might have had a bloody mess to clean up." Peters enters the garage, collects both guns, checks their chambers, then places them carefully in the patrol car's boot. Goldsmith produces an infringement book from his back pocket, flips the cover and begins writing. Now we know which cop is the reader and which is the writer.

"You giving me a *ticket*?" idiot asks incredulously.

"Prob'ly him shooting before," Brendan offers.

"It's up to a five thousand dollar fine," Goldsmith says, "and/or time inside. Per weapon."

Exhaling angrily, the guy runs a hand through his greasy hair. His own stupidity, but of course he won't see it that way.

Brendan stirs the pot further. "Might as well check his attic for hydroponics while you're here, sergeant. He looks like a home cultivator to me." He lifts his can for another swig.

"Ask him what the first day of the week is," I say.

Brendan and I laugh.

The sergeant stops writing. "Maybe you two should go home."

It is getting late. We have tickets to see Status Quo at Twin Towns Club in a few hours, and we've decided to try and drink ourselves sober.

"This is the fourth time I've told you," Brendan says to the Father. "Your dogs chase my cattle again, I'll fuckin kill them."

As we turn to leave, the five-year-old boy gets out of the family car. He strolls over to his old man, looks with quizzical eyes at the policeman holding the infringement book, and says in loud redneck style, "What's that fat fuckka doin, dad?"

6

The world's turning to shit when you can't get a drink in a pub.

Maybe in these days of every-participant-receives-a-trophy and no personal responsibility I'm expecting too much. In the not too distant future I might be forcibly removed from the premises for interrupting the barman's conversation.

I dial a number and a hotel phone rings at the far end of the bar. The gormless wonder stops his chat with a couple of slappers and wanders down to answer.

"Hello?"

"Got a minute?"

Reecognizing my voice, he turns, smiles. Then, constantly flicking gold locks from his face, he swaggers down my end.

"What's up, Myers?"

Vanity thy name is dickhead. I take a breath and look down at the beer bottle that's been empty a few minutes. Beside it, a pile of change.

"Oh, you want a beer? Why didn't you holler?"

"Sorry. My fault entirely."

He retrieves a fresh one from a fridge yet to be stocked from the night before, puts it down, leans in and winks. "I'm gunna fuck both them tonight." He takes my money and returns to his powwow with the only other people present.

How does someone completely clueless get through life so effortlessly? His looks. He's the archetype of Hitler youth. Tall, tanned, blond, blue-eyed, square jawed. He's so good looking *I'm* thinking about fucking him.

Leaving no gratuity, I pick up my beer and exit a side door to motel units. My friend is home from work, sitting on an uncomfortable wooden chair at a long picnic-type table abutting a railing outside his unit. I kick out a chair to sit opposite. On hotel grounds below, five overweight tourists lounge on deckchairs around the pool.

"Myers." He puts down a book of poetry and sips red wine from a fine china cup.

"Fastlove."

In gigantic hands his cup appears small. Badly scarred, cauliflower ears attest to a rugby forward's physical past. Now, at fifty, it's chain smoking and nicotine stained fingers, along with a perpetually butt-filled ashtray always within easy reach. Two fingers are bandaged together. Probably whacked them upholstering a car in his friend's workshop. He won't mind the pain. It's the willing price paid for putting English tenure behind him to live easy in a sub-tropic climate, spitting distance from a dozen golden beaches.

He lights up, leans back. "So what's the latest installment?"

As usual, I ignore his first question. Crossing my ankles on the next seat, I ask the question to which he always offers a different answer.

"Tell me again why you gave up teaching."

"One day I was explaining the reasonably straightforward concept of adverbs, and that by adding an L-Y to a word, it generally turns it into one. To wit, one little shit immediately sticks his hand up and says, 'Does that mean *jelly* is an adverb, sir?' "

We chuckle. We chuckle often.

"Saw a new blonde running round the kitchen area inside," I say. "What's her story? Slinky?"

"Enjoys being pushed down stairs by the husband? Don't know. She moved in around the road a few days ago. Four kids. Happily married."

"Was she bawling her eyes out while telling you this?"

He tops up his cup of red. "What a wonderfully unique outlook you have on humanity. Now, let's have it."

I convey the record producer and sponge episode, along with the insertion of same while seated on my passenger seat.

"Ah," he says thoughtfully. "The epitome of class." He stubs out his cigarette and immediately lights another. "Told you, Myers, you should write a book. I've edited a few hacks in my day, so I could help you with it, give you pointers. You could have called that little story *Blood On The Tracks* if Bob Dylan hadn't beaten you to it. People couldn't dream up these stories, let alone live them."

Because he so enjoys my tales, I favour him with another. The larder overflows.

"Took a girl to another job the same night, and when it's time for her to ring out, the receptionist calls to see if she's already in the car. I said no, so she rang the john. After about five minutes, he answers and goes ballistic because he and the hooker fell asleep as soon as they finished screwing. So she comes out of the job sixty dollars light. I ask where the rest is and she says the guy took it back because she nodded off. I rang the house to ask if I should go in and retrieve it, but they said no, tell her it comes out of her share." I grin. "Wasn't she happy."

Fastlove flicks his hand flippantly and says in his usual, colourful tone, "Hey, pal, as long as you get paid."

"That's all that matters."

"Book," he says again. "You could end up in the celebrity race at Formula One or Indy. Get to play dodgems with Elle MacPherson or Sam Worthington. Or maybe ram some awful, moronic TV personalities like The Wiggles."

Awful. Fastlove's favourite word.

"Don't knock The Wiggles," I say. "They make squillions."

Fastlove sips his wine enthusiastically, as if it were the day's first. Dee, another indolent staffer, joins us for a smoke break before the lunchtime rush. She swears her twentieth birthday was last week, but Fastlove and I reckon a fake I.D. was used somewhere down the line to obtain the job. Sixteen is more like it. We've had many a stilted, childish dialogue with this one. She's breaking in a new boyfriend, telling us a few days earlier how she keeps him in line with her pussy.

"Dee," Fastlove says.

She sucks in a gobful of smoke, looks at him, then me. "Fastlove. Myers."

Fastlove, as is his way, dives straight in.

"So, Dee, what exactly are you looking for in a man?"

Dee blows out a puff of smoke and says without hesitation, "A big dick."

At least it's different from the tired 'millionaire' reply. Then, as time passes and female clocks tick, millionaire expectations turn into an employed guy, with the hope he doesn't knock them around too much.

"Must be nice to have such high and clear-cut expectations," I say.

Fastlove's eyebrows go up. "So this new man wields a big dick?"

"Not bad," she says. "But I'll flick him if I find someone bigger."

"So you should," I say positively. "No woman should put up with mediocre dick."

Unaware of implied cheating, she continues with conviction. "I know. The bastard talks a lot of dribble, too."

"Drivel," I correct her.

"No, he talks crap, so he dribbles."

"Fastlove." I look to him while pointing an open hand at her.

"Depends," he chuckles. "Depends if he's dribbling while he's drivelling."

"See," she says to me.

I give up easily. "What can I say? My mistake. Thanks for clearing that up, Fastlove."

"Glad I could help." He lights another cigarette.

"Why do people call you Fastlove?" Dee asks.

"Myers here gave me the moniker."

She glances at me, expecting a comment.

"Ever hear George Michael's *Fastlove*?"

"Yeah. Course."

"Well listen to the words next time."

"Why not just tell me."

Fastlove's an enigma. A honey magnet. I suspect he sits out here reciting poetry to his much younger, starry-eyed targets on hotel work breaks. Fresh, untaxed minds, he calls them.

"Can't remember the words," I lie.

"Still thinking of a holiday?" he asks me.

"Constantly."

Dee's ears prick up and her voice rises with excitement. "Ooh, where you going, Myers?"

"Thinking of doing a five day white-water trip down the Colorado."

She becomes even more worked up, as if an invitation to join me is imminent. "The Colorado what?"

"Jesus. River. What else does one white-water down? Or maybe I shouldn't ask."

"Where's that?"

"Arizona. It snakes down the inside of the Grand Canyon. And for your sake you better not ask what *that* is."

She looks at me like *I'm* the idiot. I thank Saint Christopher, patron saint of travellers, that at least I'm not being asked the familiar question that's been flogged to death since the invention of travel.

"Want someone to carry your bags?" she asks.

Yeah, that one.

I stretch backwards, arch my back over the chair, scrunch my eyes and pretend to scream. Fastlove looks at me with gleeful mock-surprise.

"Something the matter, chum?"

I swipe my empty bottle and walk back into the main building. Gormless is still deep in conversation with those two girls. He catches me out of the corner of his eye, straightens and moves back an inch from tonight's sexual escapades. But he still can't quite bring himself to leave them.

I give him loud sarcastic. "Any chance of getting pissed around here?"

He strolls up to me with a big cheesy grin. "You're only drinking lite beer, Myers. What you want?"

"How about the same thing I've had the last fifty thousand times you're served me." I finish with a sickly snarl. "With a dash of speed and civility."

His happy demeanour begins to wane. He doesn't know whether to be offended or laugh. Give me a big-breasted dumb blonde serving wench any day. She may be as thick, but at least one has something to ogle while being ignored.

I take the unopened drink alfresco and resume my uncomfortable seat. A new cigarette burning, Dee blows perfect smoke rings with expertise unfamiliar to this establishment. It's probably the one clever thing she learnt at school. Kindergarten.

"Saw a bumper sticker today that sums up this town," I say. "Describes it to a T."

Fastlove stabs out his cigarette. "I'm listening."

"Masturbation is not a crime."

His silent nod conveys agreement.

"What's the worst sticker you've seen?" he asks. "And you can't say Jesus Saves, or anything religious. Too easy."

"There is one I've been seeing a lot lately. It's really getting on my wick. *Magic Happens*. It's blue, with sparkly little stars all over, like Tinkerbell just touched her wand to the damn thing."

He nods again, on the same wavelength.

"Every time I see one I feel like ramming the bastards. They live in a dream world. Away with the fairies."

"Yes," he agrees. "Pathetic."

Dee says the sticker may advertise the Disney Channel. At that moment I have an inspiration. I pick up my phone and ring a friend who happens to be a printer.

"Aspro, mate. I need a sticker made. And I don't mean a namby-pamby, wishy-washy cheap job where the glue lets go or printing fades after a decade exposed to the elements. I want a top-of-the-range bastard that lasts and sticks real good." I tell him what I want and hang up.

"What sort of a name is Aspro?" Dee asks. "Nobody's called Aspro."

"Obviously at least one person is." I say. "I've got to pick up my car from the mechanic. Then I'm going for lunch."

7

Car air-conditioning repaired, I walk into Brendan's bar, then up the stairs to his seafood restaurant overlooking a Southport marina. Recognizing me as a friend of the boss, a minion ushers me to a balcony table. The place is three-quarters full of diners enjoying lunch. Brendan appears from the kitchen with a couple of beers, and sits.

"What brings you here, buddy?"

"Lunch. How'd you go with the mission?"

"Calls were made. The concert is invite only. Or win tickets. But I'm waiting on one last guy to get back to me." He leans back, plucks a menu off another table and holds it my way.

"Steak," I say without taking it. "Medium."

"In a seafood restaurant. Peasant."

"You don't serve steak?"

He screws up his nose.

"And mashed spuds," I add, just to piss him off.

"Don't have mashed spuds."

"You have potatoes? Fucking-well mash them."

He goes into the kitchen. While he's gone, I finish my beer then pull his in front of me. Down on the piers yuppies ponce about, gearing up for an afternoon at sea, or just sitting aboard moored boats. Cool hangers-on front wearing white gear because individuality doesn't exist on the water. *Masturbation Is Not A Crime.* The rest are probably idle rich with nothing better to do. Great life if you can marry it.

While eyeing a couple of almost dressed blondes loitering below, my phone rings. It's Sally, asking if I can work tonight. Daryl wrote off his car and doesn't have a backup. At this stage there are no pick-ups, but of course that could change by kick-off.

With little else on, I agree. As I place my phone on the table, an unfamiliar voice speaks my name. I turn and smile.

Skirt just above mid thigh, Vanessa's light blue professional suit projects lawyer or office manager. However, she wears no blouse. Stylish *and* sexy.

I start to rise but she places a hand on my shoulder, leans over and kisses my cheek. I invite her to sit. She does, placing her purse on the table.

"Dining alone?" she asks.

She's almost too good looking to be real. If this is through sober eyes, when we met the other night it's a wonder I didn't jump on her them and there. Maybe I did.

"Having a bite with a guy. But I hardly know him. I can soon brush him off."

Brendan exits the kitchen, spots us and does a U-turn. He returns with an open bottle of Italian chardonnay and three glasses. He sits and begins pouring.

"None for me," I say. "Sally just rang."

"Myers, Myers, Myers," he says. "You've been hiding this one."

"Vanessa, Brendan."

"So, Vanessa," he smiles, "how long have you known Myers?"

"We met the other night after a concert. Did he not brag that he picked someone up and spent the night at her place?"

"Alas, Myers doesn't give much away." He looks at me, then back to her. "So how well did he perform?"

"He slept on the sofa."

So she doesn't remember me in her bed. I wasn't supposed to be there. She just went up a couple of notches in my estimation. Brendan gives me a pathetic losing-your-touch look.

"I hope you like fresh flounder," he says to her. "I took the liberty."

"I was meeting four friends, but I suppose they can get by without me."

"Myers would rather I ordered you spaghetti bolognaise, or something similar. That's one of his tests for prospective . . . partners. If you can eat spag bolognaise with your mouth closed, without getting it on your chin, or sucking it in, cutting it off with your teeth and letting the excess drop back on your plate, or—"

"I think she gets the idea," I say. "Thanks for pointing that out."

"My pleasure, buddy. Just trying to give her a running start. Let her know what she's up against." He clicks his teeth playfully. "Hope you don't have any tattoos, Vanessa. That's also a big no-no. But you don't look the type" He leans sideways and lifts the tablecloth to spy her legs. "Well, legs aren't on upside down, and there's no fuck-me anklets visible. I'd say you were off to a flier. You might actually have a shot. And that's good, because if Myers here gets himself a steady, my wife wouldn't mind me hanging around with him so much. Maybe—"

"Enough," I say.

"No," Vanessa says, "I'm finding it fascinating. You've obviously known Myers a long time."

Brendan gulps a quarter glass of wine. "Years. After school we took off in different directions, but we always keep in touch. He gadded about the planet. I went into . . . this sort of thing."

"But you're his boss now?" she asks. "I think he mentioned you the other night. Do you also own a courier business?"

Brendan smiles at the reference. "Myers doesn't work for me. He's self-employed. My company supplies the work, but I'm not his boss. I don't pay his wages."

A waiter places breadsticks on the table, then leaves.

"This conversation is getting exceedingly boring," I say.

"Yeah," Brendan agrees. "Let's talk about you, Vanessa."

"Let's not," she says.

We chat over lunch. To her credit she doesn't slobber her food once. Nor do any rogue bits stick to her face or teeth. A very refined eater. Afterward she invites me back to her place for dinner, which I regretfully decline. Had she turned up one minute earlier, before I took Sally's call, I would have jumped in. Now I must go home and get some kip before hitting the road tonight.

Before I rise to leave, Vanessa scribbles on a paper napkin and hands it to me.

"I don't know if you've still got my number," she says, "but call me. Soon."

I dislike leaving her alone in Brendan's company, but what can I do? I kiss her lightly on the cheek, as she had done to me, pat Brendan on his shoulder and head home.

8

After a couple of long weekends on the coast, I'm hoping for a quiet night at work. Two days on the piss have worn off, but I want to stay here, concentrate energies into getting on the radio. This is the night to get through. I can feel it in my bones.

I'm sitting at the kitchen table, drinking Earl Grey, reading today's paper. Brendan walks in and sits in the office with Sally.

"So what happened that Daryl doesn't have a car any more?" he asks her.

"Someone ran up his arse," Sally explains. "Got five stitches in his hand. Chipped a bone in his elbow. Airbag deployed, braking his nose. But he's okay."

Brendan pretends annoyance. "Inconsiderate bastard. Fancy dropping you in it like that, Myers, when you had somewhere to go tonight."

"Yeah. Self-centred prick" I mumble back. "Look what I'm missing out on."

"Oh yeah, I'd be sprinting round to her place as fast as my little legs could carry me."

He talks business with Sally. I go back to the paper. Nikki comes through from the girls' room. Today her hair is white with red streaks. She looks at me slyly, sending a shiver down my spine. She lights a cigarette, pulls out a chair and parks her arse next to me. White leg flesh squeezes out between the hem of her too-tight mini and elastic topped stockings. Suddenly I feel sour lemon juice in my mouth. Involuntarily I close one eye and shudder.

"What's the matter with you?" she asks.

"Think someone just walked over my grave."

"Fuckin hate it when that happens." She checks the office and lowers her voice. "The girls are all sitting up there clutching their phones and listening to the radio. I know you're offering a gorilla to be the right caller in this competition, but if—"

Fuck. Not a deal. Please don't be offering me a deal.

"Goes for you too," I say quickly.

"—if I get you on," she continues, leaning in a fraction further, "I want to go to Hawaii and meet some famous people at the after-concert party."

These prostitutes seem to have their own ideas about how a deal works. Because of that magic mirror some seem to possess, they imagine all men will fall at their feet. This one probably has the audacity to think she has something so compelling that it can turn gay guys from their Chutney Ferret tendencies. Scientists and shrinks have tried explaining homosexuality for centuries, but it seems the fucking answer is held by a prostitute in Tweed Heads, Australia. Who knew? Or maybe she thinks a music star at the concert will take one look at her and insist she be a vixen in their next video. Yeah, Good luck with that, too.

"Sorry, but I'll be the one answering questions — doing the hard yards, so there's someone I had in mind to take. Anyway, I might stuff it up, so you're better off with the money."

The bushpig's cocky. Something lurks up her sleeve.

"But I can get you on. For *sure*."

God no. Don't make me stoop to this. I finish my tea while thinking it over. I spose she isn't *that* hard to look at. But how can I possibly travel overseas with someone like her. No dress sense. Doesn't give a rat's how she looks. A shocker without makeup. But we wouldn't have to share a room. I could pay for separate accommodation. And she could—

NO NO NO NO NO! What the hell am I thinking! I shouldn't even be entertaining the idea.

"If you can get me on, *for sure*," — which I doubt — "I'll make it fifteen hundred. You can holiday for a week in a decent hotel in Hawaii for that."

"You've had a dozen girls trying every hour for what, five or six nights? and nobody's come close. And this is my chance to meet some celebrities."

Maybe so. But there's no way in this lifetime I'd meet *any* celebrity with a tart sporting a face like a farmer's arse hanging off my arm.

"Two grand," I say. "And don't tell the others."

She grins, sticks her nose in the air and marches off saying that before too long I'll be begging to take her.

I watch the door, waiting for the next prostitute to arrive and start negotiations. Mistress Jacqui's connections are fast looking like my only hope.

The contest comes on. The ninth caller will be taken. Everybody, including Brendan and Sally, try unsuccessfully to get through. It's looking suspiciously like this contest has already been decided by corrupt DJs, with these hourly visits on air merely for show. And Nikki somehow knows about it.

Daveyboy Foster is leading the way at the moment with seven correct answers. He's in front by a country mile, and there's less than a couple of weeks left. On the line we have Virginia. Last hour she answered two questions, and has a total of four. How ya feelin Virginia? Can I call you Ginnie?

Um, I'd rather you didn't, Rick. And I'm really good, thanks.

I'm pleased to hear that, Vir-gin-i-a, cause up against you this hour we have Joe. The two non-contest questions I have to start with, Joe, is do you know your George Michael? and can you and a friend go to Hawaii in a couple of weeks?

Sure can, Rick. AndI I guess I know George Michael as well as the next guy.

Yeah, well, hah hah, I wouldn't go betting the farm on that one Joe-boy. Okie-dokie then, Vir-gin-i-a, who did George do the duet I Knew You Were Waiting For Me *with?*

Um, was it Mariah Carey?

Fraid not . . . Ginnie. So, Joe, your question is, what nationality is George?

He's a Pom.

Correct-a-mundo. Now, for an extra point, what's the answer to Ginnie's question? Would you like me to repeat it?

No. It's Aretha Franklin.

So Daveyboy, whoever he is, has seven correct. Joe's on a big run of two. I've got none, and it looks like the words *Hey George, how's it hangin?* will never be uttered from these lips.

Thirty minutes later I'm watching our only Asian prostitute wander into a hotel foyer. Of course we call her Token, like the lone black kid in *South Park*. Nikki sits beside me sporting a devil grin. She's confident I'll crack. It's making me nervous. The call comes that all is well in the hotel room. To avoid sitting under a bright streetlight, I roll out and park a half block down the street. The radio's on low.

Three songs and twenty ads later the flag goes up for caller number eight. I get to work on my phone. Nikki sits there grinning her evil grin. After five or six tries, always ending with an engaged signal, Abba's *Dancing Queen* plays in Nikki's bag. She pulls out her phone, answers, then offers it to me.

"It's for you."

At last! The only person who could be calling me on Nikki's phone is Sally. Someone at the brothel is caller eight, and she's relaying it to me. With a little surge of adrenalin, I take it.

"Yip?"

"Myers? Hold on."

It isn't Sally. But the voice is unmistakeable. Rick, the DJ. I turn the radio down.

Okay, folks, we have Joe back this hour. Joe has two points on the board. You ready to do it again this hour, Joe?

You bet, Rick.

Alriiiiight. Your opposition this hour, Joe, is caller eight. And that lucky individual is Myers. Do you know your George Michael, Myers?

"A little bit," I say, staring suspiciously at my passenger.

Well, we'll soon find out. But I'm betting your biggest problem at the moment is deciding who you're going to take to Hawaii if you win, ay Myers?

Syrupy smug covers Nikki's face. It's clear I'm supposed to confirm her place beside me on the trip. Seems good old Rick is willing to fix the competition so she can get a freebie to Honolulu. I wonder what he is to her. Probably a client.

What a cunt of a spot to be in. I quickly weigh my options. It's a horror of a price, but with the fix in, this could realistically be my only shot.

You still with us, Myers?

"Yeah, sorry Rick. I'll take a friend."

Would that be a male friend or a female friend?

Nikki's smarmy, self-satisfied look is giving me the shits. All of a sudden I can't let her win. Having read plenty, and probably now knowing George Michael's music better than your average punter, I have to go for it myself. Anyway, I still haven't given up on Mistress Jacqui coming through.

"A male friend, I think. A mate."

Then I wish you luck. And here's your question, Myers. What is George's real name?

He must have been saving that one to get rid of somebody he didn't want on his show. But you'll have to do better than that, Rick with a capital P.

"Georgios Panayiotou."

Correct-a-mundo. Now, Joe, you can't get an extra point this hour, but you can rack up another one for yourself. What was the name of George's first solo album?

Um, Faith. *And I'm glad I didn't get that first question.*

Exact-a-mundo, Joe. So we'll hear from you both soon.

Rick takes my mobile phone number and tells me I'll hear from him next hour. Nikki smiles and says I'll never do it. Her brother will see to that.

Her brother. Knowing Nikki as I do, it's possible he could still be a client.

Then she asks for the two gorillas I offered earlier, just in case I do pull it off.

I don't think so, warthog with lipstick, body like a wildebeest.

Daryl's been on the scrounge. He borrowed his sister's car and wants to work the remainder of his shift. He needs money to buy a new car, as the one just written off had no insurance. Without a legitimate job to write on a loan application, convincing finance companies he can pay it back is tricky. He must save enough cash to buy another.

That's good news for me. After giving him the green light, I dig Vanessa's folded napkin with her number from my driver's door pocket and ring. She agrees to meet at a bar in town. I might get lucky tonight after all.

Within thirty minutes Daryl rolls up in a rusty 2-door Honda Civic. Nikki climbs into its front seat. I put an elbow on his roof and lean in. Black circles both eyes, a thick bandage bridges his nose, a sling holds his arm in place and bandages wrap his hand. He's sweating, seems distracted, like tranquillizers are wearing off.

"You can leave my half of this drive with Sally," I tell him.

He grunts.

"How'd you write off your car?"

Now he makes a fist of his good hand. "Don't know," he snarls. "Fuckka rammed me and took off."

I hold back a smile. "How could he drive away when yours was totalled?"

"Retard was driving a big red four-wheel drive thing, with bull-bars on the front. Don't think he even scratched it."

"He probably had a few bevies under his belt."

His fist rises. "If I find the bastard. . . "

"And you don't know what kind of four-wheeler it was?" I ask, trying to sound interested.

"Nah. But its whole driver's side was primer paint."

I tap his roof. "If it's local, one of us will spot it."

"Yeah. Thanks mate."

Nikki explains my soon-to-be-short competition career, reaches over and fiddles with Daryl's radio.

"What?" he says. "You got through? Lucky bastard."

Going back to my car, I mumble bad things about Nikki.

"Luck!" he calls to me.

I acknowledge with a backward wave.

Next hour's competition imminent, I finish parking just as my phone comes to life. When I answer, Rick asks me bluntly if I will take his sister to Hawaii. I answer politely in the negative, telling him I offered her two grand instead.

There's silence that means he's thinking things over. A counter-offer is in the works, I can feel it. Money takes precedence over sibling love.

"Sorry, it's a birthday present, and she needs someone to take her. She's never travelled overseas before, and I can't go."

Bugger. At two grand I thought he'd crumble.

"I want to take a friend. Sorry."

Lights reflect in my eyes as a car pulls in behind. When they douse, sleek lines and a round chrome Mercedes hood ornament of a new SLK Roadster remain.

"You realize," he says, "I'm going to have to make it tough for you, if only to appease Nikki."

With his tendency to rabbit on like a pork chop, I assumed *appease* might not be in his vocabulary. But at last, somebody understands the meaning of a deal. Now he must do what he must do. As do I.

"Wouldn't expect anything less," I say.

Vanessa taps my passenger window, sees me on the phone and motions she'll meet me over the road. I reach over, open the door and she gets in. I put my phone on speaker as she sniffs remnant's of Nikki's perfume, and frowns.

"What's up?" she asks.

I put a finger to my lips.

Okie-dokie. Back this hour is Joe and Myers. Joe is sitting on three points and Myers got his first question right last hour. You guys ready to rock and roll?

Sure am, Rick.

I look at Vanessa. "Yeah, Rick."

So, Myers, this is a double-banger question for you. What was written on the back of George's leather jacket in his Faith *clip, and what eventually happened to it? The jacket, not the clip.*

"Revenge," I say. "And the jacket was burned in his *Freedom 90* video."

Wow. I'm impressed. Could you have answered that one, Joe?

Yeah.

Okay, Joe. Name one male artist George has done a duet with.

The obvious answer is Elton John. They had a huge hit about '91 when George remade *Don't Let The Sun Go Down On Me*.

Hell, Rick.

I'm afraid he never made a record with anyone called Hell Rick. Do you have any idea?

No. But I'll have a stab and say Robbie Williams.

Oooohhhh. Unlucky. Thanks for playing, Joe. And now the question passes to Myers. Any idea?

"Yeah. He did a thing with Toby Burke called *Waltz Away Dreaming*."

Ah. Right. I'll have to look that one up and confirm it either way when we hear from you tomorrow night, when I'll be looking for caller number four. So tune in tomorrow if you want to jet off to Hawaii to attend a. . .

I turn my phone off and glance at the metallic silver Merc in my mirror.

"Leased?"

She shakes her head, amused.

I kiss the palm side of my fingers and pat the dusty dash carpet of my trusty Nissan. "Think it'll keep up with this baby?"

"Depends," she says. "Who'd be driving?"

"Mine, or yours?"

"Did you find what you were looking for in my purse the other morning?"

She knows I'd been in her bag but has no clue I was in her bed. Do I tell her I wanted an address for a taxi, or just leave it hanging. I leave it hanging.

"Ever been to Hawaii?"

"You going to take me?"

"I'm a third of the way there."

"Would you be asking me if the trip wasn't free?"

"Would it make a difference?"

"If you made the offer and didn't win, you'd still be legally bound to take me."

"That so?"

"Trust me."

"But if I don't win, I don't want to go."

"To Hawaii? Everybody wants to go to Hawaii."

"Maybe. But the whole point of this trip is to see a private concert."

"Oh."

"So, you'd pursue it through the courts if I asked you to come and I lost?"

"To my last penny."

"I could liberate our last penny before it got to court. I prey on women like a leech. I'm good at it, too." Once more I pat the dash. "Note the car."

"I've handled men like you before."

A twenty-three year-old with a sensible *and* pretty head on her shoulders. I give her car another look. "Thought a few times about buying a Ben-zee myself."

"Benz, darling," she says. "Nobody calls them Ben-zees."

"Course they do. Nelly, for one."

"Nelly who?"

"Nelly and his hip hop crew. You know, Murphy Lee, Ali, City Spud."

For this I cop a pitiable headshake. "White-boy-listens-to-black-rap-and-tries-desperately-to-keep-up."

I check my side mirror before opening the door. A red 4x4 with driver side primer flashes through the intersection. I jump out and look back down the street. There's nothing there. It's far enough away that reflected light may have made it appear red. Maybe it was two-tone instead of primer. Maybe paranoia's setting in.

We enter the bar without paying a cover charge, doormen and hostess greeting me by name. A reasonable Tuesday crowd listen to some guy spinning recently released hip hop discs louder than necessary from an alcove above the stage.

We sit at the end of the bar, as far from house speakers as possible. A barman places an unopened Heineken in front of me, then asks what the little lady is having. Vanessa smilingly tells him the little lady will have a chilled bottle of Dom. She turns to me and adds, loud enough for him to hear, "If that's all right with the master."

"Master says that's fine." I hold up a finger. "But just the one. Wouldn't want the little lady mulletted. Again."

"Good call," the barman says. "Can't have them getting off their face."

"Already tried plan B," I admit, shaking my head.

He looks at me piteously. Barman logic says we were both drunk and I couldn't seal the deal. I've disgraced the entire male gender. I shrug. That's the way it goes. Some are pushovers, some aren't.

A loud voice comes from somewhere close.

"IT'S BLOODY FUCKIN MYERS! HEY MYERS!"

Searching for a face to connect with the voice isn't required. The screeching belongs to Wanda. Hooker. After a disagreement with a brothel receptionist a few months back, she hasn't required my driving services. With the alternative being a nine-to-five job, she undoubtedly screws for one of the many other town agencies.

"HOW THE FUCK ARE YA, MYERS?" She and a friend drag padded stools over, dump cocktails on the bar and invasively shimmy themselves between Vanessa and me. "What the fuck you doing here!?"

The fifteen people she's inadvertently entertaining look away. I pick up my drink and twist off the top. "Having a quiet beer." The hint is ignored.

"So," she flicks her head at Vanessa, "who's the trade?"

Trade. Before I can answer, Vanessa offers her hand.

"Vanessa. Let me buy you girls a drink."

"Thanks." Wanda makes her cocktail disappear in a single gulp. "I'm Wanda. This is Ruby."

Ruby sculls her drink and crunches ice cubes open-mouthed. "Hiya."

Wanda turns excitedly to me. "Was that you on the fuckin radio couple hours ago? Who you gunna take to Hawaii? Nikki? Ha-ha-ha-ha-ha-ha-*hic*."

Her rapid-fire high pitched whinny hurts my ear. She throws a hundred down and frantically waves two fingers at the barman. Then she looks at Vanessa before slyly sliding the note back.

"Wouldn't mind going meself," she adds.

The barman places a champagne flute in front of Vanessa, carefully uncorks a Dom Perignon bottle, pours a half glass, then rams the bottle into a bucket of ice in front of her. He pours two bright blue cocktails from a pre-prepared shaker and positions them on white napkins.

The interlopers are settling in. Vanessa is curious. Nothing to do now but ride it out, hope for minimal damage.

"Never seen Myers with a girl before," Wanda says. "Tries to make out he's gay so we leave him alone. But we know better." There's an exaggerated wink. "Mind you, never seen him out and about before either. Ha-ha-ha-ha-*hic*."

A player dripping in gold neck chains saunters over and leans on the bar, the other side of Vanessa. Some gold has made its way to his fingers and wrists.

"Hey," he says.

"Hey," Vanessa smiles.

"Dance?"

"Do I, or would I care to?"

"Would you care to?"

"Thank you. No."

"I fuckin do," Wanda says. She drops off her seat, grabs Ruby and the guy by their wrists and drags them toward the dance floor.

"Yes," I say quietly to Wanda's back, "go for it, girl."

Vanessa slides to the stool next to mine and puts a hand on my leg. "He's probably a very nice guy."

"I'm sure. If you like I can call him back."

"I think not."

The barman wanders down to see if her champagne needs topping.

"How often they come in here?" I ask him.

"Those girls? First time I've seen them." He pats his pocket. "They throw money around. Good tippers."

"If they should ask . . ."

"Never seen you before either. I understand. You don't want them knowing where you drink." He leaves.

Vanessa smiles. "Those girls. . . "

"You don't want to know."

"Shall we go back to my place?" she asks. "We could get the first one out of the way. There's always something funny about the first one because you don't know each other's bodies, likes and dislikes."

The Prize!

I drop a hundred down and call back the barman. "Put a cork in the bottle. We'll take it with us."

"Not allowed to, Myers. Against the law to remove bar drinks from the premises. We're not a bottleshop. "He looks at the hundred and raises his eyebrows.

I drop another hundred. He stares at it. I drop another. Nothing. Jesus. I drop another two.

"Keep the change."

"What change?" he says. "I'll find a cork and a bag. Don't let anyone see you taking it out the door."

"Once the hideous first one's out of the way," I say to Vanessa, "we can get stuck into the second and third, better ones."

"Hmmm."

9

Word is out at the brothel. The fix is in. Hookers have been informed that Nikki knows the radio DJ, so I'll be winning squat unless I take her to Hawaii. Money is changing hands. None of it on me. Apparently a sure thing like this doesn't come along every day.

Telly covers all bets, and there are a lot of them. I can't help but wonder why he's doing it. I'd like to think it's camaraderie coupled with an indelible trust in his fellow driver. But it won't be. The only sure reason is if he and Nikki have done some kind of deal and will split the proceeds. She turned down my two grand, so bets would have to be big. We'll see.

"There's the motel, Myers."

Shit, I'm daydreaming. I check my rear-view and swerve across from the third lane. As I park up in front and turn off the ignition, a hand reaches between the front seats and points. "There's cops next block up."

An understatement. Fuckers are everywhere. A cop convention, flashing lights and all. I've seen this before. Every exit leaving Surfers Paradise has a Random Breath Testing unit. Nobody sneaks out of Party

Central unchecked. And while you're sitting here, sir, we'll give your licence and rego the once-over.

Each time leaving Surfers tonight I'll have to take a different exit. Breath testing will be unavoidable, but twenty times by the one unit, with a car full of tarts, may raise a constabulary eyebrow.

My immediate concern, however, is having swerved across three lanes. That won't have gone unnoticed. With so many brake lights coming on, plus flashing lights covering the street ahead, it's hard to make out what's happening.

"Where's the damn chase car?" I say to myself.

Three hookers in the car peer ahead.

"Chase car?" one asks.

"They always have a pursuit car hanging back, idling, ready to run down a bolter or— And here the bastard comes."

A marked car backs up flat maggot in case I'm considering doing a runner. Across the median strip another speeds to turn at the intersection and rush up behind me. They'll be licking lips and rubbing hands together. They think they've got a hot one dead to rights.

The cruiser's back end dips violently as it drops from high speed to zero in an instant. A larger-than-average cop quickly climbs out the passenger side and walks toward me carrying a portable breathalyser. The second cruiser screeches a U-turn at the lights and swings in behind. I smile innocent and wind down my window.

"Good evening, sir." He fiddles with breathalyser settings. "I noticed you pulled over before our roadblock."

"Yeah. Sorry. I'm picking someone up in this motel and didn't realize where I was." I hold my licence out between first and second fingers.

He takes it and has a gander. "Had any alcohol tonight, sir?"

"Not tonight," I say. "I'm the driver."

Laughter breaks out. Fran, in front, Babs the ear-licker and Jodi in back, think my statement funny.

"The driver," Fran repeats, amused.

The cop holds a dictaphone-looking gadget in front of my mouth and tells me to count to ten. I comply. He eyes the hookers individually, spotting Babs slightly longer than the others. One could say we appear nightclubbers, but who knows what a cop is thinking. Hopefully he won't find cause to search my car. With a couple hundred condoms, a dozen tubes of lube and dozens of credit card blanks of every ilk on board, it would soon become evident what we're up to. Plus I have four or five grand in my pocket while on the dole.

"Shouldn't laugh at that, ladies," he says. "A designated driver is always the responsible way to go."

Jodi laughs harder.

"Ignore the posse," I say. "They've had a few already." I am, of course, talking of fucks.

"What's a big boy like you," Babs asks, "doing working on a night like this? You should come out with us. Have a little fun."

Cop grins to himself while checking breathalyser readings. Negative. He nods at the cruiser behind, which backs up and takes off down the road. He passes back my licence, tells me to have a good night, gives each girl another look and climbs back into his patrol car.

They wave him off. Silly giggling smacks of alcohol. They've been drinking in hotel rooms. Not uncommon. I'm sure it helps them get through the odd unpleasant job. I take in this happy crew and wonder what their choice of drink might be. A couple drink wine, but I'm guessing it wouldn't be wine with a nose, a good year with a pleasant bouquet. It's doubtful they'd know Shiraz from Moselle. Cask wine for these lovelies. Bulk, housed in a thick silver bladder with a plastic tap. Chateau La Cardboard. Gonzo. Goon. Cardonnay. Death bag. Silver dream pillow. Auntie's choice. The ten-buck chuck. A red or white handbag.

"What time's your contest on, Myers?" Fran asks.

I glance at the dash clock. "I thought it was last hour. Maybe this one."

"Who you gunna take if you win?"

All three smirk. My losing has been prophesied.

"My boyfriend," I answer.

Jodi leans forward, elbows on top of the front seats, chin resting on interlaced fingers. "No really, who you taking?"

"Tell me what number state Hawaii is, and it'll be you." It's a safe call. Jodi's not the brightest.

She screws up her nose. "I didn't know the states were numbered."

"It's fifty," Fran says. "Admitted to the union in fifty-nine." She starts dancing in her seat. "Woohoo, I'm going to Honolulu."

I shake my head and click my tongue as if disappointed. "Damn, the bet wasn't with you."

"Then gimmie another one," she says quickly.

Babs springs to life. "You asked Jodi one, so give us all one. Just to be fair."

"Life isn't fair," I say. "Sorry."

"Come ooooon." Fran excitedly turns in her seat. "It'll be fun."

I try to recall the mountain of drivel — dribble — Fran's gushed during copious hours wasted in the car. She loathes television, so. . .

"You know the show *Married, with Children*?"

"I've heard of it."

"What's Peg Bundy's maiden name?"

"Fuck," she spits. "What kind of dumb question is that?"

"Wanker," I say.

"*You're* the fucking wanker."

"That's her name. She's a Wanker, from Wanker County."

I turn to sport-hating Babs, now wide-eyed with hopeful anticipation.

"Wanker!" Fran says in disbelief. "Her name is Wanker! Who the fuck is called Wanker! It's ridiculous!"

"Shuddup," Babs says. "He's going to ask me my question."

"Okay." I forget sport in favour of wine. "What's the name of air in the neck of a wine bottle between the cork and the wine's surface?"

Inspiring. Sometimes I amaze myself.

"Wanker!" Fran continues, now talking aloud to herself. "I'm going be looking that up on the innanet when I get home."

Babs whacks Fran's arm. "Shuddup. I'm trying to think of the answer."

"You haven't got a shit's show," Fran states.

Babs frowns. "Why would you need to name the air in the neck of a wine bottle, for fuck's sake?"

I tell her it's a mystery. "Maybe when the bottles are being filled by an apprentice, the boss can say to him, 'Hey, you're leaving too much *blank* in the bottle, put more wine in'."

Fran forgets the Wanker paradox and latches on to our fresh question. "Yeah, why *would* you need to name the air in a bottle? I mean, it's *nothing*. So why does it need a name? Maybe it's just air. Probably a trick question. Bit like asking what the gap is between your tits."

"That's cleavage," Babs says.

"No," Fran says. "Cleavage is the bit at the top of your tits that guys ogle when they're talking to you. Like when tradesmen kneel and show the crack in their arse. Builders' cleavage."

Pompeii bounds out of the motel, saving our conversation from further deterioration. If that were possible. She hands over the money, watches me count and add it to the mounting stash in my shirt pocket.

"Don't you trust me?" she asks.

She's new to the car, so receives the standard reply.

"If I'm short at the end of the night, it comes out of my pocket."

"Hey, Pompeii," Babs says, "what's the air in the neck of a wine bottle called?"

Pompeii shuffles about in now cramped conditions and pulls lipstick from her bag. "Who cares?"

My phone goes. We're off with fresh instructions. I drop Pompeii and Jodi at the same hotel suite before taking Fran to a private residence. It's a quiet, poorly lit street, so I park opposite and wait for the call that all is well. Eventually I'm informed four guys are inside, but only one is going to the bedroom with her. She'll stay.

A good girl, Fran. Most hookers would have left, job lost, or insisted the other men leave.

Babs exits to light a smoke. I lean back and close my eyes, but excited laughter pulls them open. Three teens holding beer cans rush out the client's front door, jump the banister and run around the side of the house. A minute later one runs back inside. He re-emerges with a lit cigarette and dashes back to join his mates. Fran unknowingly entertains the troops.

Another call comes. I tell Babs to get in, drive her to a hotel, then pick up Pompeii and Jodi before heading back for Fran. When she gets in, I smile.

"Fuck with the lights on?"

"Yeah," she says. "Why?"

"Curtains open as well?"

"Umm. Yeah. Why?"

"Because the other three watched through the window."

Eyes narrow, lips purse. "Little fuckers. I charge twenty dollars apiece if others want to watch."

She looks at me with hope, but she's wasting her time. I don't get paid more to retrieve her extras. Good luck to the little pervs.

While I count her money, Rick from the radio station calls.

"I was expecting a call last hour," I say.

"I make the rules on my show," he says. "You given more thought to taking Nikki to Hawaii?"

"Fraid not."

"Yeah? Well I'm going to ask about lyrics to a song that isn't on any album, and it wasn't a solo hit or duet. Ready to change your mind?"

"Do your best."

"I'm recording it to play in a few minutes. There's still time to change your mind."

"Won't be happening."

I shush the girls, turn off the radio and listen to Rick talk to the other contestant.

It begins.

Alllllllrighty. Again we have Myers on the line. And I don't mind telling you, folks, he's looking pretty unstoppable. You ready for this hour's question, Myers? Gotta tell you, it's a toughie.

"Hit me with it."

Okie-dokie. In what song does George sing. . . He rattles off six or seven colourful lines of a song not on any album. Son-of-a-bitch is mentioned, as is the word Fuck, and a hitchhiker's dubious gender.

He's got nothing. The bushpig's staying where she belongs, not in Hawaii meeting celebrities with me.

"Can you swear like that on the radio?" I ask.

Just Did.

"Can you repeat the question?"

Nope.

"Are you sure that's what he sings? I think he says—"

Just answer the question.

"Song's called *Happy.* "

Very good. Now. . .

What? No jolly correct-a-mundo?

I don't get a second question.

Next hour, Rick catches me off guard, so I pull over and kill the engine. Jodi ejects a Nelly CD, automatically bringing on the radio. I turn it off to avoid confusion.

Rick's getting desperate. Last hour I whipped his butt bad, so this time he feels me out by telling the question to be asked.

"This hour I'm gunna ask what the writing is on George's baseball cap in his *Too Funky* clip."

I'm ninety-nine percent it's KINGS. "Fine."

"Or I could ask a two-parter. The name of the Hollywood park he was arrested in for lewd behaviour, *and* the arresting officer's name."

The park isn't a problem. But who the hell would know the copper's name?

"Fine," I bluff. Recording begins.

Myers, I've got a two-parter for you this hour. For the first part, what was the name of the park in Hollywood where George was arrested in ninety-eight for a lewd act?

Fuck it! I'm royally shafted. Hideous visions of Nikki and me at the Hawaiian venue flash before my eyes. She has orange hair. Brightly coloured lei petals draped around her gruesome neck brown and shrivel at the mere touch of her skin.

But it's time to give in. At least now I *know* I'm going to Hawaii for the concert.

"I think it was Will Rogers Park," I say. "And did I tell you I've decided who I'll take on the trip if I win? It's Nikki, a friend of mine."

Girls in the back seat silently high-5 and jump about as best they can. They've just made money. Telly won't be happy. Is that him I hear screaming from the other side of town?

Well, that's nice. Now the second part of the question is, what song did he make after his arrest? Hah, hah, hah. He did the corresponding video in a toilet.

"*Outside*," I say dejectedly.

Correct-a-mundo.

"Nikki!" Jodi spits. "You don't mean. . ."

She's trying to be funny. Sarcastic funny. While the others continue partying silently, rocking the car, I shush her in case a second question comes my way. It doesn't. I hang up and begin banging my head against the steering wheel.

"I don't want to talk about it," I say to her, my forehead numbing from the abuse.

"But what if Babs gets her wine bottle question right?"

I stop my self-chastisement long enough to give Jodi a look. The two in back continue joyfully punching the air, singing, foot-tapping the floor, shoulder dancing.

"I watched *The English Patient* the other night," Pompeii says while jiving, "and I think yours is a question like when the fellah always asks what that V-dip at the bottom of a woman's throat is called." She touches the hollow at the front of her neck. "Let's face it, nobody knows that sort of thing, but it keeps going all through the movie until they finally tell you."

"So what's it called?" Fran asks.

"Can't remember."

My head resumes hitting the steering wheel.

I'm going to Hawaii.

Bushpig in tow.

10

Brendan jerks his head at me and we walk out the side gate. From his car boot he removes a slightly smaller but equally well-travelled hard plastic suitcase as the one he buried at my place.

"The restaurant kitchen's being renovated. Can't leave this hidden out there. Can you bury it with the other one?" He hands it to me. "Thanks, buddy."

"Something going on I should know about?"

"Like what?"

I secure the case in my boot. "I don't know. Maybe you're worried about something. I wonder if I turned up at your restaurant for breakfast tomorrow there'd be any workmen in the kitchen."

He laughs and pats my shoulder. "If I didn't know better, I'd say you were concerned."

"Fuck off. I've been dreaming how to spend all that money. Now I'm guessing I'll have to dream a little harder."

"It's good having a mate you trust completely. Not many people have that."

What is this? Men like us never say such things. Soppy shit like that is implied — never spoken. No communication shall be entered into. Ever. Something is definitely going on.

"Maybe this is a good time to tell you I fucked your wife."

He smiles, leans back and opens his arms. "See what I mean? We even know when each other's kidding."

"She wasn't very good, either."

"Hawaii with the bushpig." The butt of his palm smacks my forehead. "What the hell were you thinking last night?"

"Didn't have a choice. She must want someone to go with, or take her, and I'm the mug."

"Mug? I would have used something a little stronger." He jumps in his gangsta-rapper Bentley, starts up and winds down the window. "Hawaii with the bushpig," he says again, adding a laugh.

With a quiet hum his window goes up. He rolls almost silently down the driveway and speeds off. I open my boot and pop the suitcase latches. More bundles of cash. Mostly fifties, with a few wads of hundreds and twenties scattered about. On top sits an empty envelope with two columns of increasing crossed-out tallies between three and ten thousand, ending with four hundred and forty-two thousand.

I lock everything up and return inside. The girls' room must be smoke-filled, as Heidi now sits drinking coffee with Telly. I make one for myself. Tandi appears dressed in white lingerie and waits while the kettle boils again. Straight black hair touching her shoulders frames a better than average face. Weight is at the crossroads. One more iced cake and her developing middle and sides may be interpreted as fat. A short time off the booze while eating healthy would dramatically slim her down, accentuate those curves.

"What are you two perverts staring at?" she asks.

I look at Telly, who looks at me. Could be we're both making the same assessment.

"They were wondering," Heidi says, "why you get picked over other girls so much."

That has been a topic of conversation in the car on more than one occasion. Must be similar in Telly's car.

"I do anal," Tandi says casually, then grins. "*Real* well. I enjoy it. My husband and I use it as a form of contraception."

Sounds to me like her husband's not interested in her other assets. Probably gay. And if hubby's talked her into that and nothing else, she'll deserve the prolapsed anus and butt plug later in life once sphincter muscles are shot.

The office phone rings and tonight's receptionist, Double-U Double-U Double-U Dot, picks up. She leans back in her chair and looks at Heidi drinking coffee.

"She's very petite," wwwDot says into the phone, "but busty. Shoulder length blonde hair. About twenty, with a nice personality."

"*And. . .*" Heidi hotfoots it into the office to whisper in wwwDot's ear. WwwDot doesn't add to the description before hanging up. Then both hookers return to the girls' room.

"Okay, what did she say?" Telly asks.

WwwDot looks through the security mesh. "If she wanted you to know, she would have told you."

"Come on wwwDot," I add. "We won't say anything."

She's putty. Hesitation lasts less than a second before giving in. "She said she was also shaved."

Big deal. Most these girls are. Heidi must be a tad self-conscious about it. Modesty, no matter how slight, is unusual around these parts. A short time later the door opens and in she walks.

"BALDY!" I yell.

Heidi stops, shoots wwwDot a filthy look and disappears back through the door. WwwDot forwards us that same look.

"You two better not start tonight. Last time you both got going we lost a girl." She gives Telly the evil eye. "And everybody's in a bad mood because they consider the radio contest run and won, and you won't pay them out."

"The contest isn't over," Telly replies. "Plane and concert tickets don't have names on them. Nobody's won anything yet."

Two clients arrive. WwwDot greets them and returns. One is here for Tandi. I run into the office, push the intercom button and inform Tandi her arse is required down here immediately. WwwDot mumbles an outcall better come soon to split us drivers up.

Tandi enters the kitchen and Telly bursts into song.

" *Tandi takes it up the arse, do-da, do-da.*"

She ignores us and escorts her butt-fucker to a room. WwwDot spies something on the carpark monitor.

"Can one of you guys. . ." She exits the office for the open side door. "I'd better do it myself."

The next girl wanders into the lounge to meet the second client. WwwDot returns with Porsche and a new Asian girl toting gym bags over their shoulders. On holiday a couple of months, Porsche immediately spots Telly's shaved head.

"You got cancer or something?"

"Only a little bit."

"Oh. Right," she says awkwardly. An arm goes around her Asian friend. "My mate needs a working name, guys. Tried coming up with one in the car, but hit a blank."

I look back to Telly. "How many names you reckon there are? Millions?"

"Billions," he says.

"Well, it's a toughie alright. What's her real name?"

"Nir Too Son," Porsche says.

"I dub thee Phoenix."

"I like it, Myers," Porsche says. "How did you get it so quick?"

"You said her name is Near Tucson. So is Phoenix."

Porsche thinks it over. "But clients might also know that, and guess her real name. Can't have johns knowing our real names."

"Tell me you're fucking kidding."

"Why would I be kidding?" She holds a hand toward Telly. "Heard the radio last night. I've got heeeeaps of money coming."

"Not yet you don't."

Porsche's eyes spring wide with horror. "Pompeii told me she gave you my money."

"She did. You got tickets yet, Myers?"

"Not yet," I tell him.

"See. Contest isn't over. Myers may not win yet."

She stands akimbo. "I didn't bet he would win. Like everyone else, I bet he couldn't go without taking Nikki. And Myers said last night on the radio that he was taking her."

Telly shrugs. "No one's going anywhere yet."

"You hear this, Dot? Telly isn't paying out."

WwwDot ceases writing next week's receptionists' roster. "Contest isn't finished yet, sweetie. We're all in the same boat. But don't worry, Telly's going to hurt."

Mercedes joins us from the girls' room. Telly's gaze moves from her to Porsche. "All we need now," he says, "is a Honda, a Subaru or something, and we can open a car yard."

"Yeah," I say, "but would you buy something with so many miles on it?"

"Still some mileage left yet," Telly says. "Ay ladies?"

"You better believe it," Mercedes says.

Porsche removes her jacket and pulls back her shoulders. "Probably more than you two can handle."

Tonight, Mercedes' stilettos are thin black leather straps on clear plastic platforms and heels.

"What's with the Tupperware shoes?" Telly asks.

"Arsehole," she says caustically. "You wouldn't be saying that if you knew how much they cost."

"Yes. I would."

"Can't you do something about these two, Dot?" She enters the lounge to meet the remaining client. When she returns my eyebrows rise.

"Mister Right, is he?"

"They're all Mister Right," Telly says, "if they've got money in their pocket."

Mercedes looks a little forlorn. "I don't think he likes me."

"That's because you've got a handicap," I say.

She puts hand on hip. "Yeah? And what would that be?"

"You're a member of the itty-bitty-titty brigade."

"Fuck you," she says, and leaves. The others follow.

WwwDot gets a call and puts it on speaker.

"Hello."

"Yeah, how much for you to come to my place for an hour?"

"That depends on where you are, sweetie," she says. "But it would start about two-twenty."

"Um, can I do that for half cash and half credit card?"

"Sure. Give me your card details and I'll check it for you."

He becomes defensive. "Ah, I don't want to give you my card number over the phone."

"I'm sorry, sweetie, but I can't come without confirming your details."

"Umm," he says. "How bout half cash, half dope?"

WwwDot hangs up. Telly shakes his head. A missed opportunity.

Now wearing only a lacy white bra and short black skirt, Porsche comes back into the kitchen, followed by Heidi. Porsche's bra cups are definitely larger and filled out more than when she left for a break. New tits.

"So, Porsche," I say, "what have you been doing for the last couple of months?"

"You've noticed them." Genuinely excited, she approaches, unhooks her bra and lets it slide down her arms. "Feel them."

I cup both, then squeeze gently before feeling them head on.

"Magnificent, export quality bolt-ons. How much?"

She slips her bra back on. "You can get a boob-job for five or six grand. Half that if you want to travel to Asia. These babies cost sixteen and a half." She smiles. "The bank owns them at the moment, but let the bastards try and take them back."

"And worth every cent," I say earnestly.

"Jeez, tell me about it. Guys open doors for me now."

Heidi unbuttons her top and pulls it open. "These are just as good. And they only cost a third of that." She takes up position in front of me. "Go on. Tell me."

Just moving toward me they appear slightly rigid and a fraction rounder than normal breasts. Open the bra and *ping!* they could take a fucking eye out. She could almost rest her chin on the damn things. I say "Life's a buffet of grotesque choices" then massage both as instructed. It confirms my initial assessment: less pliable than Porsche's, but still nice to look at.

Leaving little to the imagination, Phoenix enters the kitchen wearing high heels, G-string and tiny bikini top. Before meeting the second client, she silently frowns at what could appear to be me groping a girl.

"What about my jugs?" Heidi says.

I shake my head. "Nice, but Porsche wins."

"Only by a nipple," Telly says. "But I really need a little feel to make sure."

"Fuck you," the girls say together. They leave the room.

"Maybe you've got clammy hands," I say.

Telly shrugs. "Must be it."

I rinse my cup and place it back on the table. Ramone appears from the girls' room before meeting the client. In her usual sullen, anti-social manner, we drivers are ignored. The snub doesn't upset us, for we know she hates all men. Dyke with a chip on her shoulder.

Sure enough, she returns, stands by the sink making a cup of tea and bitches to wwwDot.

"Arsehole thinks he can impress everyone with how much he owns and how many people work for him. Probably bullshitting anyway. They're the reason I gave up the corporate world. Pigs like him place the glass ceiling, so we get nowhere without their benevolence or having to suck their tiny dicks. Might as well screw the pricks here and get paid for doing it."

Her diatribe seems a little more full-on tonight. Could be she's pissed off that radio competition money has yet to be paid out. Who knows? Who cares? But I'm betting in her present mood it wouldn't take much to get her going.

Telly also thinks so. His smiling head rises from the newspaper and he begins his taunt.

"Stuff the glass ceiling," he says to everyone present. "Women should be made to work on a glass *floor*."

"So we can look up their dresses," I add.

"Course. Panties should be outlawed as well." Ramone hasn't bitten, so he changes tack. "Watched a great lesbian movie this morning. Like them, Myers?"

"Who doesn't like long-legged blonde horny lesbians acting in true-to-life porno flicks? Real hot lesbian babes who like men joining in as well."

We both look at her, those harsh, thin lips clamped so tight her mouth turns white. Our eyebrows rise innocently in unison.

"What?" we say together.

Tandi returns wrapped in a towel, job money in hand, interrupting our moment.

Telly looks her up and down. "Up the rectum, for contraception! Up the bum, no harm done! Up the skids, you get no kids!"

"Right, Myers," wwwDot says, "take three girls and head into town. *Now!*"

"Yeah," Telly says. "You shit-stirring bastard. And make sure Nikki's one of them."

I look at wwwDot and wait for a ruling on who goes with me.

"Just take three of the usual and go."

I stand, smile at Telly and wobble my head cock-of-the-walk style. "You know what that means, buddy."

His smile turns to a scowl. "Get a fat one up ya."

11

The remainder of my required ten points were put together that night. It was easy. Rick told me the answers before going to air. So it's pretty much done and dusted. Unless another person next week somehow gets ten points, then beats me in a playoff — an impossibility, Rick says — concert tickets, airfares and accommodation are mine and Nikki's.

I should feel sorry for poor schmucks getting excited when they make it on air, but I can't. I'm the one going to Hawaii, so fuck them.

Shift divvy-up complete, looking decidedly green about the gills, Telly bundles me up beside my car.

"What have you got up your sleeve?" he asks hopefully.

"For what?"

"This fucking competition. How are you going to go without Nikki?"

"Can't. It's fixed. How am I supposed to unfix it?"

"I figured you were smarter than her."

"It's not a case of who's smarter. I had no idea her brother was running the damn thing."

One of three girls waiting to be driven home toots Telly's car horn. He looks back and waves them off.

"You got any idea how much I'm going to be out of pocket?"

"Not my problem."

"Mate, you need incentive. If you can swing it somehow, there's a couple of grand in it for you."

"Let me get this straight. You'll give me . . . three gorillas if I go without Nikki?"

His shoulders droop. "Fuck it. Okay, three grand. So you *have* got something on the go."

"Nope. But for three gorillas I'll give it some serious thought."

Now he snarls. "Like you weren't already thinking about how to not take Nikki."

"Remember, mate," I smile and slap his bicep, "we have one major advantage."

"Yeah, yeah. I know," he says. "We're dealing with hookers."

"Not what I was going to say, but it'll do."

I head home. Driving in the open gate, Vanessa's Merc sweeps in behind and follows me up to the shack. I don't recall telling her my address. Maybe she sat out of sight at the bottom of the hill and followed me up. We get out and kiss hello.

"You following me?"

"I've taken the day and thought you might fancy an early blowjob."

"I like the way you think."

Vanessa's choice, the London Symphony Orchestra grinds out Khachaturian's *Spartacus* on my CD player. Not what I would have chosen, but after George Michael 24/7 it's a pleasant alternative.

She reclines on a deckchair while viewing giant rectangular sugarcane fields blanketing the valley. A large white 'The Dingo is

Innocent' T-shirt taken from my drawer covers her torso. Giveaway plastic yellow Budweiser sunglasses shade her eyes. My clothes tend to be stored a lot while I work abroad. I sit on a canvas chair wearing black rugby shorts not worn since high school.

"Some view," Vanessa says, one elegant leg bent slightly upward, tanning in the mid-morning sun.

"Yeah. Not bad."

Her head rolls to see the direction of my leer. "Want to make love?"

"That sounds like hard work. We could fuck."

"Hmmm."

"The minute I laid eyes on you I knew you were going to be difficult."

"Oh I doubt you remember the first time you laid eyes on me."

"So why the hell did you take me home as drunk as I must have been?"

"I knew you'd be . . . entertaining. In a good way. Totally different. My intuition is paying off beyond expectations." She smiles. "Feeling pressure to maintain your outstanding beginning?"

"Define pressure."

"Hmmm. And so it continues."

"Looking forward to Hawaii?" I ask.

She sips from her water bottle. "I thought you were taking some other woman."

"I am. But I'm also taking you, so you don't sue."

"Just the three of us. How cosy."

My microwave pings. I go inside, make up a tray of beer, a couple of forks, plates, hot macaroni and cheese TV dinners, and tomato sauce. Outside, I place a dinner on each plate, covering mine with a layer of tomato sauce. Vanessa opens a beer and tentatively accepts a fork. I dig in. She pokes hers a bit before spearing a single piece of cheese-covered macaroni.

"I could cook something," she says.

"We're eating everything edible in the house."

"Hmm."

Brendan's farm ute drives up. He parks beside Vanessa's Merc, finishes a phone call, climbs out and rounds the shack.

"What's happening?" he asks.

Vanessa sips beer. "Myers is trying to dazzle me with his culinary skills."

"One learns a lot of etiquette in the Peruvian jungle," he says. "Notice how he doesn't tip the macaroni onto the plate. Saves washing up."

"Pull up a pew," I tell him.

"Like to, buddy, but I came to see if you were using your car."

Car borrowing used to occur when either of us was having girlfriend trouble and didn't want to be spotted by the girl's friends while out and about. I doubt this is one of those occasions.

"I'm not going anywhere," I tell him. "Did you know that—?"

"James Bond drives one?" he cuts in. "Yeah. You've told me five hundred fucking times. You are aware he's not a real person?"

"Now it's five hundred and one."

He goes inside and exits twirling keys around his finger. "You take care of that thing for me?"

Shit. The second money case, still in my boot, completely forgotten about.

"They're now side by side," I lie "Kissin cousins."

He grins at me like he read my face and knows I'm lying. "It's still in your fucking boot, isn't it."

"Is that a statement or a question?"

He shakes his head forlornly while walking to the shed. Vanessa and I hear a rattly old roller-door go up, followed by a deep, throaty engine kick into life. The revving car backs out and rumbles along slowly behind the shack. Knowing it can't be my Nissan, she turns and watches an almost new metalic dark grey Aston Martin roll down the fenceline, through the gate and speed off.

"Hmm," she says. "Leased?"

"Deceased estate. They were practically giving it away. Did you know James Bond drives an Aston Martin?"

"I've heard that before somewhere. Recently."

When our ninety-eight percent fat free meals are finished, I take the tray inside and bring out a couple of fresh Heinies. I plump back in my chair and hand Vanessa a bottle.

"You never talk about yourself," she says.

"What do you want to know?"

"Tel me about Peru."

"Not very exciting."

"Tell me anyway."

"Ran a couple of gold mines. A comparatively small outfit. Employed five hundred or so locals."

"Make a lot of money?"

"Me, or the mines?"

"Yes."

I remove my own Budweiser glasses and wipe lenses on my pants. "They weren't doing much when I got there. Well, they were, but there was pilfering left, right and sideways. Couldn't really blame them, I suppose. Poor bastards only made about fifty cents a week in wages."

"So you stopped the pilfering?"

"Implemented a few changes. I hired a few Ukrainian mercenaries to keep an eye on the thieving bastards. Profits went up considerably.

Until then I had no idea so much was being stolen. The only thing wrong with that was, I figured those Ukrainians might get greedy. Plus the local go-betweens who'd been buying the stolen gold for next to nothing were also getting bitchy. So I hired an ex-SAS thug to watch my back. You should have seen this guy. The real deal. Walked the walk, guns strapped to his belt, Bowie knife in each boot, muscles up the wazoo. The Ukrainians hadn't seen anything like him either. A real killer. But loyal."

"What was his name?"

"The locals had a name for him that I was told meant Black Tiger. Don't know why. He was white as. His clothes were always really creased to shit. He turned up with four complete sets of camouflage clothes: four army shirts and pants, eight socks and four undies, and two pairs of boots. End of each day he'd hand wash his one, sometimes two, sets of clothes, hang them up, and once dry, ram them back into his duffle bag while he wore a fresh set.

"What was his real name?"

"Francis."

"Why weren't you worried about *him* getting greedy?"

"He was recommended by a friend, so I wasn't really worried about my safety. Least not from him. He gave me a gun to wear. I had it strapped to my leg like in the Wild West. It was cool. He had a good sense of humour, too, which made things easier. But what made me trust him most was, he didn't want any payment until we left. So, anything happened to me, he missed out."

I'm making light of what was, for the most part, a very serious and tense way of living. Sleep with one eye open, safety off. The second last mine manager just disappeared. The next guy was brutally gutted. Because of this I was able to negotiate a percentage of the profits for myself. But Francis and I both knew we were damn lucky to survive almost two years, isolated, the middle of nowhere.

"An SAS-trained killer," Vanessa says. "Named Francis. With a sense of humour. Living in the jungles. You, his sidekick, wears a gun — shall we say a six-shooter — on your hip like Wyatt Earp, likes Nelly, George Michael, and thinks all is . . . cool with the world. You're both living amongst five hundred-odd peasants with gold fever whom you've cut off from thieving themselves and their families a decent living."

"Ah, he was *my* sidekick. And you forgot about the local nasty gold dealers who had it in for me. And the mercenaries."

"The Russians."

"Ukrainians."

"Okay." Vanessa smiles. "So how come you've never married?"

Wow. I'm no English professor, but *Okay* seems a poor segue from Peruvian goldmines to marriage. Seems she was getting that one out there no matter what. At this point a lesser bachelor would run a finger round the inside of his collar and take an audible gulp.

"Never said I haven't been married." I go inside to answer the phone and don a baseball cap. When I come back she shamelessly jumps back in.

"Have you? Been married?"

"Nope."

She sits quiet for a minute.

"Engaged?"

"Most women I get to meet are smokers or slinkys. Sometimes both."

"Slinkys?"

"They enjoy being pushed down stairs."

"Hmm," she says to herself, almost gloomily. "And they always seem to go back for more."

This is insightfulness on a morbid subject that I hadn't expected. I hope it wasn't achieved through personal experience.

We sip our beers and stare out over the gold and green, sun-soaked valley. A trickle of sweat runs down behind my left ear.

"Whose is the academy award?" I ask.

"Father's. Got it for a documentary he made. He died."

Not big on false sentimentality, I let that pass without comment.

"This beer's still making me horny," Vanessa says after a few minutes. "You?"

"Sure."

"Want to do something about it?"

"If I must."

"Don't worry, when we get to Hawaii this horrid experience we're about to undertake will be but a distant memory."

We do it on the deckchair, straining hinges until its back gives and we drop awkwardly. I don't let it put me off stride.

12

A new, sturdier deckchair with thicker tubing and tougher joints sits on the Nissan's back seat as I drive Heidi into an old fogies' home. To all intents and purposes it's a hospice. However, nobody will call it that. Inhabitants may not be at death's door, with terminal diseases, but they're closer to it than most. And let's face it, when hygiene starts slipping, even your kids don't want you around. There should be a sign over the entrance: 'See what's coming? Save your pennies.'

The complex is so big it must be government funded. Surrounded by huge wire fences, drab two-storey brick 'dorms' fan out from an administration block and other odd shaped communal buildings. A few Nazi uniforms and this could be Auschwitz with a lick of paint.

We drive around but can't find the required building. Although just past noon, nobody we can ask directions walks about the paths.

Heidi frowns. "I thought retirement villages were nice villas built around golf courses."

"This one's on the taxpayer dime."

We pass an unloved tennis court with a drooping net.

"Wouldn't want to end up living like this," she says. "It's awful."

"Don't piss off your kids."

"Why would that matter?"

"You'll find out."

Pretending knowledge of the place, we continue our snail's pace further into the maze. Soon it's obvious we're going in circles. I'm recognizing the same weed-infested gardens around brick buildings. With so many idle geezers about, one would imagine these gardens would be the epitome of colourful Gold Coast bloom. Maybe I'm stereotyping old geezers.

Another few minutes brings us no closer to our objective. We can't go back to administration for directions without embarrassing the client, so I pull over to call our receptionist. She'll have to ring the guy for more precise directions.

Half way into the dial, a stocky smock-wearing matron rounds a building, walking toward us. Heidi grabs the john's particulars off the dash and says she'll ask her. I quickly tell her not to, but she's out the door and takes a couple of steps. They stop, facing each other, Heidi's arms crossed under her tits, matron's face neutral. Their conversation flows through Heidi's open window.

"Hiiiiii," Heidi says "Can you tell me where block four is?"

"Sure," the stern Frau says. She clocks Heidi's black mini, black high heels, tight white top. "Who you looking for?"

The return question. Merely one of a thousand things that could bring Heidi unstuck, as thinking on one's feet is unfamiliar territory.

"Allan. He's an old friend of the family."

Now I cop an eyeballing. As long as I'm stereotyping, I'd say it's par for the course all stocky matrons are nosy and can smell a rat. I flash a smile to put her off the scent.

"Allan who? We've got a few, and I know everyone here."

The john's surname already forgotten, Heidi shifts her feet, says, "Umm," then not very surreptitiously twists her wrist to look down at the piece of paper. "Allan Campbell."

Matron flicks her head, indicating a two-storey block we already passed twice, and walks on. Heidi gets back in and we roll across to the front door.

"Jeez, that was a bit awkward," she says.

"You handled it well," I lie. She smiles while exiting the car.

After receiving the All's Well call, I leave the compound to park outside. Sixty minutes later the Pick Up call comes and I cruise back in. Matron watches me pass from an admin window. I'd like to give her the finger, but in Queensland a little indiscretion may mean handcuffs.

Heidi ambles out and gets in the car. "What a nice old bastard he was."

"Yeah? How old?"

"Ninety-six."

"Jesus. Hope I can still get it up at that age."

"His chest was wired up to a machine."

"So he didn't want sex?"

Her head flips playfully from side to side. "Weeell, not really. But I sorta got it up for him and played with it for a while. He didn't cum of course. I think he just wanted some company. Got anywhere else to go?"

"If the day driver's at the house, my day's done. I'm dropping you off and getting on the piss."

Leaving via a different exit, we pass a grey marble memorial sitting just inside the gate. A tasteful, waist high semi-circle with IN MEMORY OF THE FALLEN engraved at its centre. Water cascades into a plain round pond at the base. This place must be some kind of war veterans' home.

"In memory of the felon," Heidi says. "Why would they put that there?"

"Beats me. Maybe it's a home for old criminals fallen on hard times. Must be a few of those around."

"That's a bit weird."

"Isn't it."

She puts a cigarette in her mouth, looks at me and removes it. I turn up the stereo to discourage further discourse.

Slowing for an amber light, a white van honks, swings out and overtakes us. It speeds through the red light while the driver shows me his rigid middle finger.

"What's his problem?" Heidi asks.

Blue block lettering on the van's side reads Pliver's Roofing and Tiling. I reach into the glovebox for a small alphabetized schoolbook. Under *P* I write Pliver's roofing and tiling. Under *R* I write Pliver's roofing, and under *T*, Pliver's tiling.

"What's the book for?"

"It's the naughty book," I tell her, placing it back in the glovebox. "If work needs doing at home I don't call anyone in the naughty book."

"Why not?"

"You drive a vehicle with a firm's name on the side, while on the road you're as good as an ambassador for that company. If he drives like a moron, he obviously doesn't give a shit about the people who pay his wages, keeping him and his family alive. So he's not likely to give a rat's about any work he does at a stranger's place, is he."

"Yeah, spose not."

We cruise back and enter through the brothel's side gate. Three hookers lay stretched out sunbathing topless on long pool lounges. At the timberyard next door, a couple of twelve or thirteen year-old boys sit on

116

stacks of lumber, peaking over the fence. The girls have no idea they're being watched.

Now the pervs have been sprung, they raise their heads. "Show us ya pink bits!" one calls.

Gina sits up and turns. "Why aren't you little scrotes in school?"

"At least turn your chairs around and take your knickers off."

"Piss off," I add, with little conviction.

"C'mon, mate," he says, "chuck us one over the fence."

"Trust me, kid, you don't want one of these."

"Course they do," Gina says. She stands to ad-lib a little tease. Hips gyrate and shoulders jump, jiggling her breasts. The other two girls egg her on.

The second kid finally speaks. "Fuck's sake. Time you got a boob-job, ain't it? Fuckers are more saggy than my mother's, and she's twice your age, with three kids."

Gina stops dancing. Her good-humoured smile morphs into loathing. Impulsively, she picks up a towel, scrunches it into a ball and throws it at the boys. It sails over their heads into the lumberyard. She bites her lip.

"Ahhh, shit! That was my own towel." She moves toward them. "Toss it back will you, guys?"

"Yeah, sure," the first says. "After we've wanked into it a few times." They laugh and jump from their timber pile.

"Bastards."

I enter the office and drop money in front of Billie. Phone to ear, she looks up, eyes rolling. I push the speaker button and hear Tammy doing an impression of a crack addicted pessimist.

". . .and my mother died two weeks ago, that's why I started gambling. I'm destitute. I can't find my son. I think his father's taken him. I owe over" — an audible drag and exhale on a cigarette — "four thousand to guys who'll be round here looking for it in the" — drag and exhale — "morning. Nobody gives a fuck what happens to me. I could be dead tomorrow and nobody would care. It's a full moon tonight. Lots of people commit suicide in" — another drag — "full moons."

"You know the rules," Billie says. "You missed your shift last night without word, so you don't come in tonight."

"But I couldn't get to a phone."

"How many times do I have to tell you?"

Billie looks pleadingly at me, so I reach over and press the hung-up button.

"Wish I could do that," she says. "I just can't seem to hang up mid conversation."

Good thing she's now running the small day crew. Night girls eat her alive.

"When Sally's not here and you're in that chair, you're God."

The phone rings. Billie answers, puts it on speaker. It's Lisa.

"Can you have me picked up later?"

Billie checks the long list of names on a roster pinned to the wall. "You're not down for tonight. You were supposed to be here yesterday. You put yourself on. We lost four jobs because I told clients you would be here."

"Yeah, I know. But I thought I'd come in tonight instead."

"Sorry."

Lisa's irked. Thinks she's indispensable. A poor combination.

"Well, if I can't come in today, take me off the roster for the rest of the week."

"Fine. Take the rest of the year off while you're at it." Billie breaks the connection and holds up her hand.

I high-5 her. "Who can we stick it to next?"

Nobody. After I pick up Dita from a job and run her home, I'm done for the day.

Sitting outside a massive block of units not far from the brothel, I'm wondering how Dita got here. Then I begin wondering where she is. A phone call to Billie sheds a little light. Dita rang out but is having a shower. Give it a few minutes.

"How did she get here?"

"Brian stopped in, paid for an hour, and they took a taxi to his place. I didn't think it would matter. He's in here twice a week, and Dita was going home straight after the job anyway."

"Don't let Sally know you did that."

Dita keeps me waiting. Typical. Everything runs on her timetable. The other girls hate her. She thinks she's a notch above. I'm not a prostitute, I'm an escort. One of them.

The waiting begins eating into my drinking time. I ring Billie and ask her to ring Brian's place, or Dita's phone. She does so while I wait. Both phones are switched off. I ask for his address. She doesn't know it. And this is why you don't send girls off on their own.

Anyone other than Dita, I'd consider banging on doors. But numbers on letterboxes run into the nineties. Fuck that. I could grab another girl from the brothel and bring her back to point out his unit, but Dita would undoubtedly come out while I'm gone.

Stewing nicely another thirty minutes, I notice my least favourite bumper sticker on the rear window of a mid-sized station wagon in front. MAGIC HAPPENS, with all its surrounding sparkly crap. I survey the area, surrounding buildings and street facing windows. Spotting nobody, I open the glovebox and grab my specially made stickers. I pull the top one through the rubber band, get out and walk casually to the car in front. Under their sticker, I stick mine on the paintwork, then return.

Below MAGIC HAPPENS it reads MOODY BITCH SEEKS NICE GUY FOR LOVE/HATE RELATIONSHIP.

The handiwork momentarily takes my mind from Dita's tardiness. But seeing the slack cow stumble through the gate jolts me back.

She tosses bags on the back seat, then climbs in front. Her hair's wet, she's drunk and smiling stupidly. "Heee. Sorry."

I start up and speed off. She lives the other end of the coast. I won't be at the pub for at least ninety minutes.

"Forty minutes I've been waiting."

"Well, you couldda rung me."

"I shouldn't have to ring you. Put your fucking belt on."

The drama queen doesn't like my tone.

"WHY SHOULD I?!" she yells.

Stroppy. Lovely. Nothing like a dame who can't hold her drink. It startles me so much I swing over and stop.

"Put your belt on or you'll be walking home."

I get a filthy, defiant look as she yanks the belt across her chest and snaps it in place. I re-join traffic hoping like hell she continues the lip service.

She does.

"Well you couldda rang me." It's not as loud, but a rebellious edge remains.

"You rang out forty minutes ago and said you were coming out."

That's it. A rancorous combination of booze and hot temper take over.

"IT'S ALL VERY WELL FOR YOU SITTING DOWN HERE IN YOUR CAR, I'M THE ONE WHO'S GOTTA SERVICE THE CLIENTS AND—"

That'll do it. She implies I forced her into this vocation, or I'm pimping her out against her will. Again I jerk the car over, reach across and swing her door open.

"Get out."

It takes a moment before she figures Right to be on her side. And why not, in her mind she's one of a kind. A star.

"Fuck you. You can't kick me out."

"Just did. Now get out before I throw you out."

Defiantly she sits there, nose in the air. I reach into the back seat, drag her bags over and dump them on her lap. She looks daggers at me. It's an expensive cab ride home or a couple of hours on two or three buses.

"You'll have to take me home! My phone battery's dead! Now FUCKING TAKE ME HOME YA FUCKING ARSEHOLE!"

She doesn't get it. The ride's over. I pick up her stuff and toss it to the grass verge.

"I'LL BE TALKING TO SALLY AND BRENDAN ABOUT THIS!" she yells, stumbling out. "YOU'RE FUCKING FINISHED."

Without waiting for the door to slam, I jump the car forward to close it. I can hear amber fluid calling my name.

Tomorrow it will be headlines at the brothel. Maybe it'll even stop them misbehaving in the cars for a while. But within twenty-four hours it will be business as usual.

Fastlove sips his first red wine of the day. A cheaper variety, but at least he knows the difference. I put my beer down and slump on an uncomfortable wooden chair opposite.

His book lowers and he gives the standard opening. "Let's have it."

"Remind me why you left teaching."

"At the start of each year I liked to get an idea of my students' command — or lack thereof — of the English language. So on Day One I always asked for a five thousand word essay on the Bible. I explained it could be about a person, a story, even why they didn't know a single thing about the Bible. Anything. Possibly a fable they thought was *worthy* of the Bible. The spectrum was virtually limitless. Two weeks later, after they were all handed in, I pick up the first paper, written by a sixteen-year-old young lady. Her opening line read 'Christianity wasn't very popular before Jesus showed up, and when he did, he tried to turn everyone into Catholics'."

We chuckle.

"Okay," I say. "I'll start my story, and you can finish it."

He lights a cigarette, nods slowly.

"Mesha takes a few days off to go with her boyfriend further up the coast for a dirty weekend. He can't afford it, naturally, so she's paying accommodation, gas, food, the lot. This guy's a bus driver, so he told his wife he's taking a busload of Jap tourists up the Sunshine Coast for a golfing weekend. WwwDot hears this and asks Mesha, 'If he's supposedly working all weekend, won't his wife wonder why his pay-packet's light?' To which Mesha replies. . . "

Fastlove grins. "Love is blind. So she also made up the three-day shortfall in his pay packet. Wonderful. *Wonderful.* Where the hell do you find these gullible tarts? And more to the point, where can I find myself one?"

Dee wanders out of the bar carrying a salad roll and a pack of cigarettes. She parks herself beside me and peels cling wrap from her lunch.

"Hey, Myers," she says.

No greeting for Fastlove. He's plied her with poetry and liquor and had his way. Chase over, he's no longer interested.

"Dee," I answer.

Unperturbed by her snub, Fastlove returns to his book. Dee lights a cigarette, rests it on the overflowing ashtray's lip, and bites into her roll.

"So," I say, "found any bigger dicks?"

Sipping wine, Fastlove has a sudden convulsive cough/laugh.

"You okay, mate?" I enquire. "Not choking, are you?"

He puts down the glass to flick wine spots from his lap.

"I listened to the words of that son *Fastlove*, Myers," Dee says.

I raise eyebrows. "Yeah?"

"Yeah. Seems you were right."

I spread my hands. "Usually am."

She chews some salad roll, sucks in a huge amount of smoke before swallowing the food, then looks at me slyly and blows it out. "You got a girlfriend?"

Fastlove's shoulders jump about in silent laughter.

"Boyfriend," I say.

13

Although not working tonight, Telly shows up, right arm in a sling, a fibreglass cast from wrist to elbow. In less than a day his kids have covered it with smutty graffiti. Broken in two places, a screwed-in metal pin holds shattered bone together. Removing a bandaid reveals eight stitches in his cheek. One eye shines black. His car is totalled. He's not a happy camper.

"Mate," I say, "if there was any doubt you were ugly before. . ."

He waits until four girls are huddled together, engrossed in personal matters, before conveying his sad tale at the kitchen table.

Approaching an intersection where another driver had, despite having right of way, stopped, Telly also stops. Both jump and hold, twice. Figuring the other clown will keep still, Telly inches forward, then goes for it. Wrong choice. The other guy puts his foot down and cleans Telly up big time.

"So I'm sitting there," he says, minimum gesticulation, "glass everywhere, his Roo-bars in my face, and blood's cascading out my cheek like Niagara fucking Falls. This arm's pointing north, south, east and west. Then he backs up and takes off, smacking my front fender as if driving home the point he thinks the entire accident's my fault."

"Four-wheel drive?"

"Yeah. Big blue Jap one. Fucking Mitsubishi logo on the front almost stamped my temple."

"You know Daryl was smashed by a four-by-four with bull-bars. Doesn't know what make, but it was red with orange primer."

Ears prick up. "So it could be blue now."

"Possibly. You alright to drive?"

He rubs his cast as if skin beneath benefits. "How we gunna find this prick?"

"Just have to keep our eyes peeled." I scratch the back of my neck. "You know, things could be worse."

"Yeah? How?" Then he looks sarcastically at me. "It could be *you* with the broken arm and stitches in your face."

"And a smashed up car."

Whispers and mumbles drift from the loitering prostitutes. This secretive quartet may not have the devastation of a lion pride on the hunt, but a huddle means trouble for somebody. Catching strings of words here and there I deduce they're devising the best course of action to secretly depart rental accommodation. Back rent mounting, their simple solution is to do a runner. The tried and true.

But nothing is ever that straightforward. A bug or two need ironing out. Like a bond and four weeks' rent for a new joint. Moving furniture is easy but will require at least a small van. And then there's the non-hooker roomy who gets shafted because she was trusting enough to hand over her share of the rent, which has, for the past ten weeks, been clearing credit card debt not hers. Now it's crunch time.

A voice with my name attached comes from the group, and they turn in unison.

"No!" I say before favours are asked. They wouldn't be huge favours, and undoubtedly wouldn't take long to do. But I figure I'd get in first anyway, just to make sure they know exactly where I stand on these important matters.

"But you haven't heard the—"

"Sorry."

"But what if—"

Jesus.

"Nope."

"Then can you—"

"Definitely not that."

"I'll pay you."

Hmmmmmmmmm. . . "Still no."

"Jeez you're a bastard."

"Yip."

Heather suddenly develops a gleeful, evil smile. On a hooker, this too means trouble.

"You obviously haven't been listening to the radio the last few nights. Seems your trip to Hawaii isn't such a foregone conclusion after all."

I turn to Telly, who shrugs. For somebody standing to lose so much cash if I go to Hawaii with Nikki, or indeed don't go at all, I thought he'd be more in touch.

"Yeah," Heather says happily. "A guy named R.D. already has six or seven points and is still going. You might be in a playoff yet."

All girls now smiling, they depart the kitchen.

Telly's worried. "We're fucked. I knew something was up. They've been placing more bets. Nikki's new boyfriend's name is R.D.. He's brought her to work the last couple of nights. If her brother doesn't let you win and take her, you'll lose to R.D. and miss out altogether."

For someone semi-intelligent, it doesn't make sense he'd be covering more bets. Still, it's not my money he's playing with.

"World's going to hell in a handbasket when a prostitute doesn't keep her word."

"That's what I like to hear, Myers. A bit of sarcasm. You're not worried, so what's up?"

"Nothing yet. If it looks so bleak, why take more bets you can't afford?"

"You can't tell anybody." His voice quietens to avoid the receptionist overhearing. "Brendan heard some girls wanted a lot more bets, so he's come in with me. As of yesterday we're partners. He's confident you'll turn it around somehow."

"If Rick and Nikki have brought in another player, the rules may no longer apply. That can't be a bad thing. It might be the opening I've been looking for."

I check the roster in the office before walking Telly out to his borrowed car. He drives off, I get into mine and wait for Nikki to show. Before long a beat-up old Holden rolls in, Nikki riding shotgun. It's safe to assume the older guy driving is R.D.. I jot down his number plate and follow her through the side gate. Exchanging pleasantries, she avoids eye contact. It's enough to confirm the bitch is probably doing the dirty on me. From this point on, everything I do will be aimed at fucking up her and her boyfriend and her duplicitous brother.

Remaining in the yard, I sit on a deckchair and ring Brendan at home.

"Got a mission for you. I need info on a guy named R.D.. Nikki's boyfriend." I give him the licence plate number.

"This to do with the competition?"

"Of course." I can almost hear him smile.

"I'll have it for you tomorrow."

"Hear about Telly's accident?"

"Yeah. You thinking what I'm thinking?"

That someone may be targeting drivers? Yes, I am, but I don't say that. "How did your missus enjoy her day out in the Aston Martin?"

"Go fuck yourself," he says, and hangs up.

Sally appears at the open kitchen door. "Go pick up Blaine and bring her in."

Blaine wasn't on the pick-up list, but complaining won't get me anywhere. It never does.

I drive fifteen minutes into Tweed Heads and find Blaine sitting on her brick fence. She climbs in when I pull up and we start back.

"Sorry bout the late pick-up," she says. "I know I'm new, but I do know the pick-up time. I just got back from my sick mother's house. I'm tapped out and nee the money."

A sick mother. My kingdom for a little originality. "So how was your first couple of nights?" I don't give a fuck, but must break the ice in case she's stuck in my car doing outcalls.

"Unremarkable."

Unremarkable? Prostitutes don't say unremarkable. Medical examiners and morticians say unremarkable. Heart — unremarkable. Liver — unremarkable. Brain — unremarkable. Cops working a few months' morgue duty unwittingly pick up words like that. I used to date a doctor. I've seen it happen.

"So how old is Skye?" she asks.

"Forty. Ish."

She blows out a breath. "Jeez. I won't be doing this when I'm that old."

"I'm sure Skye said something similar."

"A deposit for a house is all I'm after."

"Good luck with that." Nothing like attempting the impossible.

"Ever known any escorts save money?"

Another one who can't label herself prostitute.

"One. She put away almost forty grand in a couple of months. Valentine's Day, a Sunday, when nobody wanted to work, she stayed on after finishing her night shift. A lot of lonely guys around on Valentine's Day."

"How many jobs did she do?"

"Including the night shift, twenty-two. Had to take the next couple of days off."

"Twenty-two! So why can't we hold on to our money?"

Brendan and I have deliberated this over beers. We figure the average wage earner not worried about their future lives week to week. Cash earners live day to day. When money comes easily, it's pissed away the same. They can always make more tomorrow. So it's drunk, gambled, partied, smoked, snorted, or injected. If that isn't enough, there are plenty of people out there willing to sponge off you.

"Don't know," I say. "Past debts. Boyfriends, maybe."

"Yeah," she says, "I've got one of those."

"A boyfriend who doesn't work?"

"He did, but lost his job two weeks after we moved in together."

"He can't get another job?"

"He's a qualified boomerang maker. Makes Aboriginal artefacts as well. Not much call for it at the moment, supposedly."

I suppress a laugh. "So what's the difference between a qualified boomerang maker and a non-qualified boomerang maker?"

One shoulder goes up. "I laughed the first time I heard it, too. He's a fucking Pom, as well, so that kind of made it even odder. He's also about six months shy of any government handouts, because of some rule that he has to be in Australia a certain length of time to qualify."

So he's English, has no income, and unlikely to stumble over any kind of job unless it's sly and under the table.

"How would he get on if he hadn't latched on to you?"

She looks a little pained. "Yeah, I've asked myself that more than once."

Back at the house, I enter Mistress Jacqui's room of horrors. She finishes cleaning a couple of whips and hangs them on hooks amongst an assortment of others. I sit on a kind of padded hospital gurney and casually flick ropes and pulleys dangling from sturdy metal frames.

"I've got half an hour," she says. "Want to play?"

Don't think I haven't considered it. Looking at tonight's skimpy leather outfit, it's very tempting. Yeah, I'd risk an ultra mild session of some sort if she had sex with her clients. But she doesn't. She'll do all manner of things to them, but penetrating her while on the clock is a big no-no. Bitch.

"Unfortunately pain isn't my bag. Can't afford your prices, anyway. I'll have a serious look at your brochure when post Christmas deals are on offer."

"And what is your bag, Myers? Nikki? Hawaii's a very romantic place."

I'm surrounded by smartarses. I ignore her comment and ask if she's heard anything about Blaine.

"Not really," she says. "Didn't see much of her on her first night. But I don't see much of the girl's any night. Think she did say she was married, though, with a kid. But I could be wrong." She pulls a black and white nun's headgear from a box, carefully smoothes it down with an open hand, then slips it on. "Thank God for Catholics." Loose hair is tucked away at the sides. "Their church fucks them up at an early age. Probably lose half my income without them."

She picks up and adjusts leather straps connected to a larger than normal strap-on dildo that could double as a Chernobyl cucumber. I can't imagine anything that size going back up an orifice designed for the opposite action.

"I hope you're not going to fuck someone with that thing."

"Honey," — she makes a fist and smiles — "it won't be the biggest thing he takes tonight."

Eeeh. I slide off the gurney. Next to the door, a small brown leather saddle sits atop a metal cage. I point before deciding against a question.

"Equestrian," she says as I exit.

In the office, Sally puts cash in an envelope, writes on the front and drops it through the safe's narrow slit. I lean against the door frame.

"Know what equestrian entails?" I ask her.

She folds her arms, leans back in her chair and looks up at me. "What do you want?"

"If Blaine does outcalls and there's another driver on, can you put her in the other car."

"Did something happen when you were bringing her in?"

"No. It was an unremarkable trip."

"What does that mean?"

"Exactly."

"I swear to God you've got a screw loose sometimes, Myers."

14

After three months at sea catching fish, first thing sailorboy does back in port is dial a hooker. He must smell a treat.

For a little cover, I sit the other side of a fat pylon, feet dangling above the fishing boat. His white arse waves at me from the little wheelhouse while Gina takes a pounding. She didn't want to go below, and I wasn't about to check below decks where a half dozen blokes slummed it for quarter of a year. My guess is it'd be a little gamey. A bit on the bugle.

A gibbous waning moon floats high and bright. Almost still, low tide water slaps gently against a hundred pleasure craft. Booming bass-lines from two clubs eighty to a hundred metres away thump across marinas. Strobing disco lights radiate out into the night, while partying silhouettes dance on floor-to-ceiling windows. Voices, clinking glasses and cutlery clatter from closer restaurants, one belonging to Brendan. For all that, sitting here breathing in salt air is peaceful, calming.

I'd bet a week's drive money Pompeii and Jodi snuck away for drinks in one of those nightclubs. I'd bet a night's money they won't be back inside the hour they know Gina and I will be absent.

A large, untouched bottle of full strength beer sits beside me. In a nice gesture the john handed it up. But without realizing, sailorboy broke its top when using the deck rail as an opener. Not that I'd drink it anyway.

I push it into the water, then my phone rings.

"Yip?"

Brendan sounds pleased with himself because he already has info on R.D.. "Aren't you going to ask how I got it so damn quick?"

"It's not like I asked for Salma Hayek's home phone number," I whisper.

"If I had that number I wouldn't be wasting it on you. I'd be using it myself."

"Oh, that's real nice, *buddy*."

"Why are you whispering?"

"At the marina. So what's this R.D. individual done that I can squeeze till he pops?"

R.D. is a boring bastard. Works for a trucking firm, which is expected. Nikki has a thing for truckers. Divorced. Four kids. Has debt. Even that crappy car has a year's outstanding payments. It gives me something to work with should it turn out for sure I'm being shafted.

Brendan hangs up. I close my eyes and think of Salma Hayek in *Ask the Dust*, where she gets her gear off and frolics in blustery Californian surf.

"Myers."

"Salma?"

"Wake up, idiot," Gina calls from the boat. "Dave's going to give me a shower, then we can go."

"And I need to know this because. . . ?"

She doesn't answer. Sailorboy exits the wheelhouse in jeans filthy enough to stand on their own, followed by Gina, naked. I've never seen her starkers. Not a bad body. Hairless. He climbs a fixed ladder to the wheelhouse roof to pour water slowly on her from a jerry can. Because she showers, he avoids a twenty dollar penalty.

When water runs to a trickle, Gina takes a piece of rag no bigger than a facecloth from the rail and dabs herself while re-entering the wheelhouse to dress.

A minute later the guy climbs up to me behind Gina and hands over a plastic bag containing a couple of large, ugly, dead fish.

"There's one for you and one for Gina. Fresh caught this morning."

"Thanks." I save him the tale of pre-teen Brendan and me tripping into mounds of rotten fish so putrid and maggot-ridden that I've since been unable to eat seafood.

Walking back, I offer Gina my half. She's overjoyed. Fish is expensive. As predicted, Pompeii and Jodi are nowhere to be seen, and they're six minutes overdue. That probably means their night's leg-spreading — for pay, is over.

With no job waiting, I look around the huge carpark. People walk about, but none come this way. Two couples leaning on a car keep a wary eye on me while toking wacky, sweet marijuana smoke interrupting the salt air.

We should be moving to a more central location, but I'll wait a while longer in case they come back. Sally won't be pleased I've lost two girls.

My phone rings. I curse and pick up.

"Yip."

"You on the move?" Sally asks.

"Nope. Got back and the other two were gone."

"Leave them. Got another job. Gina can do it."

I jot down details and we move slowly to traffic lights at the exit. When they turn green I move forward, braking slightly to roll over gently sloped curbing. Just as well I did. It may have saved our lives.

Headlights off, a huge Mitsubishi 4x4 barrels full tilt through the red light. Gina gasps and covers her mouth. I point my car in the same direction and get ready to punch it. Before I can take off after him, an unmarked cop car waiting at the lights goes into action. Their siren blasts, red and blue flashing dashboard and grille lights fire up. Tyres squeal as it spins into a U-turn and hares off in pursuit. Both cars disappear in seconds. I follow the siren as best I can at a slower pace to avoid further attention.

"He must be fucking pissed," Gina says. "If that was a normal intersection where we didn't have to slow down, he would have cleaned us up."

"Yeah."

"Why are you following them? We'll never catch up. And we've got a job to get to."

"I didn't get a real good look at him. I'm hoping they've caught the prick."

Within minutes we're driving around aimlessly, the siren either out of earshot or turned off. By now they could be two suburbs away. Just in case, I begin checking sidestreets, left and right. Eventually we spot the unmarked police car on a parallel street, driving slowly the opposite direction, also searching for their quarry. Useless bastards lost him.

Not wanting cops pulling me over asking questions, I turn away and move toward our next job.

"Can't even make a complaint," Gina continues. "Fucker didn't have a number plate."

"I'll tell the prick you're upset next time I see him."

* *

While Gina shags her next guy, I ring Brendan.

"Not your night," he says. "You hear you're not going to Hawaii, lose two girls, now this."

"I have a sneaking suspicion it has something to do with you," I tell him.

"Not me," he says. "I've left a couple of things at your place for safe keeping."

'Safe keeping' means he doesn't want his wife knowing. What's he up to?

"I've got a lazy gorilla says I'm going to Hawaii."

He laughs. "Since it got out that Nikki's brother's the DJ, there seems to be a lot of lazy money floating around. All of it against you."

He hangs up. I turn on the radio competition for the first time since bagging my ten points.

So, folks, my man R.D.'s on seven points and looking pretty sharp. Looks like he might be giving Myers a run for his lei. How you feeling, R.D.?

Pretty good, Rick.

R.D's voice elevates like an excited teen. According to Brendan the guy's nudging fifty.

Allllrighty. Before we hear from Camille, your opposition this hour, I'll give you your question. You ready, R.D.?

Yip. Fire away.

Okie-dokie. In which song do we hear the phrase Death By Matrimony?

An old Wham song. Not even one of their biggest hits. There's no way he'd—

Young Guns. They Go For It.

Hey, R.D., that's so close I'm going to give it to you. The actual title is Young Guns, Go For It.

136

I close my eyes and flop my head back against the headrest. "Nikki, Nikki, Nikki."

Now, on the other line we have Camille. What do you say, Camille, should we give it to him?

Fuck off!

Hey, Camille, he-he, you caught me off guard. Not so much of the bad language, ay. And that's not a very charitable attitude to take towards your fellow competitor.

Beeep — *him. And I heard you say* — beeep -- *the other night.*

Okie-dokie, without further ado, Faith *was released as a vinyl record in eighty-seven. What was the first track on side B?*

Aaahhhh -- beeep -- you. Click.

Hmm. Never mind, that leaves the question in your court, R.D.. Any idea?

I've never even seen a George Michael vinyl record. There's no way he's going to get—

Um. Hard Day. *I think.*

Motherfuckers. Our verbal contract I now consider null and void.

I prod a Stevie Ray Vaughan disc and watch it disappear into the slot, killing the radio. Buzzing emanates from under the front fender where a little motor should be automatically retracting the aerial. It can't because of rust. In a minute or so the little electric gizmo will somehow realize it isn't going to happen, and give up.

15

Vanessa faces me, naked and cross-legged on the bed, eating chilled grapes. Also naked, my ankles are crossed, fingers interlaced on my stomach. She pops another purple grape in her mouth and looks again at the unlikely additions hanging on my walls. Four framed pencil sketches Brendan dropped off that I hung unevenly this morning after my shift.

"They new?"

"No. They're old."

"Well der, I know that. What I meant was—"

"I know what you meant."

One in particular holds her attention. "I've seen similar to that one. It's da Vinci. Is it real?"

"Nope. Drew it myself."

A thrown grape hits my forehead. She lingers on each sketch as if knowing the difference between John Wayne Gacey and John Constable. Her eyes then sweep my bedroom. Tacky grey paint peels in a dozen spots, curtains don't match, numerous screws protrude where God knows what had hung. I can almost read her mind. What the hell is a hundred-odd thousand dollars worth of art doing hanging in this perpetually unlocked little kitset home in the middle of a cow paddock?

"They're better than cash," I say. "They appreciate, and they're easily transferred into coin of the realm. And I don't like your inference that I'm uncultured."

"My look wasn't implying uncultured, it was implying *sub*cultured. And they appreciate what, hanging between glossies of Salma Hayek and a bikini-clad Christie Brinkley? No art gallery in the world would have thought of doing *that*."

Four books sit on my bedside table: *Brothel, Mustang Ranch and its Women; The Marquis de Sade, A Biography;* P.J. O'Rourke's *Give War A Chance*; and Charles Bukowski's *Women.*

"No classics? Poetry?"

"There's a Bukowski. That's gotta be worth a couple of points." I reach under my bed and drag out Martin Amis' *The Second Plane*. I wave it triumphantly to imply I'm a highbrow reader.

A smile creases her face that runs all the way to her eyes. "I'm willing to bet you can't recite a poem of at least . . . a dozen lines. And I don't mean something that uses the word Nantucket."

"So what are we betting?"

She hesitates, but thinks I'm bluffing. "Slave for a day."

"Done. This is called *A Slice of Wedding Cake*, by Robert Graves."

I rattle off all eighteen lines. A piece about women who choose poorly their men. She munches another grape and shakes her head disbelievingly.

"You're a constant source of amusement. Bet you didn't learn *that* in Peru."

"How much?"

This time a pillow hits my head.

"What's the plan of attack this afternoon?" she asks.

"I have to see a man about a rigged competition, then I'll meet you at your place about five."

"Rigged competition, ay. I've been listening to the radio and some other guy's notched up ten points. Are you going to see the man running it, or the man with ten points?"

"If you don't know, you can't be made to talk while being tortured." I lift myself onto both elbows. "Now, slave, I expect you to be wearing a tight Seven Of Nine bodysuit when next I see you."

"I have no idea what you're talking about."

"Seven Of Nine. From the TV series *Star Trek Voyager*. Look her up on the interweb."

The shack tingles. A car approaches. I sit up and spot a red Range Rover rolling slowly toward us.

"Damn it!" I jump up and pull on jeans. "It's Brendan's wife. She won't come in. She doesn't like me. Probably just wants tools or something in the shed. I'll be back in a minute."

"Do you like *her*?"

"Don't dislike her. But I represent everything her husband can't have any more."

"That's normal," Vanessa says. "She's jealous of what you two have. She can never replace that."

"Thanks, Freud."

Janet's Range Rover stops short of the electric wire. I slide my door open and walk to the corner of the slab. Janet gets out of her car and gives Vanessa's Merc a quick glance before stepping over the wire. As she approaches, Vanessa comes up behind me wearing only the dingo T-shirt and walks past with outstretched arms.

"Jan. How are you?" They kiss cheeks. "So you're married to Brendan."

Well, this could go badly. Vanessa was here when Brendan borrowed my Aston Martin. Did I mention to her those sketches belong to him? Probably not.

"Brendan said Myers' new girlfriend was Vanessa. I never gave it a thought."

"Come in," Vanessa says. "I'll make coffee."

I follow them inside. Janet says to Vanessa, "I came to get Myers' opinion about something, but I guess it can wait."

Wonderful. Why not announce 'Guess who died?' then say nothing. I'll be wondering all day.

Mumbles and occasional laughter drift into the bathroom while I shower. I'm curious as to how they know each other. Unless Janet's thicker than I figured, being held back in school nine or ten years, they can't have shared a classroom. Vanessa's my slave for the day. I'll extract it from her later.

I shave, dress, kiss Vanessa, bid Janet goodbye, then leave to get a feed and see a man about a lying, cheating bushpig and her deal breaking brother.

Two rigs towing long trailers weighed down by shipping containers slow as they pass my parked car and pull into a huge wire-meshed yard. They manoeuvre before backing up to a platform amongst five other trucks. Two workers leaving the yard, neither old enough to be R.D., wave adios to the incoming drivers. 1.30 p.m. knockoff. They started very early or their boss is away. Probably the latter. They look the type.

They talk a minute before jaywalking to a tavern across the street. For twenty minutes repetitive, monotonous country music from that establishment has been trying to ram home a country music headache. So far it's only managed a pain in my neck.

Aussie truckers enjoy a tipple, therefore it's a reasonable bet R.D. will turn up there sooner or later. I lock up and walk across to the bar. A lot of bosses must be out of town. At least thirty guys dressed in work clothes are getting an early start. Five surround two pool tables. Three play darts. The rest sit around high tables, talking, drinking.

I order a beer before carefully taking in every face. Three approximate R.D.'s age and hair colour I remember from when he dropped Nikki off at work. When the wench brings my beer I slap down a ten and tell her to keep it. From her grateful smile I assume blue collars rarely offer gratuities.

"R.D. about yet?"

She looks to the far corner " Playing darts."

Stereotyping has paid off. "Oh, course he is."

Trying to look friendly, I take my beer to a tall table by an open window not far from the dartboards. All three men wear identical green work pants. Two wear blue short sleeved company shirts with company names stitched in white over a pocket. R.D. dons an unbuttoned red and black check shirt hanging over his pants. Under it an almost white T-shirt says THE MEEK SHALL INHERIT THE INSIDE LANE in black capital letters above a big rig.

Rudolph Dominic Warner. The opposition. While married there were two cars, a business, nice house, gym membership. Since the divorce, seven years' full strength beer has gone to his middle. A two-day grey beard covers jowls and two chins. Teeth need repairing and whitening. He owes five thousand on a car worth three. Four low-limit credit cards are maxed for a total of twelve thousand. On behalf of his ex and four kids, our government garnishes his mediocre wage. Fate can be a bastard when you're chalking up the years. It can spot suckers a mile off. In the blink of a young girl's eye it's turned him into a podgy, lethargic punching bag.

He puts on a good show in front of his mates. He laughs, shouts his round, not a care in the world. Is he aware of dirty deeds afoot in the radio competition, or is this Hawaii trip a bit of a lark? A freebie promised by his new girlfriend. To estimate my offer, evaluate his temperament, I must first get him isolated.

While I've been sizing him up, they've noticed me. Nods have been exchanged. I finish my beer, buy another and return to my window table. The music stops. R.D. digs a couple of coins out of his pocket, walks to the jukebox, slots them and pushes a half dozen buttons without consulting the menu. Some guy with a southern drawl begins singing over a twangy guitar. More country music. R.D. probably couldn't sing a single line from a George Michael song if a trip to Hawaii depended on it.

One of R.D.'s offsiders asks if I'd like to play with him in a game of doubles, and I'm in. I move my beer to their table, where we introduce ourselves. I use Perry, my middle name, as they've no doubt been listening to the radio of late.

Now closer, I reckon R.D. has mechanic's hands, not a driver's. Grease lingers under fingernails and in creases and cuts around knuckles that no amount of scrubbing can clean thoroughly. His beer is completely flat, headless. The merest hint of diesel on skin will exterminate beer bubbles quicker than almost anything. Even after weekends off, away from the workplace, it still lingers. Just by shaking hands it could well flatten my own drink. He's bullshitting Nikki about his vocation, or after mentioning the company name she assumed he's a trucker, and he didn't set her straight. Oh well, no doubt Nikki told him she's a receptionist. They all do.

We play darts. Kind of. The three of them can't throw an arrow for shit. I'm not much better, and beer doesn't straighten our aim. It's strangely enjoyable mixing with ordinary people outside of prostitution.

They seem happy with their lot. When R.D. goes for a round of drinks, I make a pretext of emptying my bladder, stand inside the toilet for a couple of minutes, then exit and lean on the bar beside him.

With no idea how to broach the subject, or how he'll take the subterfuge of our meeting, all I can do is dive in, see what happens.

"My name's Perry, but friends call me Myers."

"So you want me to call you. . ." The penny drops. He frowns. "Myers. You're the one in for the Hawaii trip. How did you know where to find me?"

"You must have mentioned it on the radio. I've got a proposition for you."

A pained, insider-knowledge smile/grimace covers his face, implying his hands are tied. "I can't, mate. My girlfriend really wants to go."

"Do you?"

"There's no spending money with it, and I've been to Hawaii. I'd rather have the cash. But she's a hottie, and dynamite in the sack. She lets me put my dick anywhere. Never met anyone like her."

I could tell you why, you poor bastard. "R.D., mate, there's ways around everything."

"Not this, I'm afraid."

Crunch time. How much to get him interested? Four grand? Six? I'd go to ten with minimal pain. The trip itself must be worth three or four, so it's not much more.

"Because it's rigged? Yeah, I know it's rigged. Your girlfriend's Rick's sister."

He doesn't seem surprised I know. His head droops and does So-you-know-I'm-fucked nods. Good, evidently he's given it some thought. He's aware nobody escapes a 'complimentary' overseas trip without a hit to their wallet.

"I gotta tell you, Myers, it's not really my cup of tea. But what can I do?"

Poor bastard's looking for a way out without losing Nikki. It's going to be cheaper than I thought. The sympathy grab — telling him I want to propose to my girlfriend over there might drive up the price, so I'll keep that lie in reserve.

"Throw it."

"You don't understand. There's going to be a play-off question each, and if you're still in, I know the final question's answer."

"People get nervous and stuff up. People forget things."

'Hey, D," his friend yells at us. Even Rudolph Dominic's nickname has a nickname. He picks up two beers and says he'll be right back. He hands them over and returns with a positive attitude.

"How much we talking, Myers?"

"How much *are* we talking?" While he thinks about it, I push him a little harder. "You'll be off the hook, R.D., and with a few dollars in your pocket. Sure your girlfriend will be pissed off for a day or two, but a box of chocolates and she'll get over it."

Silent musing continues. I'm about to get things going with an offer of eight grand when I again notice those words on his shirt. The meek shall inherit the inside lane. Suddenly I'm in a non-charitable mood. Just yesterday an inconsiderate truck driver bullied me out of my lane. And how many times on the open road had an 18-wheel juggernaut arsehole tried climbing in my boot, even doing the limit plus 10, because I'm waiting for a dickhead in front to speed up? Touch the brakes — instant death. Truckers and taxi drivers. They seem to think because their living is made on the road certain laws don't apply to them. Or they have more rights than everybody else.

Eight grand? I should beat it out of him.

"Okay," he says. "How bout a month's wages. And I make over six hundred a week."

The lying prick makes less than five. Even so, his lack of backbone astounds me.

I flinch. "Jeez, I've got to have spending money myself. I was going to propose to my girlfriend over there, and I've got to buy a ring yet."

"Hawaii's a mighty passionate place to propose. Ever been there?"

"I wish. How bout two weeks? I could manage that in a pinch."

His index finger slow-taps the mahogany as he actually considers twelve hundred dollars.

"So in principle we've agreed on three weeks," he says to himself. "Lets call it two grand."

Then, suddenly, it's gone. He slaps the bar. "No, look, I really can't. Even for the month's pay. Sorry."

Is he trying to play me? It matters not, because after seeing the T-shirt again I'm unwavering in not offering more money. We're so close I think a strategy change is needed. Who can resist a shot at emerging on top, even if they lose?

"How about this," I say. "I don't know my play-off question, which will undoubtedly be hard. If I don't get it, I'll give you two weeks' pay anyway. If I *do* get it, you throw the tie-breaker question and you get the three weeks' pay. It's a win/win for you."

Returning to indecision, finger tapping recommences while he looks at the ceiling.

"Okay," he says. "I like it." His hand shoots out.

"You drive a fucking hard bargain," I protest, shaking it.

He looks over to his friends, now exiting the bathroom. "Not a word."

"I'm not even telling my girlfriend," I assure him.

However, come the day of departure, concert and airline tickets in hand, informing Nikki will be impossible to resist. Seeing pained twists on her face would be the ideal start to any trip.

16

Fact — tavern debated, indisputable, irrefutable. Any male curious to know what his present girlfriend will look like twenty-five or thirty years down the track, have a gander at her mother. That's what he'll be waking up next to in his prime.

Jackpot!

Vanessa's mother looks more like an older sister — a better looking, classier older sister. They're almost bookends, but mother has a little something extra, something captivating, enticing. It could be the few extra, wiser years, the sleeveless cream dress with matching Italian leather high heels, minimal but expensive jewellery. Or even her flawless, although forced, smile. Whatever it is, it's mesmerizing. Looking at the two of them I can't help but wonder if they'd be receptive to the idea of a. . .

No, even I couldn't be that tacky on our first meeting. But I'd bet a month's pay many school boyfriends visited Vanessa specifically to ogle her mother.

"Mother," Vanessa says, "this is Myers."

I clocked her peering out the window when I pulled my Nissan into Vanessa's drive behind what must be Mother's Merc. Her face showed neither recognition nor loathing at her daughter's current choice. I was merely expected.

For a petite woman she has a strong grip.

"Call me Grace."

"Nice tits," I say.

No I didn't. But it wouldn't be a lie.

We move to Vanessa's back patio overlooking a large, as yet unlandscaped yard mostly covered in patchy brown grass. They've been reminiscing. Three open photo albums sit beside an empty wine bottle and two tall wine glasses on a table. An ice bucket holds a full bottle and a Heineken stubbie. We sit, Vanessa pours chardonnay in both glasses and hands me the beer.

I take a big swig to hopefully dull expected photo album nausea. The only thing worse than country music is looking at boring snaps of somebody else's Aunty and Uncle Fuckwit, or numbingly tedious monkey photos of an extended family's latest addition.

Mother bypasses chitchat. "So, Myers, what do you do?"

"I'm a courier."

"And what is it you carry?" There's still no commitment in her voice one way or tother. It's like she knows the answer but is just waiting to see if I'm going to tell porkies.

"Prostitutes."

"Hmmm," she goes, in the same amusing manner as her daughter.

"You don't seem surprised."

"Vanessa has no father to look out for her, so I know what you do, that you have money overseas and how you made it. I'm very protective."

"I'm glad we got that out of the way. But what if Vanessa does something bad to *me*?"

She can't prevent a genuine smile brightening her face. Little more than curving of the lips, but with a slight head incline it smacks of cheeky youthfulness that maybe doesn't get out much.

"A sense of humour," she says. "A nice quality in a man."

"But I'm serious."

Grace is amused. "Why couldn't you bring Myers home when you were at school? It would have saved a lot of grief."

Ah, Vanessa had boyfriend trouble when younger. So I understand what Grace is getting at. But the simple answer to her question is, had Vanessa brought me home when she was a schoolgirl, that would have made me a paedo.

Grace slips off a shoe and massages her right foot. "Tell me about these women you drive around."

"You looking for a new career? You'd make a dollar."

"Hmm."

"They have a name for women like you and Vanessa, women who give it away."

"Oh? And what might that be?"

"Charity mole," I grin.

Grace removes her other shoe. She takes off diamond earrings and places them beside an album. She's getting tipsy, settling in. To change the subject, I make a point of noticing a photo of teenage Vanessa, an older man and Grace on a large yacht. Being familiar with Formula One telecasts, I recognize Monte Carlo marinas in the background.

"Nice boat. Who's the guy?"

"My father," Vanessa says. "We went sailing around Greece and the French Riviera. Borrowed the boat from a friend of mother's."

I flip a page, scan more photos, flip again and follow pictures while Vanessa gives a quick commentary. Greek landmarks turn to a backyard family barbecue.

"My cousin's twenty-first," she says.

"And who's the guy draping himself all over you?"

"Old boyfriend. Jealous?"

"James." Grace utters his name with a forlorn tone. "Still keeps in touch, doesn't he, darling."

"You know he does, mother."

Grace excuses herself and leaves as if the topic of conversation has turned irksome.

"Well?" Vanessa asks, nodding toward the door Grace exited through.

"She's hot — I mean *nice*."

"She doesn't drink in public since father died. Comes around here every few weeks, has a few and stays the night. It's her way of blowing off steam.

I consider that a quirk. A shrink might call it some kind of flaw, but they'd be playing it up to make money. There's nothing wrong with not making a fool of oneself in public. A flaw has yet to materialize in Vanessa. Maybe I'm subconsciously overlooking some because of her looks.

Grace returns, and I go to the kitchen for another drink. After opening a Heineken, I ring Telly using my bat-phone.

"Telly, mate, what are you up to?"

"Just got out of the shower. Ever tried taking a shower and not get an arm cast and bandages all over your body wet? Course not, but I'm telling you it ain't easy. Hand's throbbing, too. How's your day going?"

There's obvious sarcasm in them there words, so I tell him enthusiastically it's going pretty damn well.

"What the hell are you so happy about?" he asks.

"You'll never guess who I've just seen in a photo."

"Your mother," he says, "Blowing Saddam. I've got a framed copy on my toilet wall."

"Nope. Try again."

"Fuck you. Who is it?"

"The guy who almost hit my car, and probably hit yours and Daryl's."

"You're fucking kidding! Who is he?"

"Don't know yet, but I'll know tomorrow. We can do something about it then."

"Fuck tomorrow!" he says. "Lets go deal to the prick now."

"Told you, I don't know who he is yet. This is just a call to let you know it's in hand."

"Well give me what you've got. I'll go and straighten the cunt out myself."

"Tomorrow. No point going off half cocked." I turn my phone off.

As best I can figure, sick prick James somehow discovered where I'm working, but not much more. Why else target all the drivers? Telly and I will have to ask him. I grab a third beer and cold bottle of wine and return outside. Their conversation involves the radio competition.

"Did Vanessa tell you we have a place on Maui?" Grace asks. "You both should go over and relax after the concert. Even if you don't win you should think about going. It's beautiful."

Today's beer is creeping up the back of my head, warming brain cells. I admire Grace's shape; this wonderful, forbidden creature, and smile engagingly.

"Ever been told you have fantastic tits?"

"Thank you for noticing," she says. "They're slightly younger than I am."

"Are you familiar with the TV show *Star Trek Voyager*?"

"Hmmm," Vanessa says.

17

These Asians don't know how the game is played. According to hard-hitting news shows, Westerners go to *their* countries for sex tours, not the other way around.

Sally and I watch on monitors six of them in suits climb out of a rented minibus. She curses. This afternoon only two girls are working.

Speaking fifteen to the dozen in some fast yellow language, they press the front door buzzer. I once considered learning Japanese at night school, but after hiring the miniseries *Shogun* and watching Toshiro Mifune take deep breaths before spitting out words machine-gun-style, eyes and neck veins bulging as if squeezing one out on a toilet, I figured fuck that. My brain just wouldn't be able to translate that shit quickly enough.

When Sally leaves to admit them, I flick a monitor to the lounge. She escorts the johns in, pours and distributes six drinks. They yabber to each other, point at porn on TVs and laugh. Eventually one breaks from the pack, talking almost arrogantly in very poor English.

"Want Asian girl."

Sally shakes her head. "No Asian girl. Western girl better."

His request is perplexing. When in a different culture, sample its wares. What they're doing is akin to me holidaying in China or Thailand and living on Aussie meat pies.

"Want Asian girl," he continues doggedly.

Her hands go out. "No Asian girl. Western girl better."

He waves a finger metronome-like in front of her. "Western pussy like riding pushbike through Chunnel. Know Chunnel?" His hands shoot apart, conveying wideness. "Chunnel very big." Then his hands almost come together. "Pushbike very—" .

"I get it," she says. "You have a small pushbike."

That little pearler will undoubtedly be lost in translation. He's obviously had an unpleasant experience with a westerner. His mates, knowing no better, accept their leader's word. My money's on Sally demanding he drop his pants while she grabs a tape measure.

They're at the point where everyone's time is being wasted. After a little ying-tonging, they down drinks and head for the exit. At least I don't have to chuck them out. They may be smaller than me, but odds are at least one would hold some kind of black belt.

Once they exit the carpark, I switch the other monitor to the girls' room. Skye slouches in a chair watching TV or a video, feeding her face from a chip packet. Jodi should be close to finishing a job. A driver's presence today is almost unnecessary. Unless an outcall comes that is less than twenty minutes' travel time, it can be uneconomical to send a girl away from the house.

Contemplating this unexciting prospect, I flick back to the carpark and watch two cars pull in. Through the intercom I inform Sally, who admits two johns. Both receive a complimentary beer before Skye introduces herself to the first guy. He accepts and she takes him to a room. Sally informs the other that Jodi won't be long, and returns to the office.

We discuss Asians. The radio competition is mentioned. My phone rings but I let it collect with the other ninety-one hundred missed calls since last night. We see on a monitor Skye bringing her john back to a clients' little alcove, the other side of the office. He must be paying by credit card. Sally readies our EFTPOS handset, then unhooks and slides open a little paperback-sized door. Just the right height, he unzips, pulls out his flaccid, unusually hairy junk, and places it carefully on the tiny ledge. Sally rolls her eyes and shows me the universal 'wanker' sign. She doesn't believe he misunderstood instructions. The wanker's done it on purpose.

I turn away, trying not to laugh. Sally plays along.

"I check your credit card, sweetie. Skye will check your penis in the room."

We hear an "Oh, sorry," his genitals disappear and an ATM card comes through. Money is deducted and they leave.

Jodi, her job finished, is directed to the lounge. When she comes back, Sally returns to talk to the second man. He's willing to wait and meet Skye, then he asks for another complimentary beer. Sally comes back.

"He's not waiting an hour to meet Skye, drinking for free and then taking Jodi anyway. Or leaving. You mind, Myers?"

"Do I have to?"

Jodi leans against the office security screen. "Come on, Myers."

"Fuck it." I exit the kitchen, the side gate, then Sally admits me through the front door. I sit at our bar like a client. Jodi sashays out, pretends to give me her sales pitch, and leaves. Sally comes back to talk like a normal job is happening. She then goes to the other guy to say Jodi has been chosen, but if he wants her, he gets first refusal. Otherwise he might as well leave and return in one hour. However the girls may be busy again by then. The oft used ruse works. Jodi has another job.

Within a few minutes, towel wrapped around her, she brings the job money through while her client showers.

"Why is there a urine smell in here?" she asks.

Sally reaches down to check on her ailing, stunted runt dog Jewboy. His breath labours. He's been wetting his bed. It looks like he's on the way out. She caresses his jerking stomach while making soothing noises. Jodi leaves. I ask what's wrong with the mutt.

"He's been falling over all morning," Sally says, "and wetting himself. He has trouble breathing. His coordination's shot. All he wants to do is sleep." She slow-strokes his head. "Ohhhh, poor baby. Dot will be here soon so we can go to the vet. Any ideas, Myers? Ever seen it before?"

Dog and Mistress have been together fourteen or fifteen years. They'd probably die defending each other.

"I have. Many times. He's been in the liquor cabinet."

My phone rings, and once again I ignore it.

"How can you not answer your phone?" Sally asks. "It's pissing me off."

I explain a phone company is trying to sign me up to their network, but of course it's Telly trying to find out who it was ran him over. I'm surprised he hasn't turned up here, baseball bats or worse at the ready.

WwwDot fronts. Jewboy now rests, wrapped in a blanket on the table. Both women lean over him making sympathetic noises. I suggest a hospice.

Very carefully Sally picks him up. "I feel terrible dragging you in, Dot."

"Don't worry about it," wwwDot says. "Go and take care of Jewboy."

WwwDot and I sit in the office and watch Sally drive out of the carpark.

"We can phone around looking for doggie plots," I say.

"Stop it," she smirks.

Skye enters the kitchen wrapped in a towel and requests a beer for her client. "Arsehole wants me to keep my stilettos on," she tells us. "Then while we're doing it, he tells me how he's fucked his mother, his grandmother, and his sister."

"And probably half a dozen sheep," I add.

Jodi reappears for the same reason. "Skodie bastard," she says. "We're getting into it and he says, all wide-eyed and slobbery, 'Do ya like being fucked?' So I told him I'm a lesbian, and ate it."

"Way to get return custom," I tell her.

Jodi screws up her nose. "He's a pig. Who cares?"

They both recognize a car driving in on a monitor.

"Fuck no!" they say together. They take beers and scamper off.

Donkey Dave gets out of his car. His head droops, weighed down by a lifetime's purgatory. One would think the possessor of a donkey dick would occasionally smile, but since the death of his wife two years ago nothing seems to cheer him. I haven't seen the monster, but girls often bellyache about its length and girth. The fact he's a stayer doesn't help. He can grind out the entire hour. So after believing most of my life that a big dick is a woman's ultimate prize, what they mean is a pleasant fit will suffice. Even cock has limits.

Having conversed a few times, I offer to keep him company until the two girls finish their present jobs. I admit him and place a beer on the bar top. He sits on a stool while I stand the other side.

"Whatchya been doing, Dave?"

"Today? Been moving cattle around for Brendan."

"So how's the new security job?"

Head still drooping, a hand rubs his brow and he lets out a sigh. Grey has crept up his beard but his moustache oddly remains dark.

"Was no good for my nerves. Only lasted two weeks. Had to lock the car whenever I was in it cause half-blind drunken dickheads were always trying to get in. Almost shit myself the first time it happened. With stickers on the car doors and a spotlight on the roof, cruds assume you're a taxi and jump in the back seat. Then when I tell them I'm not a cab, they think I'm refusing to take them and they get real loud and very nasty. One bitch hit me in the head with a live goanna. I didn't even see she was carrying the damn thing. I tell you, I'd slow down for a set of lights by a club, and a half dozen fuckwits would make a bolt for the car. It's fucking frightening out there. Don't know how cab drivers do it."

Doom and gloom. If I were him I'd post a picture of my dick on the internet. He'd get dozens of takers, probably saving hundreds of dollars every week not coming here. Hell, they might even pay *him*.

Skye finishes early and gets to service Donkey Dave. She'll try practiced tricks to finish him off quickly. Hand job, prostate massage, rub his balls. Anything but an hour of *that* slamming inside her.

Sally returns, places a baby basket on the kitchen table and both receptionists fawn over Jewboy. I peek in. To me, unconscious Jewboy looks no healthier than when he left.

"Vet said he's had a few heart attacks," Sally says. "I've got tablets."

WwwDot softly rubs his tummy. "Ohhh. Poor baby. So what's the verdict?"

"Might last a week. But he could keep going another couple of years."

"Dead dog walking," I say.

I'm ignored. Sally moves Jewboy into the office to lay him in a corner on a fresh sheepskin from her car. He groans, rolls onto his back. Legs splay. I think he's been hanging around prostitutes too long.

WwwDot catches Sally up with events before she leaves. Sally settles in, answers phones and watches monitors as if she never left. I'm thinking about purchasing a laptop. I could sit here doing stuff instead of sitting around with my eyes closed.

I must have fallen asleep. Next thing I know, Skye enters the kitchen clothed, a little distressed. Her hand trembles while holding a cigarette to her mouth. She mumbles while anxiously pacing the floor. Donkey Dave has never had this effect on a girl before.

Sally watches through the security grille. All I know is, if Skye goes home sick, I'm left with one girl and little hope of going out on a job.

Suddenly Skye erupts.

"Genitals! Genitals! Genitals! I'm sick of the fucking sight of them! I'm sick of the fucking smell of them! I'm fed up having to touch them!"

Pacing restarts. That hand shakes so much her cigarette is almost a blur. Her head moves oddly in tight circles as she blubbers at the floor. It seems to me like there's some sort of breakdown occurring. Sally jumps up and puts an arm around Skye to keep her still.

"Give me a hand."

A hand? To do what? I'm not the huggy-touchy-feely type.

"I think she needs men in white coats, not a humble but good-looking hooker-driver."

"Get the doors." Sally tosses Skye's cigarette out to the grassed yard. "She can lie down in the girls' room."

Skye continues shaking and mumbling. Moving in little steps toward the hall door, Sally utters calming, reassuring words. In the girls' room she lays Skye on a sofa and gently places a hand on her cheek.

"In my handbag you'll find strong pain killers," Sally says to me. "Bring them with a glass of water."

"Dog medicine. Nice one. She won't even know."

"It's not dog medicine."

Jodi's there when I get back. Sally puts a couple of tablets in Skye's mouth and makes her sip water.

"If Jodi gets a job, Myers, you'll have to sit with Skye until she falls asleep."

Just what I need. I feel a headache coming on.

I return to keep an eye on outside monitors. Sally comes back five minutes later and flops in her chair.

"So what was that?" I ask.

"It's happened before. She's been a prostitute most of her life. It's getting to her."

"You think?"

"Husband died about a year ago, just before you started here. She didn't take it well."

"And this would be the same husband who shot one of her toes off with a handgun."

"And stabbed her. Silly cow took him back afterwards." She watches my face for a reaction. There isn't one.

"What? You expect me to go all agog?"

"She took him back," Sally continues, "cause after he got out of prison the last time, he had the big C. Doctors gave him three or four months. He had nowhere to go, so she took him in and he was an angel. Death's doorstep seemed to mellow the prick. I think he found a god. Most of them do."

Ah yes, the familiar last ditch desperate grab for a supreme being that until now they've never acknowledged, or at least believed in its moral codes of conduct enough to worry about consequences. A lifetime of snubbing one's nose at society, of abusing one's family, and *HALLELUJAH,* staring death in the face they find salvation. It shouldn't count. A desperation clause should be in effect. That same desperation clause ought to apply in prison. Find a god when you're released, not when it might affect parole. Then we'll take you seriously. So, arsehole, time to take responsibility for your actions. Thumb your nose, as always, and take your medicine like your numerous victims have had to do over the years.

"Praise be to God," I say.

"Do I detect a note of cynicism? What happened to forgive and forget?"

"I'll ask you the same question after your daughter's brutally raped and murdered. And don't forget to send in your hard-earned to keep the tax exempt ministry afloat."

A familiar station wagon rolls in.

"Shoppers are here," Sally says excitedly.

Shoppers. The *thieves* park beside the side gate and Sally goes out to let them in. Mary and her common-law partner tote two huge, bulging canvas bags into the kitchen and up-end one on the floor. Department store-pilfered booty falls in a large pile. Lingerie, children's clothes, T-shirts, toiletries, electric toothbrushes, fitted sheets, DVDs, Play Station and X-Box games, all price tags and security clips intact. Sally gets on the intercom, and Jodi runs to join us.

While I scan the pile from my kitchen table seat, Sally and Jodi sit on floor tiles and meticulously pick through everything. Mary is surprised more girls aren't working, but says it's quiet everywhere. She's endured a lean week herself. From the second bag bottles of spirits and liqueurs are stood on the floor.

"See anything you like, Myers?"

She sports a matchstick-legged, no arse, gaunt, drug-fucked appearance. Her laugh's more a nervous pant. Hubby now sits half asleep the other side of the table.

"How much for the shoulder bags?"

"Can't have those. That's how we get stuff out the shops."

Expensive malt whiskeys sit among sickly liqueurs. Two Glenfiddich, a ten-year-old Glenmorangie, plus a round cream container hiding twelve-year-old Glenlivet. A tall rectangular box I don't recognize has its back to me.

"How much for the scotch?"

"You drink whiskey?"

"Hate it. How much."

She picks up a round black Glenfiddich canister and looks blankly at its gold lettering, giving herself time to size up my interest. No point going for top dollar on the brothel circuit. Connoisseurs are thin on the ground. Scotch is scotch, to be defiled by mixing it with coke and ice.

"Maybe not," I say. "Maybe if you had some bourbon. . ."

"Fifteen bucks."

Cheap scotch is almost twice that. She needs money. I pick up the more expensive Glenlivet canister, remove its lid, pull out the bottle, read some of the label. I drink beer, so might as well be reading a knitting manual. I drop the bottle back in its round canister, push the lid back on and return it to the floor.

"I don't even know any scotch drinkers. Maybe one of the girls will take them."

"They want yuppie drinks, or vodka, over-proof rum. These are good whiskeys."

"How about fifty for all four."

"Fifty? That's only. . ." — she eyes fridge magnets hoping the answer is written on one — "thirteen dollars a bottle."

I lean forward, turn the oblong box around with its back to me and try not to salivate or bulge my eyes. Blue label Johnnie Walker. Easily two or three hundred dollars.

"Chuck in this one."

The common-law partner's mouth drops open. His eyelids have been slowly shutting every few minutes, then pinging open. But the idea of fifty dollars causes a smile as if the money is already earmarked. From her I get an unreadable look. She'd know how much a blonde teen virgin would fetch in an Arab country, so the cost of blue label Johnnie would be rattling around in her head somewhere.

"Sixty with the Johnnie," she says.

"Jesus." I click my tongue. "Take a cheque?"

They laugh, he all slow and dopey, her the nervous pant. I remove three twenties from my wallet, pass them over and put the contraband in Sally's office. In monitors, I notice a five or six year-old girl sitting patiently on the station wagon's back seat. The accomplished accomplice. The decoy while mum and stepdad do their thieving. The one who should be in school.

"What's in the huge boxes in back of your car?" I ask.

"Can't have that," Mary says. "That's an order job. An above ground pool with all the bells and whistles."

I resume my seat. "You . . . shop to order? And things that big?"

"Sure. What you want?"

"Nothing I can think of. But it's good to know."

Jodi matches G-strings with bras before setting them aside.

"Had any weird jobs today?" Mary asks her.

"What do you call weird?"

"Y'know. Unusual."

"Had one sick fucker," she says, scrutinizing a bra label, "only wanted me to blow on his nipples. Gently. How perverted's that?"

"What? Didn't play with himself or nothing?"

"Nothing. Just lay there while I breathed on his nipples."

Mary puts on her distorted lemon-sucking face and shudders. "What a wacko!"

I don't get it. Easy job, easy money. Yet she complains.

"Hey," Sally says, now leaning against the kitchen bench, "that wrinkle cream I bought last time was great, Mary. It works wonders."

Mary smiles her crooked, drug-fucked smile. "It says it's supposed to take off five or six years every few weeks of use."

Sally's tanned, weather-beaten face has fifty-five year-old lines a skilled plastic surgeon would have difficulty stretching out.

"Gee," I butt in, "can I book a romantic outing with you in say . . . six months? You should look like a teenager about then. Don't spose this magic cream restores virginity as well?"

"Can I buy a Glenfiddich off you?" Sally asks me. "I know there's no point asking for the blue label."

Dead Dog Walking remains on his back, legs in the air. The pose smacks of homosexuality. "If you promise to keep it out of Dead Dog Walking's reach, you can have one. We'll call it a birthday present."

"We'll call it part payment for all the shit I've put up with from you and Telly."

My phone goes off. Sally advises answering, because should it go off again today, she'll stomp on it.

I pick up. "Hey, Telly. I was expecting you to call ages ago."

"Fuck you. What's the guy's name?"

"It's in hand. Be ready tomorrow."

18

"Ah! Ah! A spider's in my hair!"

Telly runs on the spot while frantically slapping his bald head with the hand attached to his good arm.

"Shut up, fool," I whisper forcefully. "He'll hear us."

He switches from head-slapping to hastily brushing clothes. He tugs his shirt out and stretches to see if anything lurks back there. The only thing left is pleading like a baby if I can see any creepy-crawlies on him.

"I hate spiders," he whispers back, checking his jeans. "You lead the way."

"Put your balaclava on, ya nancy."

He pulls a ski mask from his back pocket and stretches it over his head. Then he picks up his dropped wooden baseball bat and we continue through the woods, me leading. Enough moonlight shines through foliage that we can keep up a steady pace with little noise.

"Explain to me," Telly whispers, deliberately stepping where I step, "why we don't just roll down his drive and give him a good seeing-to?"

"Because I want to find the Mitsubishi, just to make sure it's him."

Telly stops me with a hard tug on my shirt. "A half hour ago you were positive it was him smashing up our cars."

I turn around. "I saw him for a split second. And he had dark glasses on. But I'm ninety percent."

I turn to continue, but he grabs my arm. "So where did you see this photo?"

"It's an old boyfriend of the girl I'm seeing."

He holds his bat threateningly. "So this is down to you. Maybe I should be wrapping this around *your* fucking head."

"I can't control a jealous prick who's probably a stalker." I tap my aluminium bat on his cast, merely enough to jar his broken bones. "Just remember who smashed into your car."

We continue on another few minutes until a wide, sprawling, single-storey redbrick house comes into view. A shingle driveway runs into a big loop out front. Centre loop sits a three-tier fountain turned off for the night. A white Audi Cabriolet with the top up sits at the base of two wide steps to a patio. Lights are on inside but there's no obvious movement. No 4x4 Mitsubishi is in view. A closed double garage abutting the house could be hiding it.

We creep slowly and quietly along the wood's fringe to the double garage. Through a closed side window I can make out almost everything in the green glow of a digital clock radio sitting on a shelf. It's full of boy toys. Speedboat on a trailer. Two mud-caked trail bikes. A couple of jet-skis on trailers. Plus an empty spot for the Audi. It's strangely disappointing not to see the Mitsubishi. I begin questioning whether we have the right guy. If we don't, and he comes out of the house, is it possible to stop Telly going apeshit on the guy's arse in his present, primed frame of mind?

"Well?" he whispers.

"Nothing," I whisper back. "But there's no tools of any kind, so there must be other sheds somewhere on the property."

"You are aware people who live in the sticks usually have guns of some sort lying around the house?"

"We're armed," I say. "Sort of. And he doesn't know we're coming."

He pulls me back, raising his broken arm to remind me why we're here. "I want first swing."

"There's plenty for everyone. Greedy bastard."

Telly peeks around the garage toward the house. Suddenly his head whips back as if to avoid being shot.

"There's a dog," he forces out quietly, manoeuvring himself behind me. "A *big* dog. You didn't say anything about a fucking dog."

I shoot him a moronic look. "Spiders and dogs. Anything else I should know about before we continue?" I look around the corner, then straighten quickly. "Shit. Bad news. He saw me."

Manic barking erupts. It gets louder as the gap between us and it closes fast. Telly and I move apart, away from the garage, allowing unrestricted swing room. Our bats go up as we prepare for the onslaught about to round the building. Telly instantly breaks into a sweat.

A massive Rhodesian Ridgeback with T-Rex teeth skids in front of us barking and snarling. Muscular legs furiously pump as it tries changing direction but slips on grass and dead leaves. James must be moving to the front door to check out the noise.

Its back feet catch a tree root, and it springs at me. Telly swings one-handed but misses. For the second the beast is airborne, mouth open, ready to rip flesh, I make a possibly unwise decision. I drop my bat and make a fist.

As the dog knocks me backward I ram my surgical glove-covered fist into its huge open mouth, and before we hit the ground I've got him in a headlock.

My back smacks the earth. I clamp my feet around its back, pulling everything tight toward me.

Unable to close his mouth, thick neck muscles swing violently side to side. His huge size and bulk fling me about as he desperately tries ripping himself free.

Huge front paws push against my chest. Back nails dig into my abdomen as paws push against the force of my legs wrapped around him.

He's amazingly strong, but every time he moves, I pull tighter.

His breath is cut off. He knows it and goes increasingly berserk, trying to thrash and shake his head from my grip.

His frantic jerking continues to hop us about in little movements until we tip sideways.

I hang on for dear life.

The advantage is mine. I can't let up for a second.

His nails dig deeper. I cringe against the pain.

Every hysterical move I counter by tightening that fraction more, ramming my fist in harder, cramping his fight.

He's got plenty. I can't ease off and let him get a fresh go at me.

After what feels like minutes, he weakens.

Only a morsel, but I feel his resistance slacken.

Our heads are now all but touching. His black, evil eye stares menacing into mine.

My limbs begin to ache, but adrenalin keeps me completely focused.

Nothing around us exists except him and me in a fight to the death.

Suffocation imminent, he offers one last grand effort.

His head tries thrashing out of my desperately tight clinch.

Paw nails break my skin in one last big push.

I clamp that tiny molecule more, that last fraction needed to dispatch him.

Suddenly my concentration is almost broken by a hard sharp pain running through my thigh. Telly took a swing at the animal's back, but hit my leg.

He steps back with the bat poised to let another one go.

The dog's movements become less urgent.

Finally, he goes limp.

Victory is mine.

Sweating profusely, gasping heavily, I release all tension and roll on my back. To calm my pulse I take a few deep, controlled breaths.

"That was fucking impressive," Telly whispers.

I wipe dog slobber from my surgical glove on loose leaves before rubbing my throbbing leg where Telly's blow struck. I get to my feet slowly and brush my clothes.

"Piece of piss." Lungs now heaving less urgently, I smile broadly. Killing big dogs barehanded is in my blood. "What'd you hit me for?"

"Sorry. I thought you needed a hand. And I'm a righty. Swinging southpaw's difficult."

We let out a subdued laugh until a close voice nudges us back to alertness.

"Bear! Bear! Here boy!"

Bear. Another moron lacking originality. Telly must have thought so too. When the voice gets close, holding his bat spear-fashion he jumps out and smashes James square in the mouth.

Teeth fly. James goes down whimpering, clutching his mouth with both hands. I pick up my bat, step over the dead dog and look down at James, wet, a towel wrapped around his waist. Blood oozes through his fingers. He's eyes are wide with terror.

"Didnae see that comin, DID YE!" Telly yells in a Scottish brogue, need for silence now unnecessary. "Ye bin a naughty wee laddie. Bin doon things ye shouldnae be doon. Now's tame tay pay the fuckin piper, ye sorry piece a shite!"

He makes a big arc through the air and whacks his Mickey Mantle signature bat down on James' kneecap. Contact sounds bad. Bone-cracking. A pained, gargley moan shoots from his mouth as he grabs his knee. Telly lets out an evil little *he-he-he*.

Things under control, but still not one hundred percent sure we have the right person, I pull Telly off to whisper in his ear. I tell him to hold off until I've found the Mitsubishi. He nods agreement and I limp quickly to the far end of the house.

Behind lies an acre of manicured lawn dotted with mature native palms. A hammock sags low between two trunks. A large barn sits the other side of the lawn, so I jog lamely across, pull one of the big doors open and search for a light. There isn't one. A torch hangs by a cord from a screw. It flickers when I turn it on, so I bang the bulb end on my hand a few times until it stays lit. Batteries are almost shot, but there's enough light to give a general idea of what lies where before it dies.

I drop it and take a few steps to a covered vehicle. I pull off a green canvas cover, feel along the body, open the driver's door and an inside light flicks on. I turn lights on high-beam and move to the front. It's blue, and plates are missing. Blood-spattered bull-bars protect a grille with centred Mitsubishi diamonds. No doubt it's Telly's blood.

I don't bother turning off the headlights. When I round the house, Telly's boot sinks into James's side. Caught up in the moment, he carried on regardless.

Blood and mess smear James' face. A couple of fingers on his left hand point the wrong way. Looking down at him, I can't rouse any sympathy. He almost killed Telly and Daryl, and he almost killed me.

Still conscious, moaning, blubbering, he would no longer feel much. His next pain will start tomorrow, and last a couple of weeks, while he recovers.

Telly lets up. "Did ye fine the car, Fergus?"

I shake my head. "Sorry. We've made a huge mistake." Now Telly gives me a pissed-off look. "Only fucking with ya," I add. "Let's go."

Telly can't understand my attitude. "Ye dinnae wan a piece?"

"I killed his best friend. He's done."

We drop our bats beside him and walk up the drive removing balaclavas and gloves.

"What's with all the *laddie* and *dinnae* shit?"

Telly's pleased with his improv. "Been reading Irvine Welsh. I thought I'd try and confuse old James a bit."

"Who's he?"

"He's the piece of shit we just beat up." He smiles. "Only fucking with ya. He's the guy wrote *Trainspotting* and *Filth*. His characters have really broad Scottish accents. Good stuff. Wanna borrow one?"

"No." Suddenly hunger pangs hit. It's been a long while since breakfast. "Hungry?"

"Fuck yeah."

Back at Telly's car, parked off the road behind trees, we climb in and sit in silence. We're both thinking James is too far out of town to be found. Telly takes his phone from the centre armrest to dial the emergency number.

"Yeah, there's a sorry sack-o-shit lying in his driveway. Better send an ambulance to. . ."

I wait until he hangs up. "Where we eating?"

"First place we come to." He starts the car. "Still liked that move with the dog. Veeeery smooth." We roll out of our hiding place, moving toward town. "Some days I wouldn't mind trying that on a hooker or two."

I watched my minder in Peru perform the same stunt. I had the same reaction Telly's having.

"You're making me blush."

19

Next day, another afternoon shift. It's quiet, but I'm on the road earning. James' unfortunate accident happened too late to make the morning paper, but there's been no mention of it on the radio. Contrary to the pathetic, jealous, cowardly stalker that he is, maybe he's going to take his medicine. Then again, what can he say?

Street heat outside the Marriott is oppressive. Can't park in the hotel basement because someone watching monitors will toss me out like last time. So I sit sweating, twiddle my thumbs and look about the interior. Carpet needs a vacuum, but nothing new there. Pieces of paper with jottings of girls' ramblings stuffed into the open driver's door panel threaten to spill out. That book I'm never going to write gets more consideration, and the laptop I thought about a day or two ago is looking good. It would give me something to amuse myself during down time.

Thirty minutes into the hour job, wwwDot rings to say Fran and Porsche have extended another hour, possibly two. This puts a different spin on things. I can do something constructive for the allotted ninety minutes. Windows go up, air-con goes on, and I head two suburbs over to Aspro's.

His printing shop sits at the end of six businesses set back from the main road. The video shop's gone bust, but a medical centre, chemist, bottleshop and florist defy crappy economic times.

I step through Aspro's front door. A man and woman sit with their backs to the shopfront window, waiting for printed stuff. A gum-chewing cheap suit resembling a used car salesman uses a coin-fed photocopier. The pretty brunette who sold me my stickers wiggles fingers my way and calls out back. Aspro appears, eyes the seated couple, leans on the counter beside me.

"Fuck there's some ugly buggers in the world," he says quietly.

The young brunette grins at his comment as I take a surreptitious glance behind me.

"Tell me about it," I say. "Should be a law against the bastards breeding."

"So," he says a little louder, "what brings thee hither?"

"That computer you were . . . giving away. Still got it?"

He rubs his chin. "Don't recall having one I was giving away. Got one for sale." He does a follow-me sign. "Step into my office."

Out back, a couple of car-size machines click and spit out colour posters. One of three smaller jobs drops completed pamphlets onto an increasing pile. Another young brunette appears to be running things. Aspro and I step into his air-conditioned office. He kicks the mostly glass door shut and we sit either side of his desk.

"You still set type these days?"

"Isn't much that can't be done with computers. Two in every home and I've never been busier. The public are idiots."

"And ugly."

"Yeah. And ugly."

He reaches behind for a lidless cardboard box on a paper-crammed shelf, lifts it off and places it on the desk in front of him. Inside, a laptop and accessories. The tight-fisted bastard would have bought it through the business, costing him nothing. I can afford a new one, but when its only function will be as a typewriter, if it gets used at all, the expense couldn't be justified.

"I've seen your stickers on a few cars around town," he says. "Magic Happens. Pretty fucking corny."

The second big-breasted brunette opens the door without knocking. She drops a blue folder on top of an old metal filing cabinet.

"This is Angie," Aspro says. "She runs things now when I'm not here. Angie baby, this is Myers."

She says hi, smiles.

"That would mean you run things pretty much all the time," I say.

"Pretty much." She winks at Aspro before returning to her clicking machines.

"For a good deal on the computer I can make sure she doesn't file work-related sexual harassment charges."

"Bit hard when she's a willing participant," he grins. "Jealous?"

"Nothing a free laptop wouldn't cure me of."

"Still running those sluts around?"

"Fine upstanding young women. Each and every one of them."

"Yeah-yeah. Keep telling yourself that and it might come true. Magic happens, apparently."

His desk phone rings. He picks up, listens, lets out a loud *Wooohooo*, hangs up and punches the air a half dozen times. I think he's happy about something.

He claps and rubs his hands together before making a grandiose gesture of pushing the computer across to my side of the desk. If it's free, as he's suggesting, my first instinct is to grab it and run before the old Indian Giver changes his mind. But I sit quietly, awaiting a punch line.

"It's yours," he says cheerfully. "I picked up a book yesterday and I've just been told it's worth over twenty-eight thousand English Pounds. Shakespeare's sonnets. Second edition.."

"Congrats."

"Wouldn't believe it," he begins, a book-spotting boast about to be rammed down my throat. "Got it in a Salvation Army op shop. Have a guess how much. Go on. How much you reckon?"

"Five cents."

"Fucking smartarse." He holds up a finger. "One single solitary dollar. One spondooly. An Oxford scholar. A single beer token. One hundred pitiful cents. Best damn buck I ever spent." He swings a computer screen around and taps away at the keyboard. "What's an English Pound worth in real money?"

Angie must have spotted Aspro's antics through the office windows. The door opens and she pokes her head in.

"What's up? Good news?"

He doesn't even look up. "No. Bugger off."

The door closes, his mouth becomes a tight circle and he noisily sucks in air. "Wow. More than double." He leans back, satisfied. "Every Thursday, when new stock is put on the shelves and clothes racks at op shops, housewives climb out of their four wheel drives looking for labels they can buy for a song and then put straight on the internet. None of them think to look at books."

"The public are idiots," I say.

"And ugly."

"Yeah, that too."

I'm in the passenger seat, closed computer on my lap. An ice cold can of Fanta sits snugly in a Heineken stubbie holder on the dash. Ham and cheese deli sandwiches lie on the driver's seat.

Where to begin? What to do? I'll try writing a chapter. See how it goes.

Fuck it. I've no idea. At 34, for me this reading game's a new lark. At school when we were told to read *Animal Farm*, I didn't bother. It got discussed during English class, making the storyline easy to pick up. Its main tagline virtually explained the book. All animals are equal, but some are more equal than others. Shit, I could even stick my hand up and answer the odd question. Animals revolt, the farmer is ousted, pigs are in charge. Head pig is Napoleon, and for obvious reasons horses become barnyard enforcers. So why waste time reading when there're empty tennis courts nearby?

Where to begin? No good asking Fastlove for tips. According to him just about everything published these days is glug. Mountains of it, by people with nothing to say. Angst-filled rubbish by scribes who suffered childhood problems nobody cares about. But he's overly pedantic.

I just need to pick a story to get started. I can always change it later. Nothing.

There must be something interesting these hookers do. Stories I tell Fastlove get a laugh. Others hearing them want more. So. . .

Nothing.

I pop my new secondhand laptop open, press the ON button. If it can smell fear, I'm fucked. An image of a big-dicked male shagging a woman on all fours pops up, Michelle Pfeiffer's head, as a brunette, superimposed on the female body, Aspro's on the man's.

I dial his work number.

"I've just seen the tasteless, over-the-top picture of you giving Michelle Pfeiffer one on my computer," I say. "You're a sick, perverted individual. Can you do something like that for me?"

"Easy. Salma Hayek? I'll send them over the airwaves. Expect them tomorrow."

"You need to get a constructive job."

When he cuts the connection, I punch up a Pages-type program and go back to my dilemma of where to kick off. The first notes jotted down were of Phoebe exiting a job with wet shoes she'd worn in a shower. No, maybe something simpler, like the first time I met Vanessa. But that's still a blur. I'd have to make shit up, and my imagination isn't that good.

Peru. Now that was an experience worth writing about. How to secure one's future while surviving the most strenuous, bizarre, life-threatening circumstances. Also not good. This will be about a guy driving prostitutes, which he doesn't do in South America.

Fastlove. There's a character. Clever, witty, larger than life, rugged, reader and writer of poetry, plus a real lowlife Romeo Rat.

Still my fingers won't work. Writer's block. Can it be called that if I've never written?

A different frame of mind is needed. I'm doing this merely to fill time in the car. It beats sitting staring at Jap tourists walking about with cameras around their necks. Just then, Heather's hubby speeds his heap in the opposite direction, four lanes over, and I have my start.

It'll be him, sitting in the brothel carpark, smoking dope, waiting for Heather to finish her shift. From there to the incident with Sean's vibrator, the unemployment office, the tit-less wonder at the takeaway, ending my first chapter with Brendan burying a case of money in front of my ant-infested shack. But I'll change Brendan's name to . . . Bob, so he doesn't get in the shit with Inland Revenue. Same with Telly and myself. Hookers use aliases anyway, and if they don't, they can deny this shit themselves.

* *

By the time Fran and Porsche call out, only one rough page is completed. Pecking away one-fingered seems to take an inordinate amount of time. However, even with typing skills it's doubtful more pages would have eventuated. It doesn't seem to be my cup of tea. I close the laptop, tidy up, slide over and drive up to the Marriott's front entrance.

Fran and Porsche climb in. I roll down to the footpath, stop and hold out my hand. Fran places money in my palm without a word. After counting, it's three hundred and eighty dollars light.

"Where's the rest?"

"Bastard," she says. "When we get there he paid for the first hour in cash, then later he paid for the second. When he booked the third we were in the Jacuzzi, but he said it was all there, so we didn't get out. At the end of the third hour he goes through his pants and comes up short."

"He didn't have a credit card?"

"Said he didn't." She shrugs. "What could we do?"

Porsche talks from the back seat."Don't spose you'd go up and. . ."

Prostitution one-O-one: *Get the money up front*. The only time it doesn't happen is in shit movies and unrealistic 'tell-all' books by women claiming to be ex-hookers. It's similar to getting booze on tick. Nobody likes paying for last night's consumed piss.

"You suppose right," I say. "How long you been doing this?"

"But the way he talked, he was loaded."

I ring wwwDot for guidance. There's a moment's silence, then she tells me to come home. Upon our return, I hand the short stack to wwwDot and watch proceedings from the kitchen.

WwwDot counts the cash before looking at Fran and Porsche. "This is just stupidity on your part. How long have you been in this business? Ten years? Well, Myers gets paid for three hours, the house gets paid, and you two come up short."

They come up plenty short. Less than an hour's payment for a three hour job. That won't be happening again for a while. My hat goes off to the client, easily conning a couple of veterans.

"Myers could have gone in and got it," Fran says.

"Running escorts over the border is illegal. And if Myers went up he'd probably feel obliged to thump the guy. Anyway, this has absolutely nothing to do with him. You rang in and said the third hour was fine. You lied. It's on you."

Fran and Porsche slink away dejectedly to their room. They fucked up, and know it.

20

Chloe's eyes dart frantically about the prostitute-filled kitchen. "Where's my phone? I left it on the table. Sally, there's a thief in the house."

Sally steps out of the office to placate her. "When you went into your last job I put it in your box."

Chloe makes a funny, surprised, relieved face and covers her crotch. "Ohh, I didn't feel a thing."

"That's cause you're so loose," Heather says, "I can hear your nether regions clappin and slappin as you're walking around."

"Well," Chloe says, "I wasn't going to say anythink, but this guy went down on me last night and said he heard an echo. Said it was like talking into the Grand Canyon. . . canyon. . . canyon. . ."

"Hey, Myers," Porsche says, "not long now before you lose your trip."

"Looks that way."

She turns to Mercedes. "Told you he had something up his sleeve. Wanna make it fifty?"

"He just said he's going to lose," Mercedes says. "And we all know the other contestant's Nikki's boyfriend. Make it a hundred if you like."

Now they're making side bets. When shit hits the fan, there will be a lot of pissed off hookers running around. Hopefully.

Mistress Jacqui watches proceedings, me in particular. "I'll have a hundred on Myers," she says. "Want it?"

"Okay," Mercedes responds confidently. "Make it more if you like."

"Five?"

"Sure."

"It'll be a pleasure taking your money." Mistress Jacqui winks at me, finishes her coffee and places her cup in the sink. "But now, ladies, you'll have to excuse me. I have to nail a company CEO's scrotum to a piece of wood, then stick a fish hook through his foreskin."

My legs involuntarily close. Telly's face contorts in imagined agony.

"Jesus Christ," he says. "Must we hear details."

"While you're out tonight, Myers," Chloe says, "don't spose you'll be going to a Kentucky Fried Chicken?"

"Hadn't planned on it."

"It's just that I need a toy. It's the last one in a set and I promised my daughter. The promo finishes tonight."

"Then if I'm close to a Kentucky Fucked Duck, I shall get you one."

"You're a prince. Wish I had one at home like you, stead of that lazy shit I got now."

I feign a blush. "Stop it."

"Can I come out in your car tonight, Myers?" Sean asks.

"No." However it's not up to me. Sally has last word.

"What, just like that?"

"Just like that."

"But why?"

"Cause you've just eaten. Now you'll spend the next hour and a half sucking your teeth, picking them with your tongue, accompanied with some seriously gross sucking noises. It gets on my wick."

"Fuck you." She turns to Telly. "Can I come with you?"

"Nope."

"Why the fuck not?"

"Same reason," he says. "Now he's pointed it out, that's all I'll be hearing all night. Kinda like a song getting stuck in your head."

"Sally," Sean says, "can't you—?"

"No," Sally says, pressing a phone against her ample breast. "Already decided who's going out tonight. We're short of girls so you're staying in." Then, to me, "Fran's on the phone. You were supposed to pick her up."

"Turned up," I say. "On time. Waited ten minutes She didn't show."

"You didn't come out," Sally says into the phone. "You want picked up now, you'll have to pay twice." She hangs up and turns to Telly. "You can pick her up and keep her tonight." Then, again to me. "You could toot or something."

"They all know we don't toot, because most of them don't like the noise and the nosy neighbours it attracts. Can't ring, because most of the time they've got their damn phone switched off, so we end up talking to a machine. Can't go in, because they don't like it, and why should we anyway. They get told when we're going to turn up, and half the time they can't even look out the damn window. Or they're not even there. So tell me, how long do we wait before assuming they're not coming out? Ten minutes? Thirty?"

"A real prince," Telly says.

A hundred dollars is a hundred dollars. That's tonight's price to get me into a hotel room to watch a guy fuck Babs. I shouldn't complain. Some people would pay *him* to watch. Everything's about-faced and missed opportunities.

While his twenty-five year-old sheathed dick slides in and out of her, he seems more interested in watching me than concentrating on what he's doing. Therefore I can't look away. Got to give him his money's worth.

His pace varies, probably trying to stretch it out. The end of every downstroke brings a hard push Babs is starting to find uncomfortable. This adds to his pleasure, broadening his lecherous leer. Babs stops for more lube, but I think it's to give herself a break. After forty-five minutes he doesn't seem close. Air-con isn't on, so he's covered in sweat. Odd shaped black moles dot his badly freckled back. They look cancerous. The money he's pissing away on this hour might be better spent on a cab ride to a skin clinic. No excuses. Fucking things are all over the coast, and free.

But, of course, I'm not telling him that. My hundred equals a cosy meal for two, with a bottle of wine, in a Waikiki beach café. He'll have to live with his cancer a little longer. Let it take hold, making it a long involved chore getting rid of it.

Babs lets out a little squeal that's supposed to sound pleasurable, but there's a tinge of pain mixed in. Any wonder some females turn to women from the Isle of Lesbos for their intimacy?

Last time I got paid to watch was in a guy's house. He wanted me positioned in his wife's closet, door ajar, eye noticeable at the opening. He shagged Destiny, a looker with skills. Once she started working it, doing things to him that made my dick real hard, real quick, unzipping was all I could do to relieve the pressure. Then, of course, cock out and fully erect, I had to jerk off. Very slowly, to the rhythm of her bobbing head. Getting paid to masturbate. That's the way to make money. And not a sperm bank within cooee. I think I exploded into a hanging dress before dripping copiously on to his wife's shoes. It was dark in there. I couldn't be sure.

Watching this one trick pony is actually boring. So much so I can't prevent my mind wandering. How much spending money should I take to Hawaii? Doesn't matter, I've got plastic. On leaving this hotel I have fifteen minutes to pick up Phoebe from another hotel. After that we can hopefully meet Telly for coffee. Still need to swing by for Chloe's toy, but there are twenty-four hour fast food joints in Surfers Paradise.

Arse jerking up and down, his thick dick continues pumping. I wonder what Vanessa is doing. And how is James coping? He must be in hospital. One doesn't get over a beating like that at home. One needs a few weeks' care. Bear is no doubt still lying where I choked the poor big bastard. Insect fodder. I tenderly rub my stomach where the dog's nails tore and scratched my skin.

Finally, seven minutes to spare, Casanova groans, arches his back, gives Babs a few last deep pumps, then rolls off looking pleased with himself. He grabs a cigarette from the bedside table, lights it with a soft book of matches, takes a big drag and watches his dick go limp, the half-full condom drooping like a sick, wilting flower.

For an extra ten dollars I could clap, cheer, yell bravo, but he didn't request it. Babs hops up for a shower. I merely leave the room.

Babs hands over the money and thanks me for coming upstairs. For allowing me to watch, melanoma-man paid her an extra fifty.

"Only too pleased to help. You bring lingerie? You've got a two hour booking and he wants lacy knickers."

She rummages in a bag at her feet. "Always come prepared."

On the short drive, with zero bashfulness Babs replaces her underclothes with lace-trimmed accessories and stockings.

"You want to go for a drink some time?" she asks, slipping into her shoes.

Jesus, is she asking me on a date, or just to have sex? I pull up outside the hotel and give her a light-hearted smile. Drivers get sacked for fucking the hookers.

"My boyfriend wouldn't like it," I tell her.

"No, I'm keen. No one need know if you don't want them to."

"Thanks," I say. "I would, but there's no way I could hang around with a smoker. I've tried a couple of times and" — I squirm about and look sorry — "I couldn't stand it."

"Oh well. Keep it in mind." She smiles, pulls a white vibrator the size of a large index finger from her bag, then turns the base until it hums. "I'm pretty handy with one of these. You might enjoy it."

Telly and Fran, Phoebe and I meet at a 24-hour kebab shack. We sit at a small round table on the footpath. I take in the blackboard menu high behind the counter.

"Lasagne's good," Telly says. "They'll put it in a plastic tub in case we have to leave early."

I scan down until spotting the item mentioned. It reads LASAGNA.

"Don't think so. I prefer my lasagne spelt with an 'e'."

The obese woman Telly yelled at waddles up to the counter blissfully unaware of who we are. I nudge him and raise eyebrows her way. His eyes light up as he looks across.

"Hey look. It's the salad dodger back for another sugar hit."

She turns, registers who it is, then turns back, nose defiantly in the air.

"When you've ordered," Telly continues, "come park your wide butt with us and have a chat."

"Arsehole," she says without turning.

"Come over here and kiss me, honey," Telly says. "Nothing makes *me* sick."

"I'm not putting up with this garbage," she mumbles, retreating down the street without ordering.

"See you next time," Telly calls, waving a friendly goodbye. "You'd think someone that size would have grown a thick skin by now. I mean, she didn't get that big over night."

A waiter fronts. We order four coffees, with toasted sandwiches for Telly and myself.

"So when's the big night, Myers?"

Fran finishes a conversation on her phone and slides around in her seat. "Yeah, Myers, when's the big showdown?"

"Tomorrow night. Leaving a few days later."

The girls smile slyly at each other. They have money on me losing. Or something like that. It's hard keeping track. Telly remains as deadpan as I've ever seen him.

A few hours later, twenty minutes into an hour job, Babs exits a house without ringing out. Behind her stomps a pissed-off, well built Maori or Islander of some description wearing only a pair of faded jeans. He comes straight to my side of the car and looks down menacingly. I crack the window slightly. Babs moves in beside him.

"I checked him," she states. "He's got things on his dick. When I said I was leaving, he said he'd settle for hand relief with a condom on. Half way through, he changes his mind and says he wants sex."

This is awkward. He's so close I can't open my door.

"I want my fuckin money back," he spits, baring teeth nastily.

"I told him he couldn't cause he's seen me naked. But he said 'Lets go see what Guido's got to say.'"

He flashes his best intimidation face. His shirt was doubtless left off for effect. Tattooed, moulded dark skin ripples in the moonlight.

"So, Guido, you're the hard man?" he says. "The one I talk to about my money?"

"Me?" I say calmly. "I'm just the dummy with the car."

Babs starts speaking again, but he turns, pointing at her face.

"Shut up. I'm talking to ya pimp."

Guido and pimp. We're not off to a spiffing start. While he talks to Babs, I quickly plug my phone into a short charging cord perpetually dangling from the dashboard cigarette lighter socket. When he turns back, I pretend to dial a number before holding up a polite finger.

"Just ringing the boss. I'll see what she has to say. Won't take long." I wind down the window, then hold my phone close to the door sill. "Wants to speak to you," I say nicely.

He's big, but not too bright. When he leans over to speak into my phone, I give him an elbow to the face. The perfect shot, right on the button. He staggers back and drops to the grass verge the other side of the street. *Once Were Warriors*? Not this one. More like Once Were Wankers. His proud ancestors would be disgusted.

I tell Babs to get in. She hurries to the passenger side and we take off. We get away clean, but I'm far from pleased. The situation shouldn't have ended with a man lying in the street. When Babs saw he was . . . flawed, she should have left.

"We showed him," she boasts.

Unplugging my phone, I can't help but wonder if Salma has nights like this.

Unlikely.

7.30 a.m.. Everyone's being paid. Telly emerges from the office and hands me ten dollars for the pick-up that didn't show.

"Another routine, successful night at the orifice," I say.

He snickers at my comment. "Not the way Babs tells it."

I put the note in my pocket. Sally then calls me into the office, where she counts and apportions tonight's girls', house and drive money I collected. I exchange ten fifties for five hundreds. When one doesn't spend much, larger denomination notes are preferred, as stashing money seems to take up a lot of room. At home, these and three others are added to the biscuit tin behind the stove.

I pop a beer in the squatting Polynesian God's mouth atop the stereo speaker. I open my laptop sitting on the breakfast bar and go over my opening page. For a first draft, it now doesn't seem too bad. But, of course, it could be monumental crap.

What's needed for inspiration is a title. I turn sideways, lean back against the wall, lift feet on to another stool, use the clicker to turn on the stereo radio, close my eyes and sip Heineken.

David Bowie's *Young Americans* comes on, forcing me to sing along out of tune as best I can without having heard it for what must be fifteen years. Lyrics were indistinguishable then, and things haven't improved. Something concerning an un-American, then *idle sin* blah blah blah *loud*, followed by something about leather and ghetto I can only mumble to.

Idle sin.

I ring Brendan. "You near the internet?"

"What do you want?" Endless moaning about my lack of on-line amenities has thankfully ceased.

"Lyrics. Bowie's *Young Americans.*"

It takes a minute. "Okay."

"There's a bit, You and your idle sin, something, something."

"There's nothing about idle sin. It goes on about idle singing falsettos."

"Is that supposed to mean something?"

"Who knows. It's not an official website, so there's every possibility it could be something completely different. And it's Bowie. I heard he used to write words on pieces of paper and pull them randomly out of a jar. For *Suffragette City*, I used to sing 'The smell of fat chicks,' instead of 'This mellow—' "

"Yeah yeah. Good story."

I hang up, slide page one back to its beginning and type *Idle Sin* in big letters. Then underline it. I smile at its originality. No royalties for you, Mister Bowie.

Vanessa will be here in two hours. Then I can 'idle sin' her.

21

The heavy bag dangles from a hardened steel butcher's hook slung over a tree branch beside the garage/shed housing my Aston Martin. It swings back, I dance sideways and give it a speedy one-two. Breathing's hard, hair's wet, shorts drip with sweat running down my uncovered torso.

Twelve cows watch from their side of the wire, possibly thinking I'm no boxer. I show them a little Ali shuffle, but they don't seem impressed. I jog on the spot, hands above my head, humming the *Rocky* theme. They're a tough crowd. I add a menacing "YO!" Still nothing. Maybe they've seen *Rocky VI* and know the show's over. I could tell them my preferred brand of cheese is Laughing Cow, but they might gang up on me.

I resume pounding the bag, but Vanessa's car driving toward the shack means quitting time. She's an hour early. I remove sparring mitts and walk down to open the wire. Brendan and Janet's red Range Rover is behind her.

They drive in and I reconnect the wire. Avoiding my sweat-covered body, Vanessa gets out and leans in to kiss me. She notices the deep red welts where Bear's nails tore into my chest and abdomen.

"What happened?"

"Had a workout with Telly. He's another driver." We move toward the shack door. I'd call it the front door, but that implies there is another. "You're an hour early."

She says a hospital visit finished early, then Janet rang and it was decided to come for breakfast.

"Hospital?" I say. "Not your mother, I hope."

"Remember the photos of James, my old boyfriend? Someone beat him up badly. He looks terrible. Broken teeth, spleen, ribs, smashed kneecap. Oh it was awful."

Brendan's eyes lock with mine for a half second, and instantly he knows it was me. He would also know there must have been a reason other than the fact he is Vanessa's ex.

"Sounds nasty," I say. "He be all right? Get in any good shots of his own?"

"Says he was blindsided. Never saw it coming. One was an Irishman, but he didn't see their faces or even know why it happened. They also killed his dog. Bear was a beautiful animal."

Not to mention a strong bastard. I'll enjoy informing Telly his Scottish accent sounded Irish.

"Maybe he's been a naughty boy," Brendan says.

Vanessa stops. "What . . . what do you mean?"

"Y'know," he says, continuing walking, probably wishing he hadn't opened his mouth, "a guy takes a beating like that, then says he knows nothing. It just makes you wonder if he's been pissing somebody off. He won't say anything now because he was maybe doing something, I don't know, a little less than legal in the first place. You said it happened at his house, and he wasn't robbed. Sounds a lot like he'd taken what was coming to him."

Her eyes widen and her bottom lip disappears. "Good God. Do you think so? I couldn't imagine James doing anything to get beaten up over. He's got loads of money. He has no reason to do anything illegal." She glances enquiringly my way, perhaps seeking confirmation of Brendan's theory.

"Who knows," I say. "Could be he cut someone off on the road, then showed them his middle finger. People take umbrage at the slightest thing these days. So who's making breakfast?"

Brendan steps over the wire to check his beloved cows. Toting shopping bags, Vanessa and Janet make their way inside. I head into the bathroom for a shower. While rinsing my hair, Brendan walks in.

"Only me," he says.

Visible through the thin shower curtain, he drops the toilet seat cover and sits. I brush my teeth, turn off the water, slide back the curtain, lift a towel off the toilet cistern and buff my hair.

"So, does James being out of action solve your problem too?" I ask.

He leans forward, elbows on knees, fingers interlaced. Low stereo music drowns our voices.

"Probably not," he says. It's the first time he's admitted something is wrong. "So how'd you find out about this guy James?"

"Bit of luck. Telly would still be laying into him if I wasn't there."

"Could have called me. Bastard. I miss *all* the good shit these days."

"You're a semi-respectable businessman. If it went pear-shaped you wouldn't have wanted to be there." I wrap the towel around my waist, step out and sit on a wicker clothesbasket. "Anyway, married men don't do that sort of thing. If anything happened to you we both know who Janet would blame."

I know his look. There's genuine disappointment he wasn't the first person I called.

"It was Telly's and my problem," I tell him. "A driver thing. It was us he was putting off the road."

He accepts my explanation. "So why was he trying to give it to my drivers?"

"Jealous prick. Doesn't like the idea of me slipping it to Vanessa. Nearest thing I can figure, he knew what I did and where I did it, but for some reason didn't know the car I drove."

"Telly know this?"

I spray on deodorant. "Oh yeah."

"So when's the big play-off, buddy?"

"Tonight. You good to go?"

"Yeah. Confident it'll come off?"

"Yip. It's almost a done deal. I know the last question, so as long as I can get past my first one, they won't know what hit them."

"Nikki have any idea what's going on?"

I grunt. "What do you reckon? If R.D. mentioned it to her, something would have been said."

"She's going to be pissed off."

"Good, isn't it."

He shakes his head. "Lot of damn trouble for a trip to Hawaii."

"It's not the trip. It's the concert and party full of celebs afterward." I squirt Armani *White* on my neck. "Never know, might even treat it as a pre-live together. Get to know what Vanessa's like to be with day and night."

The idea appeals to him. His wife is now amicable toward me. He and I can do things like we used to without her thinking I'm corrupting him. The four of us can also gad about together.

"Bit quick for you, isn't it? You've only known her five minutes."

"Never met anyone like her. And she doesn't know how much moolah I have."

"I'm sure Janet's told her you're not short. I don't think that would be a consideration, anyway."

"She's got plenty?"

His head bobs about. "Yes and no. Wouldn't have at the moment, but she's an only child. Daddy's dead. He invented some technical attachment thing for movie cameras. So mum's got oodles. Thirty-five, forty mill, maybe."

"No shit." We move to the door.

"*You* won't be bashing people with that kind of money, either," he says.

I slap his back and slide the door open. "All the more reason to bash arseholes who deserve it. Wouldn't want to end up a hog-tied dullard like you."

He sneers. I enter my bedroom to throw on shorts and a T-shirt. Vanessa and Janet are giggling already. On empty stomachs expensive champagne goes to work quickly. I liberate a cold beer and join them at the breakfast bar.

"Beer?" Vanessa says.

"This is my dinner, not breakfast. Why can you sup champagne at this hour and I can't drink beer?"

"Breeding, darling."

For the first time in my life I feel kind of warm inside. Since deciding to ask Vanessa to move in, her endearments have that much more meaning. Or maybe I'm reading too much into it. I'm in uncharted territory. I've yet to find that flaw. There must be at least one. Nobody's that perfect.

I never thought Brendan would settle down. Before his wedding I reminded him of our motto. Some things are plainly too expensive. If you fly it, fuck it, or float it — rent it. At the wedding chapel, those wise words had no meaning. That's what love does, I suppose.

Brendan's fingers snap in front of my face. "Myers, we're drinking to you two." He holds up his glass. "Hawaii."

I click my Heineken bottle with their glasses. "Hawaii."

"You okay?" Vanessa asks.

I smile at her, then Brendan and Janet. He's grinning. He knows my thoughts only too well.

"Couldn't be better."

She places a hand on my thigh. "I have every faith he's going to win."

22

In it's male slut style, Jewboy lies on a sheepskin on the brothel's kitchen floor, feet bent in the air.

"I think Dead Dog Walking's carked it."

Sally stops writing. "Don't you start. I'm not in the mood."

She's usually pretty tolerant. She may expect trouble tonight after the competition has been decided. Either way, there will be a few pissed off punters. Or it could just be her time of the month. If she still has one. Maybe it's what comes after that. Hormones, or whatever. That mysterious female anatomy again.

I take coffee to a spot at the kitchen table where I can watch office monitors. A car swings into the carpark and an unfamiliar girl gets out holding a sports bag. Sally punches a button to release deadlocks, allowing foyer access. Guest lounge empty, I trot out to admit her.

Seated back with my coffee, I look her over while she waits for Sally. Body's good, but there's something not quite right about her face that I can't pick. She's pretty enough, blonde locks to her shoulders, a long fringe partly obscuring one eye. I don't know. . .

Sally steps out of the office. "I'm Sally."

Keeping her head slightly bowed, the new girl smiles sweetly.

"I'm Patsy. We spoke on the phone."

"You said you were twenty-one, blonde and good-looking. You're thirty, and look it."

Then comes a quizzical frown as Sally notices something's not quite right. She cranks her neck to peek through Patsy's fringe.

"Are you on something? You're not a fucking smackie are you?" Sally moves a bit closer. "What's wrong with your eye?"

Patsy turns a tad sheepish. "A little scarring. I lost my eye in a car accident."

"Oh! So when you describe yourself on the phone, it doesn't occur to you to say, 'I'm twenty-one, blonde, good-looking, and oh yeah, I'VE GOT ONE FUCKING EYE!' "

Telly should be here to witness this. I'm close to wetting myself. This could be an entire book chapter all its own.

A phone rings and Sally steams into the office. Not sure whether to stay or leave, Patsy, somewhat awkwardly, just stands there.

Sally answers in her seductive schoolgirl voice. "Hello, can I help you?" Then her voice turns normal. ". . . Yes, I'm always looking for new girls. What do you look like?. . .Yeah?. . .Well that sounds good. How many fucking eyes do you have?"

Patsy shoots me a one-eyed idiotic look while Sally finishes her conversation. I consider asking if she's heard about the one-eyed Japanese prostitute who, after her sailor client had given her one in the eye socket, waves him goodbye saying, 'I'll keep an eye out for you!' But I decide against it. Only because Sally might overhear, and in her present mood. . .

I make three trips to my car, each time retrieving gear I hope will give me an advantage for tonight's radio play-off. The third time, I shut the side gate behind Patsy. I don't know what happened, but she's leaving.

"Cyclops not staying?" I ask Sally.

A cross between a growl and an angry moan comes from her mouth as she returns to her phones. I begin setting up my gear. Chelsea appears from the girls' room flashing her crooked, cheeky smile from that pretty face I haven't seen for a few weeks.

"Three weeks up already?" I ask. "Good to see you're back."

"Thanks, Myers."

"But I'd rather see your front."

"Ah," she says sarcastically, dropping a teaspoon of decaf into a cup. "I've missed you and Telly. The girls say you almost won a trip to Hawaii."

"Twould seem they're a trifle premature. The play-off's tonight. I haven't quite lost yet."

She smirks at the TV and DVD player I'm setting up atop the bench. "Yeah, you have."

Before going on holiday her hair was natural honey blonde. Now there's a light brown tinge running through it. She catches me looking.

"It's called copper something." She swishes it about. "Like it?"

If I didn't know better, I'd say a dog pissed on her head.

"Yeah, suits you."

The competition comes on early. Girls listen in their room, leaving the kitchen to Sally, Mistress Jacqui and me.

Allllrighty, this is the ultimate night for two big George Michael fans. Going up against each other is R.D. the trucker, and Myers the self-employed courier. One of these lucky gents will be taking a partner of their choice to Hawaii to an invitation only concert, and then attending the star-studded party afterwards. And I can tell you, folks, that there is no media allowed at the after match function, so you can bet the stars will be letting their hair down. Are you ready, R.D.?

Yes, Rick.

Myers?

In front of me, on the table, lie fifteen CD covers, removed from their cases so I can read them quickly. Lyric sheets printed from the internet sit in piles according to their originating albums. *Wham! The Official Biography* is open and skimmed again before this afternoon's sleep. On the bench, a TV/DVD player I've loaded with one Wham and two George Michael discs. I'm about as ready as I can be. Unlike R.D., who has the answers, I still have to get past my 'easy one' before we get the separator.

"Aloha," I say into my phone. Mistress Jacqui winks at me.

Okie-dokie. I'll ask you both a couple of questions, and if you're still locked together, I'll ask a question that's answer is a number, so closest will win. Allllrighty, we're off and running. R.D., in the song Wake Me Up Before You Go-Go, *what is put into George's heart and what is put into his brain?*

Two questions each? It was supposed to be one. Fuck it.

Um, I've misplaced my notes, but I'm pretty sure boom-boom goes in his heart, and, a jitterbug goes in his brain.

Ho-ho. Correct-a-mundo. You've been studying up, R.D.. Okay, Myers, in the video clip Kissing A Fool — I pick up the DVD clicker, hit disc two, track thirteen — *what time does the clock in the background show?*

You've gotta love this modern technology. The clip is running before he's finished asking his question. Skimming through at eight times normal speed, a clock springs up, and I freeze it.

"Bout sixteen minutes to ten."

Ho-ho. I can see someone else has been studying. Okie-dokie, R.D., continuing the video theme, who's the very first face you see on the Freedom 90 *clip?*

Ah, that's an easy one. Linda Evangalista, the supermodel.

Hah. They're all easy when you know the answers, R.D..

Smart prick's rubbing my nose in it. But last laughs can be mine if I get the next one right. Mistress Jacqui and Sally look nervous.

Here we go, Myers. George recorded a song with Mary J. Blige called As. — Not a problem, I rummage through single CD covers and hold it ready — *This was a remake of a Stevie Wonder song. From which Stevie Wonder album did the song originate?*

Stevie fucking Wonder! Who the fuck would know this?!!! I can't name *one* of his albums. I've never *seen* one of his albums. I flick the cover over to check credits and acknowledgements. No miracle today. Stevie Wonder gets a nod for writing the song, but there's nothing about an album.

I'm sunk.

It's over.

I've lost.

I sink back and throw up my hands. Sally's nervous grin turns to a smile.

"*Songs in the Key of Life,*" she says. Just like that. "And you didn't hear it from me."

Back from the brink! "*Songs in the Key of Life,*" I repeat into the phone.

Well, well, that's absolutely CORRECT-A-MUNDO. So, it comes down to a tie-breaker. The exciting finale, folks. Here's the big question; and remember, closest to it wins the trip of a lifetime. In the song of the same name, how many times does George sing the word Faith? R.D., you want first shot? Better be quick, cause I'm sure Myers is digging out the CD as we speak.

I actually had this written down, Rick. But like I said, I've not got my notes with me.

Have a shot anyway, R.D.. You've only got a few seconds before I go to Myers.

Okay, I'm pretty sure I remember. He says it a lot. So I'll say thirty-six.

Wow. Not bad. Do you know how many times he says Faith, Myers?

"Well, suck me dry and call me dusty," I say "What's the odds of being asked this?"

Pardon?

"Twenty-seven."

Nikki's scream pierces the kitchen. Rick is silent, no doubt wondering what the hell went wrong.

Well, well, — Rick finally says flatly — *seems you've hit it on the head. Congratulations, Myers. Who was it you said you were taking with you to Hawaii?*

"I made a deal with a friend, but she broke it, so now I'm taking my girlfriend, Vanessa. She's looking forward to the trip as much as I am, Prick — sorry, Rick.

Telly fronts thirty minutes later. Not only are high-5s exchanged fifteen times, we add a little jump to each one. He's made a lot of money. Unbegrudgingly, he hands over three grand.

"We kicked arse, ay," he beams.

"Yeah, I spose *we* did."

"Going to tell me how we managed it?"

Telly enters the office to press the girls' room intercom. "Aloha, ladies." We listen to a minute's abuse before he turns it off. "It really makes getting up in the evenings worthwhile."

Sally finally sits back in her chair and eyes me with suspicion. "How the hell did you do that? Nikki was dead set positive she was going to Hawaii with this R.D. guy."

"It was you gave me an answer," I say.

"You know what I mean. It was you or Nikki, and I didn't have any money on it." A car pulls in. "Brendan's here."

I greet him at the gate.

"Any trouble?"

He shakes his head. "R.D. didn't want to let me in his house, but when I showed him the cash he opened up okay."

"Think he was going to double-cross me?"

"Don't know. Could have. Once he saw the folding stuff he was hooked. Took a cold carton of piss with me to break the ice, just to make sure. Can't believe you got him so cheap."

"Pathetic, isn't it."

Brendan cups an ear to pick up sounds from inside. "Is that blubbering I hear?"

"The girls are shitty. Nikki's not so popular at the moment. Telly's handing out money. Enjoy."

23

"What are you doing?"

I cease removing CD covers painstakingly replaced after the competition. "I was going to ask George to put his moniker on them."

Vanessa shakes her head, clicks her tongue, *tsk*. "George? Well there's no way you can ask him to sign them. Apart from it being bad form, you'll embarrass yourself."

"You mean I'll embarrass *you*."

She says nothing. I give it more thought.

"Bad form, huh?"

She pulls a camera from her bag. "*If* we get to meet him, you ask for a photo of the two of you and I'll take it. That's quite acceptable."

"No shit. How many celebrities have *you* met?"

"Obviously a lot more than you, darling."

"Don't go getting smart." I playfully wag a finger. "We're not on the plane yet. It isn't too late to call Nikki."

She tosses me her phone.

"I'm very, very sorry." She opens the towel wrapped around her naked body. "Can you ever forgive me?"

"I can only promise I'll think about it. Is that what you're wearing to the function?"

"Could be," she says cheekily.

"Well that'd be a bit stupid. There's nowhere to put the camera."

I duck a thrown pillow and leave to shower. On my return, Vanessa, now dressed, rummages in her suitcase on the bed.

"I knew we should have left from my place."

I buckle my jeans, pull on a golf shirt, slip on socks and new white Reeboks. "Anything you've forgotten we can buy in Hawaii." I kiss her neck. "I'm sure they'll have at least one shop amidst all the grass huts and spear-chuckers."

She hands me a wrapped parcel hidden in her bag.

"I was going to give you this when we got back. But you might as well have it now."

I tear off the glossy wrapping. Inside, a couple of framed 8x10 signed George Michael promotional photos. In the first he leans against a brick wall, short stubble first deemed cool in the eighties, jeans, white T-shirt, mirrored aviator glasses. In the second he sits holding an electric guitar in a red convertible, same glasses, stubble, jeans, T-shirt, but with a black leather jacket. I can't say what I think of them because it may be a serious gift.

"Bidded for them on eBay," she says, pointing proudly at the first. "That cost seventy English pounds, plus postage. The other cost a hundred and twenty American. Both have certificates of authenticity."

This is almost disturbing. Signatures on both photos are completely different. One is flowing grandiose circles, the other, large, overlapping, almost individually printed letters. Yet she stands there evidently pleased with her purchases. Items to be cherished for the rest of my natural. How can an intelligent person not notice something so blatant.

The first chink in her armour?

"Something wrong?" she asks.

"Is 'bidded' a legitimate word."

"I just made it one. Why don't you say what you were going to say."

"I love them, babe. Thanks." We kiss. "You didn't notice the signatures are miles apart?"

Vanessa takes one in each hand for comparison. "Shouldn't he do something about this sort of thing? People using his image, making a fraudulent buck off it?"

"He's probably, like, the tenth richest man in Britain. Why would he give a rat's what people do with his photos on the internet?"

Both photos drop onto the bed. "I'll toss them when we get back."

I place them flat on the bedside table. "They cost too much to destroy. One might be authentic. And who knows, in years to come we might look at them and laugh ourselves silly."

"When are Janet and Brendan picking us up?"

I point at the window. "Speak of the devils."

"Oh, God. I'm nowhere near ready. How long will you be?"

I swing my palms up. "I'm done. Toothpaste, shaving gear, undies and socks in a bag. Easy."

"Jesus. Men!"

"Time for sex too, if you like."

I'm pushed out of the bedroom. I go outside to greet Brendan and Janet. The electric wire is open, cows in the bottom paddock. Janet goes inside to see Vanessa.

"I'm having a beer," I say. "Want one?"

Brendan consults his watch. "Why not."

By the time he finishes checking something in the shed, I'm seated, sucking a Heineken. He sits on another director's chair, accepts and raises his bottle.

"Hawaii."

"Yeah." Laughter floats out of the windows. "Know what they're happy about?"

Brendan looks a little shrewd. "Could be they're talking about you two."

"You told Janet what I said about Vanessa moving in?"

Now he grins. "We do talk occasionally, buddy. It's all very well going out with lookers, but although it's a nice thought, you can't fuck them twenty-four hours a day. You've got to find someone you can also converse with. Especially if you live together."

"Wow, that's deep. Advice for the ages. Tell her about the drawings in my bedroom? Mention suitcases of cash keeping the worms warm at night?"

"We've got a little bet going," he says. "Jan reckons you won't ask Vanessa to marry you. I do."

"Haven't you got that the wrong way round?"

"Nope. She says you're too independent to tie yourself down."

"And what do you say?"

"Independent? Yes. But specimens like Vanessa don't come along every day."

I remember him saying the same thing about Janet. But they've had their share of bickering and yelling. That must be another thing married couples do. I watch him looking down at his cattle and wonder if he is truly happy. Does beckoning fatherhood eradicate past differences and name-calling, or just hold them at bay until the first kid becomes a routine part of parental life and old nuances come back out to play?

"Four whole days," he says. "Looking forward to it?"

A stupid question. I nod and say No.

"I can see you're jumping out of your skin."

"I'm excited about the concert."

"Charlize or Salma be there?"

"If they're not—"

"You'll still say they were. That goes without saying."

"I'd expect the same from you." I say.

"And get it. Halle Berry may also be there."

"I've heard she's going," I lie.

"Yeah," he says. "I thought you might have heard that. And you'll have an inappropriate story about her when you get back."

"Of course. By the way, because you've been acting funny lately, I re-buried those cases next to the trough by the shed. It's often muddy and cows trample it constantly. Can't tell anything's buried there. I did it at night in case someone was watching."

"Good call. But I haven't been acting funny."

The biscuit tosser brings our airline meals, along with another can of almost cold beer for me. I've had a few. They're working, warming my head from the inside. Although she's getting on, that curvy butt of hers is starting to look okay.

Vanessa peels the aluminium foil cover from her chicken dish. "You seem deep in thought."

Her motley chicken looks like it died of dropsy. Gravy appears a week old. I peel back my lid and smile at more attractive veal.

"You think I'm overly independent?"

"No. It's normal to refuse help of any kind; to want to take a rented DVD back yourself, even though I go past the shop; to pay for computer discs and sticks after I've offered them for free. Want more?"

I poke my meal with a plastic folk. "Rely on people and they invariably let you down. Likewise, if you do something for someone and do it the way you yourself would do it, but that's not to their liking, the lazy bastards bitch about it when they should have done it themselves.

My parents always got us kids to do simple things for them, and it pissed me off. My alcoholic old man would sit on his arse, smile drunkenly and hold out his glass so I'd fill it with whiskey and water. When I made coffee, he'd complain it looked like dish water."

"Hmmm. You get Brendan to do things for you."

"That's different. And it's only stuff I can't do myself." A forkful of mashed potato I wash down with beer tasting of aluminium.

"That's the first time you've mentioned your family."

"You don't want to hear *that* shit. We're on holiday. We're supposed to be getting drunk." I sip her white wine. It's warmer than my beer. "And renewing our membership in the Mile High Club."

"Renewing?"

"I meant joining."

"Sure you did."

After a second can I fall asleep watching some movie. Somebody should move Hawaii closer to Oz, or invent faster transport. Ten and a half hours is too long sitting in a plane twiddling your thumbs.

We clear Customs without being arrested and step into Waikiki sunlight with expectant thoughts of Waikiki pleasures. Palm trees. Hula girls. Exotic cocktails in coconut shells with colourful little umbrellas. Surfboards. Souvenirs. Elvis memorabilia. Panhandlers. Overweight, lily-white holidaymakers on beaches and lounging around hotel pools. Drunk, puking tourists urinating in shop doorways in the small hours. Sounds suspiciously like where we were eleven hours ago.

We snag a cab to our hotel. A receptionist hands us a key and points toward the elevator. Twenty stories in this hotel, but we only manage one above street level, directly above the hotel laundry.

It's not a room like in their brochure. Television, bedside lamp, phone sitting on a bedside table. The bed doesn't seem wide enough to be called double. A tiny balcony has a solitary chair made from thick white plastic tubing covered with interwoven thin strips of green plastic moulded to resemble some type of grass. When seated, one can't see over the solid concrete balcony wall. The view isn't much anyway: tall commercial building opposite, noisy street below. In the bathroom, the most worn white floor tiles have darker edges. Set in a wall beside the main door, a thermostat and red button for air-conditioning. I push it, wait, nothing happens.

"I think the balcony door has to be closed before air-conditioning will work," Vanessa informs me.

I tell her I know that, then close the glass door. Presto, our noisy air-con rattles to life.

Vanessa kicks off her shoes and begins flicking through hotel information booklets fanned out on a small table. I take a good long discerning look at her legs before moving in behind.

She continues reading. "What are you doing?"

"Checking you for breast cancer."

"Thank you, but that's not the recommended technique. If you like, I can show you."

"No thanks. I'll work it out myself. Eventually."

"You could at least remove my top first."

She lifts her arms and quickly spins around as I pull off her top.

"Why is it," I say, "the first thing people do in a hotel room is screw?"

Her arms go about my neck. "They do?"

"Well, yeah."

"You're making this up as you go."

"It's probably written in that booklet you were just reading. Put cases down; check out room; screw."

"I have a sneaking suspicion it doesn't say that at all."

"Trust me."

We screw, then lie naked looking at the brown-spotted roof that isn't supposed to have brown spots.

"Want to hire a car tomorrow and do the island?" Vanessa asks. "Saw a Viper and a Ferrari for rent on the way in. Always wanted to drive a Viper."

"While here we'll do it the tropical way. Saw a sign, back a few streets, off Kalakaua Avenue, advertising open Jeep-type sports vehicles. We'll get one of those."

She turns to me quizzically. "You told me you've never been here before."

"Haven't. Being in the car a lot I've developed a thing for street names. See them, can't forget them."

She says ah, then voices what I've been thinking since we opened the door.

"We should get another room. In a better hotel."

"You're a snob."

"This is a budget tourist's room. We're not exactly tourists. My shout."

Children's dirty handprints cover the balcony door's bottom half. "You're right, we're not tourists. We're lower than tourists. We're competition winners."

"My god! That's right! I'll never live it down." She playfully pushes me and jumps toward her suitcase. "I'm having a shower. Then we can—"

I'm taken aback. Two huge bruises cover a patch just below her right shoulder blade.

"Jeeesuus!" I sit up. "How did you get those bruises? They're fucking huge."

"It's nothing," she says, moving toward the bathroom.

I leap off the bed and stand in front of her. When I gently run a hand over the blue and black marks, she flinches. I consider the way she's been moving since last night, the quick spin when I removed her top thirty minutes ago. She's been purposely keeping them from sight, but had a momentary lapse.

"Bullshit. You've been hiding them."

She brushes me off. "It's nothing."

I follow her into the bathroom. "Tell me how you got them or we'll go home now and I'll ask your mother."

She turns shower taps above the bath and studies my resolve. "No you won't. You've come all this way to see the concert. You won't leave now."

I turn them off. "Try me."

She sits on the bath's edge, eyes floor tiles, then looks up. "It was James. He didn't mean to. He's not a bad person. He just didn't want me coming to Hawaii with you."

And there it is. When it turns, it turns quickly. Why did it have to be in Hawaii, where I'm stuck with her.

"I thought he was in hospital."

"I took him home yesterday. He's got a nurse."

I hold back as best I can. "Right. When we get back we'll take out a violence order or stalker's thing to stop the bastard coming near you."

"No," she says matter-of-factly. "I can't."

"If you want to stay with me, you will."

"He only hit me because he thinks you're dangerous. He doesn't think I should be with you. He's not a violent person."

I can't believe what I'm hearing. This isn't right. This is slinky talk. Next she'll be saying it was her fault.

"He's a stalker who can't accept that you and him have split. He spies on you. He's a fucking nutter."

Again she considers my face, if I'm being truthful. "He does not."

"Trust me. The guy's fucked in the head."

"Why would he think you're dangerous? You didn't have anything to do with his beating, did you?"

"I wish I did," I say without hesitation. "I might have to organize one when we get back."

I punch the air and walk out. Vanessa follows, pleading for my word I will do nothing to harm James. When it isn't forthcoming, she grudgingly relents.

"All right," she says. "We'll sort it out when we get back."

"Just so there's no grey areas, what exactly do you mean by sort it out?"

"I'll get a restraining order to make him stay away from me."

I know she won't. I'm far from happy.

24

While Vanessa showers, I try ringing Brendan. He'll get a kick out of this. I can hear him laughing already.

I'm unable to get through because of the ridiculous hotel phone system. I dress and go down to reception, where I purchase a fifty dollar phonecard that supposedly works when slotted into our room phone.

It doesn't. When I try ringing out, some guy on the line informs me he's working on the new phonecard system. Dialling codes have yet to be programmed in. It will be a while. Probably tomorrow morning.

Vanessa exits the bathroom. I shower. After alone time, when I come out my demeanour is somewhat calmer. She's dressed, ready to go walkabout. I throw on jeans, T-shirt, sneakers, and we leave in a slightly better mood. She must think I'm accepting her word something will be done to rectify the James situation when we get back to Australia. But I know how this will end. It will end poorly. She has a victim mentality.

At reception I ignore the queue waiting to check in, approach the idiot troll who sold me the phonecard and slap it down in front of her. She smiles apologetically at the person being served before turning to me.

"You didn't require it after all?" she says, patronizingly.

Her shoulder length perm doesn't suit that long, thin face. It looks like she recently exited a shower without bothering to dry the straggly mop on her head.

"Of course I required it," I say coolly, "otherwise I wouldn't have bought it. But it seems I can't use it. Programming the phones will take another day."

She gives me a superior look, accompanied with a frustrated blow through her nostrils. "Can't you make your call tomorrow?"

"Are you a fucking moron?" I say a little louder. Suddenly everybody in the busy little foyer falls expectantly silent and turns our way. "You could have said something when I bought it."

Her eyes shoot past me to a big Hawaiian gum-chewing security guard swaggering our way. His shoes are black, polished. A gun strapped on his hip offers backup. Thumbs are hooked behind his belt buckle. His presence gives her more confidence, attitude, lip. What ever happened to Suck it up, smile politely and deal with the public in a courteous manner?

"Are you saying I'm below average intelligence?" she asks.

"I'd put money on it, sweetheart."

Our audience shuffles about, allowing the guard to move in. He takes up position in front of me, arm resting on the counter to prevent himself falling over. For some naïve reason I can't fathom, she addresses him like he's her boss.

"This . . . *gentleman* is saying—"

As if following a high tennis lob, Muscles lazily arches his head from me to her, stopping with a slack I've-got-better-things-to-do sneer.

"I heard what he said. Why don't you just give the guy back his money, honey."

I'm reimbursed, with an embarrassed blush. Vanessa and I exit the foyer happy. We decide to spend the afternoon looking around, drinking and eating. Emphasis on drinking.

Strolling into a bar/restaurant, we park ourselves on stools at the counter. A wench in a loud Hawaiian shirt ambles over and informs us Mai Tais are two for three dollars. Cheap in anyone's language. I slap a twenty down and order a couple. She mixes liquids in a cocktail shaker, pours the brown concoction into four glasses with ice, adds a pineapple wedge to each and places the delights on napkins in front of us.

Mother's milk. They're gone in seconds. We order two more and take them to a window table. From here we pick holes in gaudily clad tourists strolling the footpath. Finding fault gets easier the more we drink. Another round and most holidaymakers have morphed into ugly hunchbacks who shouldn't have been handed day passes from the asylum.

After three rounds we up-stakes and mosey into the next bar. Same deal here. We tell the barkeep to bring us a round. Vanessa complains about weight that drink mixers will be putting on, but protests soon slide away with her sobriety. I'm not used to rum. After these I'm going back to beer. She can drink what she likes.

"Before we get too much steam up," Vanessa says, "and as long as we're walking around, shall we look for another room?"

"If you must."

"Down by the beach. Overlooking Waikiki and the ocean."

"Why?" I say. "We live by the sea. Why spend six or seven hundred a night on a room to look at what we look at every day?"

"Hmm. We'll see."

Beginning the search for another suitable watering hole, we don't have to look very hard. Bloody things are everywhere. Like ABC shops, with all their general goods and souvenirs. Damn near one on every corner.

We meander through a maze of reception areas and shop fronts until stumbling into an Outrigger Hotel foyer. While I check out one of three large jewellery cases housing locally make crafts, Vanessa sneaks to reception for a room key.

We ride the lift up nineteen floors to a newly refurbished, clean and spacious room. The balcony's tiny, but has a metal railing. We can sit on chairs and look through. Diamond Head is on the opposite side, so isn't visible, but in our direction we can view the ocean. Across the way, an expanse of hotels curve around a huge tree-lined park. If the impulse grabs us we can toss coconuts in three or four hotel pools below. And the tariff is half what I expected. However, giving a shit is a problem when I'm not paying.

"Okay," I joke, "since this has a minibar, I'll wait here until you've booked in and fetched our bags from the dump."

"Once we've moved in," she says, "it's a new room. You'll have to perform again."

"Reckon?"

"It says so in the brochure."

"Bloody brochures."

We don't bother checking out of the other hotel. Fuck 'em. They can figure it out themselves. The room is pre-paid, and we hadn't chalked up any room service — if there was such a thing there.

I perform again in our new room, which all but sobers us up for another Honolulu assault.

Sun sets on Waikiki beach. I'd say the vista is spectacular, but it's the same sun we watch set on the Gold Coast, so. . .

We hit a couple more beachside public houses before heading in a few streets to Kuhio Avenue. Spotting lights and hearing laughter from low, open window shutters, we amble up a one way side street to a busy little establishment full of locals. The name Shots either reflects what it sells, or past trouble. Hoping it's the former, we take up position at the counter's far end, under a couple of large TVs showing American sport with the sound down. I order a beer, Vanessa a dry martini.

Two thirds full, everybody appears to know each other. Topped-up with jungle juice, they call to friends across the room, causing more laughter from previous conversations or private jokes we aren't privy to. Even our barman's drinking. He adds to conversations while mixing Vanessa's drink. When they're placed in front of us, he asks from whence we hail. Australia, we reply, and he's called away before he can chat. Fifteen minutes later, I finish my beer and motion him back.

"Another beer for me."

"I think I'll try a Manhattan," Vanessa says.

A minute later, he puts both on the bar top. "Tell me who the first Manhattan was supposedly made for," he says, "and this round's on me."

A group of four beside us halt their talk to listen. Maybe the barkeep's tried it before. Vanessa sucks a mouthful through a straw and looks hopefully at me.

"Winston Churchill's mother," I say. "Jenny, or Jennifer. Something like that."

The listening locals begin laughing. Vanessa, grinning widely, endearingly strokes my arm.

"That's never happened before," the barkeep says.

"Cheers." I drink a mouthful of my freebie. Nice. Everybody knows freebies taste better.

We're dragged into the conversation beside us, so decide to stay a while. Other bars would be full of tourists, and I don't want to drink with tourists. Definitely not lowly competition winners. Anyway, this day is catching up with me. Lasting more than another couple of hours could be a stretch. Vanessa's also looking a little peaky.

It quickly deteriorates into a drink fest. The more we imbibe, the more we want. Maybe it's Hawaiian air. Perhaps being isolated in the middle of the Pacific requires everybody to get along. Well, almost everybody. Our first hotel receptionist doesn't appreciate living in constant sunshine, the middle of nowhere.

Vanessa trots off to the bathroom, only to be dragged into a powwow half way back. I push my empty forward, and it's replaced with a full one. A young couple in our conversation explain they have a stall in the International Markets flogging semi-precious stones, and I feel a sales pitch coming on. I take the opportunity to use the bathroom. On my return, Vanessa hasn't moved, but now holds a new green cocktail.

Remembering our new hotel's location may be a problem.

Remembering our new hotel may be a problem.

25

Hawaii. Day Two.

I park the car curbside, top down, fuelled and ready for action. Vanessa's dabbing final touches to her war paint as I enter our room. She swears there's no hangover, but slightly red eyes tell a different story. She says it's the change in time zone and yesterday's extra long day. I think if she had changed to a more familiar drink, such as wine, instead of staying on those concoctions, after ten hours' rest she'd feel as good as I do.

The upside of drinking away from tourist traps, we've been invited tomorrow to a once a year Hawaiian piss-up at some place called The Ranch, forty-five minutes along the coast. Fifty bucks each covers drinks and transport. I can drink twice that myself.

8.05 a.m.. We walk to an alfresco cafe at the corner, sit at a table for two under a wicker umbrella beside the footpath and order pancakes.

"Why is holiday food so unhealthy?" Vanessa asks. "Even cocktails."

"Why do they bring coffee first?" I counter.

"Hmm."

Tourists appear a little healthier during early hours. Brighter eyes. Springs in their freshly showered steps. Diners arrive and depart. Pigeons relocate, flapping noisily from table to empty table. Large signs ask eaters not to feed them, but two female salad-dodgers in wide straw hats do just that. Hoping a bird might crap on their plates would be asking too much. Can't tell anyone anything these days.

Ten minutes later, maple syrup covered pancakes arrive, two big ice-cream dollops on the side. And bacon. Vanessa takes one look and grumbles about going on a diet the second we get back. I feel like telling her not to bother on my account. We'll more than likely be calling it quits on our return. She can pack on as much weight as she pleases.

We eat, I tip the waitress, pick up our gear, walk to the car. Vanessa climbs in and smiles slyly.

"What?" I say.

"You got a Jeep Wrangler."

I start it up. Top off and no door windows, we're completely open to the elements, as all cars should be in a tropical climate.

"What's wrong with it?"

"Nothing, if you're gay."

Her short cream skirt rode up enough to expose white lace knickers. Two white silk squares, one front, one back, held in place with shoulder and side spaghetti straps, don't come close to covering her top half. She's right about extra weight. It wouldn't suit her. Back bruises are partially visible, so she's comfortable showing them. Does this mean a Violence Order slapped on James after all? Doubtful. Victim mentalities are ingrained. It'd take twenty years of shrink sessions to even get close to fixing those problems.

I pull away and we head off. With no itinerary, we'll follow road signs to make our way around Oahu. It isn't so big that we'll get lost.

First stop, Pearl Harbour, see where Japs dragged the US into World War Two. Yanks were choking Japan's oil supply. Seventy-odd years later and everybody still fights over the same shit. Nothing changes. It's tedious.

Vanessa wants to drive the gaymobile, so before entering the Nimitz Highway we swap places. I sit back, plant a bare foot on the dash and tell her if we follow signs we should end up at Pearl. She doesn't think that's right.

"We're not going to Pearl Harbour?" I ask. "See the Arizona?"

"I don't think it's Pearl Harbour we go to."

"Now you're being silly. Everybody knows it's at Pearl Harbour."

She's right. We roll up to a Naval Base boom gate and are greeted by a Navy woman with a smile on her face. When I ask for admission to see the sunken wrecks, we're politely informed coming here is a common mistake. She then offers directions to the Arizona Memorial. The woman has patience. I couldn't smile all day at idiots like us. Okay, if they looked like Vanessa I probably could. We head off in the right direction.

"It's been a while since I was there," Vanessa says, "but I didn't think it was at the naval base. The site's administered by the National Park Service, not the Navy."

"Why didn't you say?"

"Hmmm. I believe I did."

"Yeah? Well why do these signs say Interstate Highway? It's not like anyone can drive interstate."

"It manipulates a law that forces the federal government, not the local government, to pay for roads."

"You know that too, huh."

"Sure do."

"Whoever told you everybody likes a Wisenheimer, lied."

She's cooing. It's annoying. Another fifteen minutes sees us parking in a sprawling carpark. Upon entering the main building we're handed numbered blue tickets. Green ticket holders are just entering the theatre to watch a movie. We're next.

"It's free?" I say.

"We can make a donation on the way out."

"Economy's in the toilet and this is free. I don't get it."

"It's not always about money."

"Like I said, economy's in the toilet."

We wander about inside, checking out model ships in glass display cases and other exhibits. Photos, sailors' memorabilia, a scale model of Pearl Harbour with ships anchored in their original positions at the time of attack. It's an odd place, like visiting a tomb or library. Everybody talks in hushed tones.

Avoiding souvenir shops, we stroll outside to take shots of open fifty- or sixty-seater boats standing ready to run people over to the memorial. Across the water, resembling a Madison County Bridge, a white arch spans the sunken USS Arizona. It's quiet out here, too.

After taking photos we meander about the lawn for twenty minutes. People begin emerging from theatre side doors, walking toward the boats. Over speakers, blue ticket holders are requested to make their way to the theatre entrance.

We're ushered inside with a few hundred others. A white-suited navy guy takes the stage and gives a little speech before we watch a twenty-three minute film of the attack on Pearl Harbour. Footage not seen outside this theatre. Then it's boats over to the memorial.

It's even more churchy over here. Hallowed turf. Everybody roams slowly in quiet, reflective contemplation. Probably the same at Ground

Zero, New York. Far end, at the base of a wall of fallen sailors' names, large vases hold freshly cut flowers.

"Not many Japanese about," I whisper.

"No," Vanessa whispers back.

"You'd think with a million of them in Waikiki, more would make their way here."

"I get the picture."

"They've got their own newspaper in Honolulu, TV channel, but Pearl Harbour doesn't interest them? Strange."

"Enough."

"They should get over it. Everyone else has."

"Mention the Japanese again and there'll be no sex for the remainder of the trip."

"You mean the trip today, or the entire—"

Vanessa's finger shoots up and I get the evil eye. Maybe she's a godbotherer and thinks we should be quiet.

I point to a spot half way along. "I'll just trot over there. They say oil drops still rise to the surface after all these years, you know."

"A wise move."

"Are they still called 'drops' if they rise?"

"One more word. I dare you."

Masturbation or sex. A no-brainer. I amble away quietly.

A large metal circle, remains of a gun turret, pokes up just above the waterline. Floating close, small rainbow-coloured oil pools sit almost motionless. I watch them for a while before moving to the wall of names. No fallen sailors had my name. I suppose most people look for their own moniker. Nothing much else to do here. Brendan's name also isn't there. Nor Vanessa's. There are no women's names at all I can see. After snapping a dozen photos we hop a boat back.

Exiting to the carpark, I drop a hundred in the donation box.

"Ease the conscience a bit?" Vanessa asks.

"Those white officer suits must take a lot of cleaning."

Off we go, Vanessa driving. We cruise the Kamehameha Highway and stumble into the Dole Pineapple Pavillion. Pineapples, as far as the eye can see. There's a tour, which we forgo. Spiky green fruit heads growing out of the ground by the square mile hold little interest for me. I see acres of them back home driving to Cabarita Beach.

We enter the huge Dole shop. Three busloads walk about buying souvenirs, tasting pineapple flavoured everything, adding to already ample, middle-aged girths.

I make my way to an ice-cream stand for a pineapple cone. Jesus, I had no idea ice-cream could taste so good. I scoff it down and buy a couple of larger one's.

Vanessa's enduring a chat-up from a native bus driver. I take her the cone, stand beside her, and the driver gets the message and leaves.

"More calories," she says.

"If I could have sex with this stuff I would."

We walk around licking ice-cream, then hit the road, me driving. We roll further along the uncrowded Kamehameha Highway, past Chun's Reef, Waimea Beach Park, until reaching the Banzai Pipeline. I feel we should be listening to *Hawaii-5-0* theme music to set the scene.

It's a fizzer. Barely a ripple. If I were paying, refunds would be demanded. In the water a couple of rented jet-skis speed about. On the sand a few tourists walk among a dozen sunbathers.

"Where's the pipeline, the surf competition, TV cameras, hot chicks?"

"Wrong time of year," Vanessa says. "They're probably in Australia, or Brazil."

We get back in the car and continue on past a few small shopping centres, a Mormon Temple, then the Polynesian Cultural Centre. Vanessa shows little interest in dropping in to watch indigenous dancers in hula skirts, and I can only think of stopping to buy a second Polynesian God to sit on my other stereo speaker back home. We continue on without stopping.

Vanessa gazes out to sea. "People watch whales around here somewhere,"

"Somewhere?"

"I was a kid. I can't remember. Since buying the house, mother and I go straight to Maui."

At the next little village I swing in and buy a few packaged sandwiches, a couple of beers and carry on until finding a place to picnic. The sign says Kualoa Point. A spacious green park dotted with palm trees and lawn stretching to the water. Behind us lushly covered volcanic mountains look suspiciously like they were on TV's *Lost*.

Sitting at a picnic table, we twist tops off the beers and open the stale sandwiches. They may have been put together yesterday, possibly the day before. Eight or nine couples, independent travellers like us, stroll while taking photos. We dump our rubbish in a bin and walk slowly to the water's edge, close to a small island Vanessa calls Chinaman's Hat. Behind a knee-high concrete wall we lie on the sand and go for it. A few people walk within earshot, but we don't let up. Shagging in public seems to invigorate her, squirming about more than usual.

When we finish, I pull her up and brush sand from her clothes. She wraps arms about me and administers a tight hug. I flash false romantic eyes.

"What are you doing?" she asks.

"Nothing. Why?"

"What's with the stupid look?"

"That's my suave double-o-seven."

"It's more like a sleaze on the prowl."

It's a tough gig pretending to still be interested. She brushes sand from her legs and looks about.

"I think people are surreptitiously staring."

"If they are, they're just jealous. Of me, of course."

She looks longingly into my eyes, removes my baseball cap, teases my hair. "You know just the right things to say, Myers. Sometimes."

We drive toward a turnoff that should take us to the Pali Lookout. Brendan told me it's a must. If I do nothing else this trip, he said, going there is a requirement. So we travel a long road up to the entrance, weave through tour buses and park among other rentals.

Walking up the rise, the valley drops away in front of us. At a railing, the expansive valley spreads below like a giant fan to the ocean, kilometres away. Volcanic cliffs on our left drop vertically to the valley floor, golf courses, homesteads, parks. In the distance it's now obvious how Chinaman's Hat got it's name. I take a series of photos.

"Wow," I say. "Ever seen anything like this?"

"You mean as impressive? You've never seen the Grand Canyon. How high up do you reckon we are?"

"Twelve hundred feet." From behind, I wrap an arm around her waist, rest my chin on her shoulder, point left to the sharp cliffs. "In seventeen-ninety-five King Kamehameha threw his vanquished enemies off there."

She grins. "Read those facts on a street sign?"

"No. A plaque behind us."

"So you have a thing for street signs *and* plaques."

"Just street signs. Plaques occasionally."

"Okay, what was on the plaque on the giant anchor as we went into the Arizona Memorial?"

"This anchor is from the USS Arizona."

"Hmmm."

Driving again, we backtrack toward the sea to follow the coast. We pass more beaches and a famous blowhole. It's not so famous that I've heard of it, but I think it featured in an episode of *Magnum*. We pull into a carpark above Hanauma Bay. Disney couldn't have invented a nicer spot. Palm trees, golden sand, clear green water, snorkelers swimming about shallow coral and floating turtles. It's almost too nice for this garbage strewn day and age. Suddenly I want to hug a fluffy koala. I take more snaps on Vanessa's digital camera.

"Want to walk down?" she asks.

"Nope. We'll keep going.

"I've seen *Magnum P.I.* discs at your place. His house is a short distance."

"Goodie."

Her eyes roll. "Settle down. Unless things have changed, it's not posted or anything. Nobody's allowed in there. They cover streetside trees as well, above the fenceline, to stop people slowing down to gawk."

"Bastards. I'll write a shitty letter when we get home."

"You do that, darling. I'm sure it will force a complete rethink of Hawaii's tourist industry."

We miss Magnum's house because I have no idea where to look. It's been a long day, covering a lot of ground. Getting on to 4.30 p.m., Diamond Head is now off the agenda. We drive straight back and dump the gaymobile, walk back to the hotel, shower, then head out to hit a few different watering holes.

Drinking, while staring at the ocean, gets boring mighty fast. After two hours of this, we follow crowd noise into a mall and fight our way into what could be a gay joint. A lot of guys wear muscle shirts and singlets. Around the periphery of tables, it's standing room only as all eyes watch some smooth guy talking on stage. Behind him, three couples appear eager for whatever is about to happen. One of each couple sits behind a desk with a centered quiz show buzzer, while their partner stands behind. I'd bet Vanessa's Merc two couples are pillow-biters. On the end sits an empty desk. It's difficult hearing what's being said on stage over crowd noise, whistling and yelling.

Vanessa gestures to a spot near the edge of the tables, and heads off. I inch my way to the bar for drinks. There's no cut price happy hour liquor while the action happens, so after paying through the nose for beer and a champagne cocktail, I elbow my way to where Vanessa stands deep in conversation with two forty-something women from Wisconsin. Amongst the crowd it's even louder, forcing me to merely nod and smile when I think it appropriate. They're here trying to win whatever's up for grabs.

I'm guessing everybody wants the last spot on stage. As Vanessa takes her champagne flute, the emcee holds up what looks like two tickets.

"So," he says into his microphone, "for what are likely to be the last two seats to see George Michael, who can tell me his first hit as a solo artist?"

What are the odds? Come all this way and end up watching a George Michael competition. The place goes postal. The two Wisconsin ladies join in, desperately trying to attract the emcee's attention. Giving it their all, they jump about, arms flailing frantically. Not one seat has a bum on it.

Finally, he points to a leaping male and female in front of the stage's far side, and a hush erupts.

"*Careless Whisper!*" the couple yell together.

"Sorry," the emcee says. "In America that was released as Wham, featuring George Michael."

Again the place explodes. Emcee looks about, milking his moment. Standing behind Vanessa, I rest my chin on her shoulder. She lovingly pats my cheek and asks if I know the answer, which I yell in her ear.

Emcee settles on a guy at a back table, and points. "With the blue neck bandana."

The guy goes gay-hysterical. "*Faith*!" he yells.

"Oh no," emcee says. "Sorry. Does anybody else want to try?"

From silence to ear-splitting screams. Emcee casually steps right of stage, picks up a water bottle, unscrews the top, takes a sip. When he looks up, Vanessa's arm shoots into the air, breasts jumping in her low-cut bright red top. Emcee likes what he sees, and points.

"In the red top."

Unbelievable. Want to know what it's like struggling through life ugly and unnoticed? No fucking point asking her. Keen to know the price of a nightclub drink, the cost of a restaurant meal? Ask muggins escorting her, as she wouldn't have the foggiest fucking notion.

Again the place falls silent. All turn to Vanessa.

She stops leaping and calls, "*A Different Corner!*"

Everybody turns as one to the emcee. Taking a minute, he pretends to consult an answer card.

"Correct!' he says. "Come on up, beautiful. And bring someone with you."

We force our way to the stage, Vanessa beaming. She sits expectantly jittery at the last little school desk, buzzer and microphone on top. I stand behind, checking our opposition, beer in one hand, rubbing her shoulder with the other. There's two male couples and one boy/girl. They appear more eager than bright. I'll try to make this as quick and painless as possible, so they don't suffer.

We're the only ones with drinks. Emcee offers to delay proceedings so we contestants can refresh our beverages, and I'm the sole combatant who trots off for more, keeping everybody waiting. It matters not if Vanessa and I are tipsy. We already have tickets. No pressure on us.

Emcee jumps down to walk among people seated at tables in front. The three standing contestants crouch over their seated partners to place hands on buzzers. I pick up my beer and lean to Vanessa's ear.

"When I tap your shoulder, press the buzzer."

She nods, excited, so I pat her shoulder to calm her and instil confidence before we start. She bangs the buzzer. *Beeep*! Everyone looks. I sip from my bottle and shrug at the others on stage. Sorry. Blonde. Alcohol probably isn't helping.

"Right-o," emcee says, walking amongst tables. "Here we go. This shouldn't take long. All couples ready?"

Nobody speaks. Emcee consults his cards. Contestants check each other out. Two of the determined-looking three crouched behind partners have one leg back as if awaiting a starter's gun. Maybe they expect to pounce on answers.

Emcee puts the mic to his mouth and begins. "A river is mentioned in which—"

I have no idea what rules we're playing, but can afford to pre-empt questions. I tap Vanessa's shoulder and again she slams the buzzer, *Beeep*! stopping him mid-sentence.

I lean down to the microphone. "Hopefully the song's called *To Be Forgiven*, from the album *Older*."

"Wow, that's exactly what I have here." He makes a show of looking at the back of his question cards. No, we can't see through them. "Okay. On we go. Question two. Where was George's father born?"

Vanessa looks up at me. Once more I shrug. "I think it's something like Malta, but I'm not—"

The clown two desks down pushes his buzzer and answers he was a Greek Cypriot.

Oh yeah. Now I remember.

"That's right." emcee says. "So, to question three. How many people are on the *Listen Without Prejudice* album cover?" He's trying to be funny. It's a crowd scene. There must be thousands. He has a little chuckle, playing up to his audience, accepting applause and laughter. "Only kidding. Question three. In what song does he mention Ricky Martin's name?"

I tap Vanessa's shoulder. She hammers the buzzer. *Beeep*!

" *My Baby Just Cares For Me,*" I say into the microphone.

The others on stage look worried. And no brighter.

"That's two correct. One more, couple four, and you're winners." Emcee waves concert tickets toward the other three couples to gee them up. "Okay, name this song from the first line. I'll read the words one at a time. Let. . ."

Shit! Cut me off at the knees and call me tripod. Bend me over and bugger me backwards. This is one of my favourites. I tap Vanessa, who almost breaks the buzzer slamming her palm down. *Beeep*!

"*Heal the pain,*" I say in her ear. She repeats it into the mic and begins screaming, leaps from her seat before it's confirmed, and hugs me while jumping about.

How easy was that! I feel like asking somebody what the hell just happened. I smile broadly at the others. For some, it could be interpreted as a gloat. Couldn't help myself.

Emcee finally says yes, that's correct. Vanessa continues jumping and hugging. She says she's never before won anything in her life. I find that difficult to believe. The bitch won the gene pool stakes at birth.

Emcee leaps on stage and wraps an arm tightly around Vanessa's shoulder. "What would you like at this moment, beautiful?" He holds his mic in front of her mouth.

"Tickets to see George Michael," she beams.

He looks at me and asks the same question.

"Sex," I say. "But I'll settle for the tickets."

The mob laughs. But not the losers on stage. They persevere with sour. And stupidity. Emcee hands Vanessa the envelope containing concert tickets and turns to the others, who won't leave empty handed. T-shirts and caps emblazoned with his radio station's logo he distributes from a cardboard box dragged from behind a stage curtain.

We jump down and join the two ladies from Wisconsin, where Vanessa smilingly hands them the envelope. They can't believe it. *I* can't believe it. She didn't even ask me if it was okay. Those seats may be closer to the stage than ours.

Drinks finished, half the crowd dispersed, we make our way to an exit. One of the shirt-lifter losers witnessed the handover and stands in front of us. He's a sissy, but vain, defined. Hangs out at the gym three or four times a week.

"Hey, if you planned to give away those tickets, why did you play?"

I look back. The Wisconsin ladies have left. "It was rigged," I tell him. "Everything's always rigged. It's the way of the world. How else could I have known the answers so quick?"

He eyes the emcee on stage packing away gear while chatting up a couple of teen girls too young to be in a drinking establishment. The guy and his partner mince determinedly toward him. Vanessa and I make our escape.

"That was mean," she says.

"Yip."

She slips her arm through mine and leans in. "We did a good deed tonight."

I picture us walking into George's concert spotting two Wisconsin ladies out front scalping our tickets.

"Spose so."

26

Hawaii. Day Three. One day until the concert.

We eat a big breakfast at Denny's before walking a dozen or so blocks to Shots Bar. Rounding the last corner, ten huge blue and red eskies full of ice, assorted beer cans and wine casks, sit by the curb waiting to be loaded onto a bus yet to appear. Of twenty-five expected day trippers, half loiter on the footpath talking. Uniform of the day: colourful shorts and skirts, T-shirts, straw hats.

Within minutes of our arrival, bar doors and window shutters open. Two people remain outside to protect our booze, the rest wander in for a heart starter.

Mary and Greg watched us win those tickets last night.

"I couldn't believe our luck," Vanessa says, "just walking in and being chosen like that."

"Amazing," Mary says.

Greg's smiling to himself. He knows why Vanessa was chosen. His eyes have hardly left them.

"Are they good tickets?"

"Don't know," I say. "We already have some, so we gave them away."

Their jaws drop in unison.

"Myers won those as well." Vanessa says. "On the radio back home."

"Oh, God," Mary says. "You *are* lucky."

"Luck had nothing to do with it," I correct her. "Nor did any god. Well, maybe Bacchus. We'd had a few before the comp last night."

"Bacchus?"

"Roman god of wine and intoxication." Once again crosswords make me appear intelligent.

I empty my beer and get another. Other travellers arrive over the next fifteen minutes. Half I haven't seen before. Vanessa, social butterfly, does the rounds while I tag along. I'd never meet anyone, otherwise. The men all smile and welcome her. Even anti-socials like me wouldn't tell Dracula to fuck off if Vanessa was on his arm.

When a yellow school bus pulls up on the No Stopping area out front, a half dozen men go out into rising heat to help load. I may get in the way, so watch from inside, standing under a slowly rotating ceiling fan.

Bus loaded, we climb aboard. Every window is lowered. Our driver cautions that drinking alcohol is strictly forbidden on the bus within city limits, then everyone who doesn't have a drink is handed one. I sip from a can. Vanessa settles for a chilled wine in a throwaway plastic cup.

Our bus moves slowly through town before following the coast road. Travelling faster on the highway, warm breezes flow through windows. Vanessa moves about talking to anyone with an empty seat beside them. I walk to the rear for another can and converse with guys guarding the grog.

It turns out Vanessa and I are this year's only first-timers. A few regulars do pilgrimage from the mainland. Since boarding, one man has talked constantly on his phone to a business partner in New York who this year couldn't make it.

Forty minutes on, our bus swings off the highway and circles a double-storey Tackle & Sports shop. Leaving drinks on ice, we file disorderly from the vehicle, walk up stairs to a bar. Another drink, more socialising. Return to the bus. Twenty minutes of the Pacific rolling past on our left, the driver pulls over beside what could be a grassed sports ground.

The other side of a wire fence, spreading trees shade a wide, open stage. A band plays folk music to a couple thousand Hawaiians drinking at long tables under an expanse of corrugated roofs. All in our group disembark carrying bins of alcohol and a small bagged-up marquee, and we congregate at an empty space beside the stage. Five of us drag a picnic table over, park our arses and watch the usual suspects try to raise the marquee while we sup drinks. Their task proves embarrassingly difficult. After thirty minutes everything still lies in disorganized stacks. Even the aluminium frame hasn't been put together. Between acts the celebrity emcee elicits laughter pointing out our ineptitude.

Juicy smells from a dozen large gas barbecues being set up behind the masses stirs my hunger. Behind them, a couple hundred four-wheel-drives and sedans sit in rows at the foot of more *Jurassic Park* mountains. Kids run about everywhere.

Two stage acts, four more beers, and I need a toilet. There must be some somewhere. Everyone can't be pissing in bushes. I pick up my can and walk between the barbecues and main crowd toward the other side. The further I walk, the smell of animal shit increases.

Three rows of twenty-five portable toilets point to a couple of large corrals holding horses of varied size. Ignoring strong animal odours, a hundred rowdy kids play or line up for supervised rides.

I finish my can, squeeze it in the middle, drop it in a drum and open the door to a toilet about half way along the front row. Wow, reasoning behind positioning toilets close to corrals becomes clear. Outside, horseshit overpowers all other smells. Inside, a different story. I sit sunglasses on my baseball cap visor and look down to see where I'll be aiming. They slide off my cap into the hole.

Bastard! Six hundred dollars.

I bend and look inside. Was this crapper transported here without first being emptied? There's a hill of faeces — runny and hard, toilet paper, urine. Glass lenses stick face down half way up the mound, the farther stem poking up, daring me to reach in and bring it home.

There's no damn sink in here to wash them or my hands afterwards. This must be payback for telling those gay guys the competition was rigged.

Forced to assume there's a tap somewhere outside, donning my best revolted face I hold my breath and inch fingers slowly into the abyss. It's deeper than it looks. My entire arm almost goes in, preventing me identifying the last few centimetres of my objective because I must turn my head to avoid kissing the seat.

Nudging something, reluctantly I clamp my two longest fingers on it and begin reversing. Disgusting job almost over, my bare arm touches the seat rim, and I automatically spring back. The glasses catch the edge and drop back in. Fuck it!

I hesitate looking down. They just have to be in a worse spot. Peeking in confirms it. Lens bases sit partially buried in runny shit, both bent stem ends rest below the urine line.

So that's that. Six hundred dollars isn't enough to break an invisible toilet seat barrier a second time. I no longer spit in the eye of germs. As a kid I would have braved Ebola viruses to save *six* dollar glasses. Priorities change.

I empty my bladder on top of them and return to our picnic table. Six hundred dollars down the toilet. Literally.

Vanessa notices me squinting and interrupts the person talking to her. "Where are your nice glasses?"

"Swapped them for a blowjob."

The obvious lie draws a grin. "Expensive blowjob." She produces a pair of free promotional plastic Budweiser sunglasses from her bag, taken from my shack. "Use these."

"Why do you have. . . Never mind." I put them on. At least I won't be squinting the rest of the day. I take a scented baby wipe from her bag and thoroughly wipe my hands.

Five young guys take the stage and begin playing a mixture of acoustic and electric guitars and banjo. People dance, not just in front of the stage. Thirty minutes later a gong rings. Clutching cash, groups make their way to barbecues. Vanessa joins a different queue than me, no doubt hoping for something healthier than whatever I choose. On a paper plate, a thirteen year-old roughly plops a couple of burgers hastily slapped together with little imagination or feeling for the cow that gave up its life for this once a year dining extravaganza.

Back at our table, culinary delights are compared. Her steak sandwich actually looks edible. I lift off my burger's top to expose blood red hamburger meat sitting all alone atop another unbuttered half bun.

"A good vet could have that back on its feet in no time," she says.

I take a couple of bites. Without alcohol in my stomach it would be dog food. An unloved dog. But I get through it and start the second while checking out Hawaiians stuffing their faces.

"There's some big *wahines* around."

"It's a Polynesian cultural thing," Vanessa says. "Big women used to be a sign of wealth and prosperity, so men tended to like their women a little larger."

Some are fucking huge. Nightlights burning in every kitchen. Telly would have a field day throwing insults.

"A little larger?" I say. "That's very magnanimous of you."

She playfully slaps my arm, unintentionally knocking my burger to the ground. Her eyes widen with surprise and she bites her bottom lip. "Sorry, darling. I didn't mean to." There's a tipsy giggle at the end.

I dump it back on my plate and eye forlornly the dirt-spotted remains. Those bastard germs again that once I would have ignored. Maybe I'll buy a steak sandwich.

Vanessa opens her mouth to take another bite, but stops short. I follow her eyes to a ten-year-old Hawaiian boy carrying stacked plates of food back into the seated crowd.

"Aren't they your. . .?

"Glasses," I finish. "Yeah."

He disappears behind people when he sits. Brave, dirty little bastard. Probably hasn't washed his hands. If he's lucky, somebody will tell him what he has. Put them on the interweb, make a few hundred.

Vanessa is asked to dance. She leaves me at the table, so I get up to buy more food.

The marquee was never erected.

At 8.30, seated in a little outdoor beach restaurant, we sip fruity Spanish chardonnay. Two inch Pacific ripples roll rhythmically up the sand, close to our feet. Flaming wicker torches amplify what she considers a romantic evening atmosphere. I'm still playing along until we touch down on Australian soil. I'm getting good at it, approaching Academy Award proportions.

Our non-intrusive waitress only wanders over after we look her way. Vanessa munches a seafood platter. Unlike today's burger, my steak is cooked to perfection. The ideal night.

Then it falls apart. Bad news comes via a couple talking at the next table.

"Excuse me," I interrupt. "Did I just hear you say tomorrow's concert is cancelled?"

"Yeah," the man says. "Mr. Michael tripped on a cord while rehearsing today and broke a bone, I think. Was it a bone he broke, honey."

Honey's eyebrows lift. "I think that's what they said. We weren't going, but it's never nice to hear things like that."

"Thank you," Vanessa says. She sympathetically squeezes my hand resting on the table. "Disappointed?"

Okay. It's official. Vanessa's an idiot. Does she really think there's a chance I'll say No? She'd suit journalism school. Learn to ask people exiting a courtroom who've just won a case how they feel. The answer's bleedingly obvious, but they ask anyway, because they're *fucking morons*!

I empty my glass and pour another. Where's Springsteen when you need him?

"Yip," I say calmly.

"I thought you'd be a little more upset."

"It's par for the course. Murphy's law. Nothing I can do about it."

We finish our meal and start back for the hotel. A few blocks shy we stop outside one of Honolulu's many twenty-four hour markets. Vanessa wants to nip in for some stuff.

Stuff. What could she possibly need?

"There's only tomorrow and a bit of the next day left, which we'll spend drinking or shopping."

"Just a few items. You can wait out here."

"Shopping's fun," I lie. My head droops and I follow her in.

Each aisle must be inspected, Vanessa leading, me trudging behind with a basket. Labels on picked items are minutely scrutinized before being placed back on shelves. Each passing minute is like an hour under Chinese Water Torture.

Beside a half empty chicken rotisserie sits a stack of white, foil-lined bags, the top one showing FRESH TASTING CHICKEN in large red lettering.

"Look at that. Fresh *tasting* chicken. Does that mean it's *not* fresh? Just *tastes* fresh? Who's the plonker thought that up? Or maybe he's taking the piss, bringing back truth in advertising while laughing at the clueless consumer."

Vanessa smiles indulgently and continues slowly up the aisle. I pick up a toilet bowl cleaner shaped roughly like a duck.

"Same guy wrote this. Cleans and kills germs. Why would anyone want to clean a germ before they kill it?"

She turns my wrist to read the label. "It means as well as killing germs, it cleans."

"I know what they're trying to say. But a comma should come after cleans. Cleans, comma, and kills germs. Seems pretty basic to me."

She takes the bottle, places it back on the shelf. "Look, there's a bar across the street. I'll finish up here and be over in fifteen minutes." She takes the basket and gives me a shove toward the exit. "I'm sorry about tomorrow's concert. Think happy thoughts."

I mumble a few slighting names under my breath.

"Who are you taking about?"

"No one you know."

"I think I get the idea, darling. I'm sure he's heard worse. A guy who can take the piss out of himself as brilliantly as he did on *Extras* wouldn't give a hoot about names." She pushes me again. "Go."

"Never liked his stuff." I turn toward the street. "They'd have to beat me senseless and tie me to a chair to watch him perform. Again."

Four people sit at the bar. I take a stool at one end and order Heineken. Local news plays on a TV. The barman places a bottle on a napkin in front of me. A picture of George Michael appears on screen while the newsreader says his concert is still on, postponed one day.

Well, maybe it isn't so bad after all. There are worse things than spending another heavenly day in paradise, drinking cheap Mai Tais. Somebody break out the Jimmy Buffett records, get a conga line started.

Vanessa fronts empty-handed and takes the stool to my right. Purchased 'stuff' has been taken to the hotel, giving me alone time.

"No need," I say happily. "Concert's back on. Just postponed a day."

"But I've got an important meeting. I have to be back in two days, no matter what."

There's always a killjoy in the bunch. I order her a Manhattan. "Have a nice trip."

"You know I don't like travelling alone. You wouldn't make me go on my own, would you, darling?"

"Crawling doesn't become you," I smirk. "And I can't give up a once in a lifetime chance like this."

"What happened to 'You'd have to beat me and tie me to a chair'? Along with all the name calling?"

"Hush thy mouth. This is one of the great artists of our time you're talking about. Elton John called him the Paul McCartney of his generation."

"I'm not going to win, am I?"

"Not a hope in hell."

27

Day Four. An unplanned day of leisure. Once again Vanessa's a tad blurry-eyed, so today it looks like shopping, not drinking.

Exiting our hotel, the receptionist hands us a handwritten note asking me to ring Sally at work. It's not Brendan asking, so it's duly ignored. Probably wants directions to a client's house, or something equally trivial.

The International Market maze zigzags a few blocks around Waikiki buildings. Before entering we're accosted by a man with two huge, tropically coloured birds. Tails, longer than the birds' bodies, point straight down. He places one on each of Vanessa's shoulders and pressures her into an instant photo. Tourist rubbish.

We walk into an IMAX theatre foyer and study a brochure taped inside the ticket window. A thirty minute doco on Hawaiian scenery starts in ten minutes, so we pay and enter. I've never seen an IMAX screen. It's very tall, more square than wide. And close. We sit centre on steeply banked seats among a handful of people.

It comes on immediately, no ads. A guy swings on a rope around cliffs, hand-pollinating rare Hawaiian flora. Colourful scenery fills the huge screen. With such a massive canvas I wonder how porn would look up there.

I whisper to Vanessa. "Looking at this big screen, are you thinking what I'm thinking?"

She says no, whacks my leg and tells me to take my mind out of the gutter. At its conclusion we stroll back into the markets. A different guy, with different tropical birds on his arms, zeroes in on Vanessa. I pull the original photo from my top pocket and flash it. Undeterred, he places a bird on her shoulder and begins criticising the previous photographer's work. Colour is bad. Birds aren't as pretty.

"Unless you fancy strangled chicken for dinner," I say, "remove it."

He nudges the bird's legs, forcing it to hop back on his hand. "No need to get nasty."

"Apparently there is."

He leaves. We continue on. Vanessa soon has a dozen plastic shopping bags in her hands. My purchases are crammed into two. Some souvenirs are so tacky they must be bought. She asks why I'm grinning whenever I exit a stall, wants to know what's going on. I tell her we can compare crap over lunch.

Through an arcade toward the beach, one level up, we stumble on Duke's bar and eatery. We luckily snag a table up front, where there are no windows or walls obstructing Waikiki beach views. Spread out in front of us, sunbathers lie everywhere, along with umbrellas, deckchairs, families, posers, picnic blankets, long surfboards, short surfboards, inflatable floating devices of all shapes and sizes. If you don't have a board, a yellow one can be rented a dozen paces to our left. Directly ahead, in the surf, paying tourists board a beached, orange jumbo catamaran for a sail around Diamond Head.

Below us, a very happy young guy kneads a bikini clad honey lying face down on his massage table. A half dozen other lovelies sit patiently on the sand awaiting their turn.

"There's a guy with nous." I say.

"That's just what I need."

"A young guy with nous, or a massage?"

Vanessa grins cheekily. "Maybe both."

"Enjoy your trip home tomorrow."

"Hmmm."

Over my pizza and Vanessa's semi-healthy salad, purchases are placed on the table for display. She cringes at my inventiveness. Sally gets a deck of cards sporting a twenty-stone lily white fugly mouthing *Aloha* while lying provocatively in a one-piece on the beach. I have four towels with horrible scenes of dragonboat races and pukey sunsets. There are little Hawaiian shirt fridge magnets, plus one of a cigarette packet that screams 'No smoking, fuckface,' when the centre button is pressed. A disgusting blue miniature surfboard clock has Elvis' smiling head on its dial. Pièce de résistance — Brendan's hula doll. A hideous little thing that sticks to a dashboard, holds a ukulele and wiggles its grass skirt when the car moves. I can see it on his Bentley, lowering the value. He'll love it.

Vanessa's stuff is boring crap. She doesn't think like me. She buy's things she would enjoy receiving. I say buy lots of shit to hand out. It may be loathed, but they won't forget who gave it to them.

She frowns at Brendan's dashboard hula. "I can imagine mother's face if I gave her something like that."

"I've got something very special for your mother."

"Oh? Let's see."

"It's a surprise."

Two burly deckhands push out the big orange catamaran before jumping on board. Sails go up and it moves slowly away from the beach. At this moment, I think of Sally's note. We changed hotels. How did she know where to find us? Strange.

"So, what will you do tomorrow after the concert?"

"Have you forgotten the piss-up afterwards?"

"Oh. Yes."

"As Bart Simpson would put it, time to *par-tay*."

"Hmmm. And what are you going to do with my ticket?"

Little intuitive alarm bells begin ringing. She's done something I'm not going to like.

"Um . . . I was going to put an article of your clothing and a photo of you on the seat next to me so you'd be there in spirit. I'm only joking. I was really going to pick the best looking bimbo hanging around outside — with the nicest tits, of course, and invite her in."

"Well, darling, as long as I know it's not being wasted." She smiles before delivering her punchline. "But I'm only joking too. I went back to our first hotel and gave my ticket to that wonderful receptionist you got on with so well."

Yeah, right. That's a stunt worthy of Brendan. But her devious leer doesn't waver.

"You look a little pale," she says.

"Tell me you're kidding."

"I'd be lying."

A second message from Sally is waiting at our hotel, this time hinting it's urgent. I drop it on the bedside table and pick up a *What To Do This Week On Oahu* book.

"Want to see a show tonight?"

"As long as there's no luau with it. Pick a show at another hotel."

I lie on the bed while Vanessa showers. Might as well ring Brendan, let him know I'll be returning a day late.

He doesn't answer. Probably at the brothel. I can get both calls done in one hit, so I ring, and Sally picks up.

Our conversation is brief. Vanessa comes out of the bathroom naked. I must look odd.

"What's up?"

"Brendan's dead."

28

We fly home next afternoon, as originally planned. No point staying for the concert. I wouldn't enjoy it now.

On the way back I crave silence, but must endure useless reassurances and sympathy. *I'm here if you want to talk.* Talk? About what? Fuck off. Let me deal with it in my own way.

After picking up our bags, we grab a taxi to my place. I want to shower before dropping in on Sally for more details of Brendan's death. All I understood through her blubbering was that it was a single vehicle accident. I don't want to speak to Janet until I know more.

I pay the cabbie. Vanessa throws bags on her Merc's back seat and I open the driver's door.

"I'll come over tonight."

We kiss lightly.

"That would be nice." She gets in.

"I know someone we can ring about James," I say. "Best do it today. Get things started."

Her head drops. Here it comes.

"Look," she starts weakly, "I've given it some thought. I don't think I can do it." Her eyes plead for understanding. "We grew up together. He's not a bad man. Brendan's death sort of helped me to this decision. We need all the friends we can get."

Friends? Brendan's death should have shown her that life's too short to put up with arseholes like James. I close the car door softly and watch her window lower.

"That your final word?"

"Yes. It is."

"Thanks for the ride," I say. "It was nice."

She looks up at me, a tear running down her cheek. I pick up my bag and walk off. She doesn't start her car.

I unlock the shack door, throw my case on the bed and get a cold beer. Still she sits there. I enter the bathroom to shower. When I come out, her Merc is gone.

I sit on a stool beside the untouched beer and stare blankly at the wall. Two rows of ants — one going, one returning, run from a ceiling crack to somewhere behind the fridge. They've found something to drag home piece by piece to munch on. Probably a cockroach or spider.

I need to hit something. No, I need to *pound* something.

Windows open, Lou Reed's *Rock And Roll Animal* blaring, I give the heavy bag a beating for fifteen minutes until legs and arms ache. I then collapse exhausted and frustrated in the tree's shade. My bare chest heaves as air fights to fill my lungs.

Sitting there, forearms on knees, I recall a trip to Paris with Brendan, before leaving for my first stint overseas, a dozen years ago. We fucked different women every night. Sometimes two. One drunken evening we fell into the Seine from a tourist boat, causing chaos. End of the week, we missed our return flight. Gendarmes advised us not to return. We thought that only happened in old movies.

My breath regains some normality, and I stand. Speaking of gendarmes, a couple of guys loiter on the concrete slab, hands in pockets, amused. Arrogant fuckers in generic detective suits. Any normal person would have said something, called out. These two jerks just watched as I took out my frustration on the bag. Now I've noticed them, they exchange amused looks. They're on Brendan's case, and he was connected to a brothel. Brendan always said when the law deals with things brothel-related, you're treated as a second class citizen. Everyone knows people in the prostitution racket are scum. I'm best friends with Brendan, therefore I too must be scum. They'll treat me accordingly.

My hands tremble after removing sparring gloves, lactic acid pulsing through muscles. In five minutes I'll steady.

They remain silent as I walk slowly toward them. If TV shows are anything to go by, one will want to use my bathroom so he can have a nosy inside.

Before I reach the door, eyeing my torso injuries big cop says loudly over Lou Reed singing *White Light/White Heat*, "We come inside for a talk? I'm Detective Sergeant—"

"I'll come out."

I close the door behind me, turn down the music, liberate two cold beers and return outside with a towel around my neck. I snap open a canvas chair and sit.

"Like I said," the bigger one continues, now a little miffed, "I'm detective—"

Motioning him to stop talking, I drain an entire beer without coming up for air. I then wipe sweat from my face and chest with the towel, twist the top off the second bottle and roll my hand at the wrist for him to continue.

"We thought your girlfriend would be here. Vanessa Rayford."

Both are thirties, not overweight. Blond hairdos a fraction long, combed flat but ratty at the ends. Nicotine stains big cop's moustache, which would render him virtually redundant if things got real physical for more than thirty seconds. Little cop is skinny, boney, but the onset of fleshy jowls means he doesn't work out either.

"I know her name," I say.

"Okay. We're just following up a few things on Mister Bagley's motor vehicle accident."

Smaller cop produces a couple dozen photos from his inside suit pocket and hands them to me without speaking.

"Mind telling us when these were taken?" bigger cop continues.

I glance at the first few snaps. Brendan, Janet, Vanessa and me, inside and outside this shack and at the airport. Vanessa and Janet took them on one of Brendan's digital cameras before we left for Hawaii. I hand them to big cop because he's closer.

"Four days ago."

"Vanessa Rayford confirm this?"

"You'll have to ask her."

He looks perfunctorily at a few snaps, keeps one, passes the rest back to smaller cop. "What was the occasion?"

"A few drinks before Vanessa and I went to Hawaii."

"Good concert, was it?"

He knows a lot already. Something's fishy with Brendan's car accident.

"Didn't see it."

"Uh-huh." He holds out the photo: Vanessa and me standing in front of our cars, inside the electric wire. "So there was no damage to the Range Rover the night you left?"

Conclusion: the Range Rover has marks inconsistent with a single vehicle accident. Maybe it was nudged by another vehicle.

"No. There wasn't."

"Uh-huh. You in Brendan Bagley's will?"

"Be surprised if I wasn't. He's in mine. I'd imagine his missus will pretty much get the lot. There's also a kid on the way. He was the type of guy who would have sorted that out with lawyers right away." I wipe my face again and glance down to their plain car parked just inside the gate. "Anything else?"

They share sheepish glances before smaller cop's gaze drops, embarrassed for some reason. Big cop carries on.

"You haven't heard then. Mrs. Bagley was also in the car. And you say she was pregnant?"

Was pregnant. That kind of knocks me sideways. I hadn't given her a thought. She must also be dead. I drink some beer, anger at talking to these two dicks suddenly replaced by sadness. I stare blankly at the golden valley Brendan will never see again.

"Yeah," I say. "Brendan had a couple distant cousins in . . . I'm not sure, Argentina somewhere last I heard. But . . . I don't know how his will would look now."

"Seems you get this piece of land," big cop says. "The restaurant on the—"

"If you know this, why fucking ask me?"

"Restaurant on the marina. Quarter million dollar Bentley. One or two other sizeable chunks." He adjusts his pants a fraction higher on his hips and takes in views as if estimating land values. "So how long had you planned this trip to Hawaii?"

"Didn't. Won it on the radio. Left a few days later."

That answer wasn't expected. They seem to search for their next question. It brings back the drunken conversation weeks earlier on this very spot, and I figure maybe they should have brought a police dog along to speed things up.

"On what station?"

I tell him, then ask what happened to Janet's Range Rover.

"Went over a cliff. Had black paint scrapings along the side like it may have collided with another vehicle. I'm afraid," he goes on," it may end up one of those things we'll never know for sure what happened. Nobody saw the accident, and unless somebody comes forward, or we find the other vehicle. . . Well. . . "

He thanks me for my time and hands over a business card. They step over the electric wire. Smaller cop then points down to where Brendan buried the first suitcase of money. A shovel sticks out of the ground that I hadn't noticed. I stop myself looking over to the water trough where I reburied both cases.

"That's freshly dug," the cop says. "Know who did it, or why?"

Freshly dug? They've already been sniffing around. Good thing I locked the shack. Maybe I should jump up and appear surprised. No point.

"No idea."

"Uh huh."

They leave, but I feel someone may still be watching. I walk down to inspect the freshly dug ground. It's the exact spot. Somebody watched Brendan bury the case. I take the shovel back to the shed. On entering, I glance quickly at the ground around the trough where cows dribble water and turn earth to mud. Hoof prints but no digging. The money's safe.

I re-enter my shack and look about. Everything seems in place. Same in the bedroom.

Once again I shower.

* *

I drive to the brothel to see how Sally is fairing. The extra day has calmed her somewhat, but she can't say Brendan's name without her voice quivering. Cops have come to see her a couple of times, asking if she knew Brendan had left this building — ergo the business — to her. She had no idea, but is worried they don't believe her.

Seems strange to me, too. Why leave her the business?

"Just doing their job. I wouldn't worry about it. They've been to my place as well."

"They didn't say anything to you about me? They asked about you a lot."

"No. Nothing. How's business?"

"They never mentioned . . . Brendan . . . *and* me . . . at all?"

What the fuck?! Those two? Come to think of it, Sally does look a lot like Brendan's mother. Maybe there was something incestuous he needed to get out of his system. The dog.

"Nothing," I repeat.

She looks relieved, and a little embarrassed now I know. "Money's getting tight. The yanks have a new black president about to spend a billion to hopefully kick their economy along. But we're doing all right. Want me to pick you up for the funeral?" she asks. "I'd like to go with someone who won't break down."

"Don't do funerals."

She frowns.

"Won't set foot in a church. Like all cops are dirty, all priests are paedophiles."

"Jesus, you can't tar everyone with the same brush like that."

"Okay. Fair enough. But can you tell the paedophiles from the good ones?"

On any other day she would argue the point, vigorously. Her mouth opens to berate me, but she thinks better of it. I turn to leave.

"You driving tomorrow? You're still rostered on during the day."

Heather arrives from the girls' room to make coffee. Last time she was in my car it was stinking hot, windows were down. Her phone rang, she answered. Beside us, stopped at a red light, an 18-wheeler idled noisily. Carbon monoxide plumes washed through the car. In-between coughing spurts, she yells into the phone that she's in an important corporate meeting and would ring them back later. After my four days away, she doesn't appear any smarter.

"Okay, but try and get the night driver in early. I want a few days off."

She kisses my cheek. It's the first real sign of affection from her I've seen toward anyone other than Dead Dog Walking. I hope she's not eyeing me as a possible replacement for Brendan in her bed. Not happening. I don't have mother issues.

Grace's silver Merc sits beside my shack. That she knows where I live isn't surprising. Checking out Vanessa's boyfriend, she told me on our first meeting, is standard procedure. Wealthy people can afford to think differently than the less fortunate.

I park beside her car and spy a shapely pair of legs with white high heels. She sits on the canvas chair I left outside after my cop visit. If she's come to plead her daughter's case, things may deteriorate quickly.

I step over the wire to the slab. She rises and we kiss cheeks.

"Cold chardonnay in the fridge," I tell her.

She follows me inside and sits at the breakfast bar, but it's not like she has a choice where to sit. I uncork a bottle Vanessa left behind, pour a glass, sit opposite with a beer. Her sleeveless white dress and bling are likely to be the classiest things this paddock shack will ever encounter. Odds are she'd look even better out of them. I'm over her daughter, I can think what I like.

"Vanessa's distraught," she says sadly. "What happened?"

"What did she tell you?"

"You couldn't accept the fact she was keeping an ex-lover as a friend."

"You obviously haven't seen her bruises," I say. "I couldn't accept the fact she has as a friend someone who beats and spies on her, and refuses to do anything about it. Ex-lover had nothing to do with it."

"Ah," she says with a sullen and private recollection of times past. "That's what broke them up in the first place. Vanessa promised me since they split, he hadn't touched her. I see now she was being less than truthful."

"She. . . " I stop. Nobody enjoys listening to other people's problems. Well, I don't. Buck up and deal with it.

"Is there any hope?" she asks.

"None."

She finally takes a minute sip of wine, waits a moment, then stands. "I hope this won't make it awkward if we pass in the street."

I stand to see her out, thankful she hasn't offered condolences on Brendan dying. "Of course not."

She moves closer to administer a sympathetic, parting hug. I put my arms around her lower back to reciprocate the gesture. Her hands press against the back of my shoulders. Her hair smells of jasmine.

We continue hugging fractionally longer than a goodbye embrace should last. Her body is warm and taut and compact. When detaching, my hands slide to her tiny waist, her hands rest on my shoulders. I smell chardonnay as we stare into each other's eyes.

"I bought you something in Hawaii."

We kiss.

Passionately.

"I'm sorry," she says. "I should go."

I pull her closer. We kiss again.

"No, you shouldn't."

She didn't.

We did.

It was nice.

It was better than nice. It was so good, I wouldn't be surprised if I looked out the window and saw cows in the bottom paddock breaking their own non-smoking rule.

29

The mood in the office is better than I anticipated. But wwwDot didn't know Brendan that well. Girls on today, for the most part, also seem okay. They didn't know Brendan other than as a guy who sometimes spoke to Sally.

I can't get Grace out of my head. Last night was . . . different. Talented hands.

A car pulls into the carpark, and WwwDot gets on the intercom.

"Heather, your little retired army guy's coming in."

Heather appears and sits at the table waiting for her client to be admitted. Sally hasn't told them of all past days events.

"Hey, Myers. How was your trip? Meet any celebrities?"

"Yeah. A few."

"Gee. Who did you meet?"

"Music people mostly. Met George Michael, of course. Bono was there. Elton John. You know. Music people."

"Wow! Was Jennifer Lopez there? See her?"

"Nope."

"Nope she wasn't there, or nope you didn't meet her."

"Both, unless she was there and I didn't see her."

"Was Taylor Swift there? See her?"

"Yeah," I say. "Danced with her at the party afterwards."

She jumps up and down in her seat like an excited schoolgirl, holding in screams with both hands. "God! What was she like? Was she as nice as on TV? What did she say to you? Did you get her autograph? I bet she was a good dancer." Her eyes roll up to the ceiling and her mouth turns on a dreamy smile. "Oh, God, I wish I was there."

Get a grip. Taylor Swift's a woman, just like you. Well, maybe not quite like you, but she's still just a female doing a job. Admittedly a highly paid job, plus, for the most part, she's loved the world over, mingles with other celebrities on a daily basis, probably has an entourage of six hundred and fifty at her beck and call, receives tens of thousands of fan letters daily. . . Yeah, maybe you should be jumping up and down. You and her are about as far apart as two people can get.

"She was a great dancer," I say. "And nice. She gave us her number. Said to ring if we ever get to Nashville."

She slaps me hard on the shoulder, and gasps, "No!"

"Yip."

"I would have died. What's her number?"

"Don't know. Got drunk with Van Morrison and left it on a table at the party."

Horror contorts her face. "Ring this guy Van. Maybe he picked it up."

"Van didn't give me his number."

"This is important. Can't you get it somehow?"

"This is Van Morrison we're talking about. You don't just look up guys like him in the phonebook."

"So who is he?"

"You've never heard of Van Morrison? He's Bob Dylan's brother."

"Then ring this guy Bob. You've got to get Taylor's number back."

Fuck me. If I didn't know her better I'd say this little exchange is a put-on.

"Ever heard of Montgomery Clift? Fred Astaire? James Dean?"

Her face is blank.

"What about Marilyn Monroe."

"Dah," she says. "Everyone's heard of her. Was she there? I thought she might have been dead."

Like this conversation.

WwwDot opens the lounge door. Heather stands.

"Can you believe it, Dot?" Heather says. "Taylor Swift gave Myers her number and he left it on a table with some plonker named Van."

"Yes, I can," she says. "Sounds like the sort of thing Myers would do."

Heather departs shaking her head at the floor.

"Why do you and Telly do it?" wwwDot asks.

I shrug. "She was asking stupid questions. I couldn't help myself. It'll put a little something in her drab life. She'll be talking about it for weeks. Her vicarious brush with stardom."

Phoebe appears from the girls' room. WwwDot tells her a regular has asked if she's available. I'm driving her in a few minutes.

Phoebe's nose scrunches, cheeks go up, eyes squint. "Oh, that guy's sick. He's a schoolteacher. Not only that, he's the headmaster. You wouldn't believe what that guy can take up his arse. I mean anything and everything goes up there. It's gross. And he jerks off to pictures of his male students."

"Why do you suppose there's a silent O in Phoebe," I ask her.

"Is there?" Phoebe says. "There's no F either, so I spose the P's silent as well."

"Ah," I say. "A silent Pee, as in swimming."

"There's no P in . . . ha ha, I get it."

I'm happy for her. Stepped into any showers with your shoes on lately? Why are the thick ones on today? What the hell am I doing here? For certain Sally will drop driving fees to a par with other Gold Coast agencies and brothels, virtually more than halving our money. Multiple-hour drive money for the one job we will no longer see. Sixty dollar drives out to places like Beaudesert will probably be the standard twenty. It will all now go to the house. And knowing Brendan won't be walking through the side door again, for me this place has lost its pizzazz.

When I pull over outside the headmaster's house, he jogs out his front door and slides into the back seat without invitation.

"You'll have to take me to an ATM," he says. "Don't have any money."

"You can use a credit card, sweetie," Phoebe says.

"Nope. Machine or nothing."

Cards are probably maxed out. Cash is his only option. I get the usual questions while we roll down the street. How does one get a job like mine? Get to try the girls? He smirks continuously. Cool dude. Man of the world.

At the ATM he tries unsuccessfully four or five times to obtain cash. When he gets back in the car, there's no embarrassment. He's too suave for that. It's the morons at the bank who fucked up. They're always fucking up.

"I can wait if you want to go in and sort it," I offer, knowing he won't.

"Nah, fuck them," he says. "I'll give them a blast when I get home. There should be fifteen grand in there."

"So I'll take you home." Before he says anything I start up and head back. He'll have to jerk off drooling over photos of male pupils.

When he climbs out, Phoebe says, "Jeez, can't really trust anyone these days." She lifts her top and juggles her huge bare breasts. "These are the only two suckers I trust."

I stretch her top out, and down. "Not in daylight, ay."

"Sorry. Wasn't thinking."

WwwDot rings and says Skye wants to be picked up from her house. A ten minute detour and we spy her waiting curbside, smiling, the mental breakdown, or whatever it was, obviously behind her. She hops in the back seat.

"Hey, guys," she says. "How was your trip, Myers?"

"Fantastic."

"Yeah? That's good. It costs ten dollars to be picked up like this, doesn't it?"

Odd question. She knows it does. "The receptionist can deduct it from your day's tally, as per."

"Can I suck your dick instead? I've got a mountain of bills at the moment."

"No."

"Don't worry bout Phoebe. We can swap seats. She won't tell anyone. Will ya Pheeb?"

"As long as I can watch," Phoebe says.

"No."

"Won't take long," Skye adds. "It's my specialty. Best you've ever had. Guaranteed. I won't use a condom, so you'll be done before we get back."

A compelling sales pitch. However a *free* blowjob wouldn't interest me at the moment.

Heather and Skye are in a job together. Gina, Phoebe and wwwDot lounge about the kitchen. Gina wears sunglasses. Indoors.

"Tony went to court yesterday, Dot," Gina says proudly. "Y'know, for bashing and robbing that old bag in the supermarket carpark. The judge took into consideration he was drunk at the time, so he got time served."

"Ah," I say. "Yet another sorry piece of shit who isn't prepared to face up to his responsibilities. Sorry I raped your wife and slit your mother's throat, but I was drinking heavily and my shrink tells me it may go back to that one time I had to wear a pink T-shirt when I was seven."

The three women stare silently at me.

Three hours to go. I move to sit alone in the office and watch nothing happening on monitors. In low tones the women discuss my attitude. Maybe I am a little down, a tad punchy. I tap in Brendan's computer code and play a couple games of solitaire. Computer games aren't my thing. Never have been. Now the brothel has a new, as yet unofficial, owner, I probably shouldn't be on this computer at all.

I open a file named Janet that has nothing to do with her. It contains lists of regular clients' initials, what they take pleasure in, and from whom they enjoy receiving these . . . pleasures.

Lickers. One likes his legs and buttocks licked. No sex, just tongue the backs of his thighs until squirtingly happy. Another prefers women with varicose veins. The more pronounced her veins, the better to lick.

Where are all the normal people hiding? Are there any left? Who's to say what's normal? Is shagging my ex's mother weird? Compared to what's on the screen in front of me, it doesn't rate a mention. Consenting, unrelated adults. Hell, our age difference is only five years. With her daughter it was ten or eleven.

Two hours left. Am I going to make it?

Just over an hour to go. Kevin, the young night driver, arrives with one girl. Sally asked him to come in early. We met once before I left for

Hawaii. Telly asked him to fill in while I was gone, and after almost a week he's still expectantly wide-eyed. Maybe a bit overwhelmed. The girls would have taken liberties until he wised-up. *If* he wised-up. Some never do.

We're the only two in the kitchen. He sits on a table seat.

"Good trip?" he asks.

"Okay. Considering."

"Yeah."

"How's the job going?"

He gives me a confused look like he's taken a blow to the head. "I don't know how you and Telly stand it. If it wasn't for the money I would have been gone on my first night. I drop a girl at a hotel, and when I go back she comes out and waits at a different entrance. I dropped another, then when she's due out I go into the hotel looking for her for fifteen minutes, only to find her drinking coffee in a café on the other side of the street, for fuck's sake. I've lost three at nightclubs while it's quiet. I can't control them. This one I just brought in, on the way here I had to drop her damn kid at the babysitter's place." Shoulders rise and his hands shoot out. "Are we supposed to do that?"

Liberties.

Heather returns to the kitchen, greets Kevin and rolls her eyes.

"He lost Taylor Swift's number. Can you believe it?" She turns to me. "Don't spose Justin Timberlake was there?"

"Spoke to him a couple of times."

My shoulder receives another slap. "No! What did you say to him?"

"Asked him who Chew is."

"Chew?"

"A lot of Hip Hoppers seem to know Chew. In their songs they want to leave wit' Chew, go home wit' Chew, or they're in love wit' Chew. Chew must be bi, and good in the sack."

"They're saying *With you,* not wit' Chew."

"Oh. I'll know next time."

I have one ear on the office. WwwDot's up to no good. Because a hooker hasn't rung out of a job, she's on the phone asking a client where her friend is. But how can that be? Normally it wouldn't mean anything. Standard procedure. However with both drivers here, and girls not allowed to drive themselves, the only possible answer is wwwDot's running escorts on the side. Every now and then, after receiving a client call on these brothel phones, she'll send an escort of her own, on standby up the coast, to the job. They split the money. I doubt she would have tried it with Brendan alive. Then again, maybe she was. Like I said, when busy, a phone call from the office asking a client about a girl's whereabouts is merely everyday brothel business.

I pick up my paper, say adios and exit via the side gate. As I'm unlocking my car, Sally rolls in, parks by my passenger side and climbs out. I lean on my roof.

"WwwDot's thieving off you."

She's been in this business long enough that her face registers neither surprise nor anger. Everyone wants a slice of the action.

"How?"

"Running her own girls from the office."

"Thanks. Keep it to yourself."

Driving out, in my rearview I see Sally making a call standing beside her car.

30

Next day. Fastlove sits at his hotel balcony table listening to Ross, a clueless twenty-five-year-old duty manager. Ross leads an unusually colourful love life. Darker colours. I join them.

". . . her two crazy knife wielding brothers are always coming around checking on their precious little sister. One's named George, but it's spelt J-O-R-G-E, so I've got to call him Haw-hey. And get this, the other one's called Jesus, but it's pronounced Hey-Seus, for fuck's sake. Last I checked we spoke Australian in this country. If she wasn't so damn good looking, and didn't have that hot little Spanish body with those big tits, I'da given her the flick ages ago."

It's doubtful Ross ever checked anything. He consults his watch, gathers his cigarettes and lighter.

"Want another drink, Myers? Fastlove?"

"Does Dolly Parton sleep on her back?" I answer.

Fastlove shakes his head, no.

"Unopened," I add.

"Technically, I'm not allowed to pass unopened drinks across the bar. That means they're takeaways and should be taken off the premises."

I lift a foot onto the railing. "Yeah? Well bring it with the top off and I'll technically stick it up your arse."

"That's a fine way to talk to someone offering a free drink."

I slide el-cheapo sunglasses down my nose and look at him. He turns toward the bar, singing, "*Hey-Seus loves me this I know, for the Bible tells me so.*"

"You ever seen his missus?" Fastlove asks.

"No."

"Ugly as sin. She could be the third brother, in drag."

We chuckle. Below us, on the grassed area, a couple hundred people drink while listening to a boy band singing to recorded music. Thirty kids play inside the fenced pool. Nobody watches them. We have the best seats in the house.

"How long has there been entertainment on outside?"

"Couple of weeks. You're probably asleep this time of day, weekends."

"Spose. I quit today. They don't know it yet."

He nods slowly, thoughtfully. "Figured you might. When's the funeral?"

"Couple days."

"Said your goodbyes?"

"Might go see him tonight."

"Funeral homes open at night?"

"Wouldn't think so."

"Ah."

The duty manager returns with a couple of unopened Heinekens and places them beside me on our table. I nod appreciation and watch him walk back toward the bar. A man I don't know passes him, and I turn back to watch the band. Next thing, Fastlove's frowning at something above me, and I look up. The guy who walked past Ross stands there, scowling.

"What the fuck were you just staring at?" he snarls.

Hey-Seus!

"Nothing," I say, as non-confrontationally as possible.

His hands turn to fists. "You calling me *Nothing*?"

An unanswerable question if ever I heard one. He obviously wants hitting, and I'm in the mood. So I spring up and give him what he craves. Get him plum in his mouth and hurt a knuckle. He sprawls backwards over a spare chair and lies motionless on the tiles for a second or two, gathering his senses.

I shake out the pain and poke the affected knuckle. Already it's bruised, changing colour. I must have clocked him wrong. Maybe hit a tooth. That'll do it to you every time. He staggers up and walks back through the bar door.

I resume my seat. "Friend of yours?"

"Can't hold his piss. He's in a room downstairs. Never shuts up. Comes out here, and if I'm sitting on my own, parks his arse and bleats in a half drunken stupor for thirty minutes about his many problems."

"You didn't answer my question."

Fastlove chuckles and lights a cigarette. Ross returns, taking the moron's spot beside me.

"What the hell happened? Guy in twenty-two says he was attacked out here."

"Technically," I say, "the guy attacked himself. Asked for it. I tried telling him I'm not a people person, but he kept crowding me." I flick dregs of my first bottle on a few brown terracotta tiles by Ross's feet. "Then he slipped. There should be a sign out here. Slippery when wet." I hold up the empty. "Problem?"

"Good job," he says. "The guy's a doofus." He takes my empty and disappears back inside.

"Seems you did what everybody else has wanted to do," Fastlove says.

"I try to please."

The boy band takes a break. A disc plays two shades quieter. People go inside to buy drinks and use the bathroom. Ross reappears yet again.

"There's a couple of guys inside looking for a little action tonight. I told them you'd go in and fix them up.

"Know these guys well, do you?"

"They're staying here. They're okay."

"Course they are. But until I hear otherwise, pimping is illegal in Queensland. Probably the entire country. Let them look under Companions or Escorts in the paper, or the interweb, like everyone else."

"Oh, it's like that. I thought I was helping."

"No you weren't. You were trying to make yourself look good." I raise my eyebrows and wait. He buggers off. Fastlove tops up his fine china cup with red wine.

"You haven't mentioned the concert." He drinks a third.

"Didn't go."

"Because of your friend's accident?"

I nod.

"Haven't mentioned the woman you took, either."

"Haven't I?"

"Oh, I see. Percy Bysshe Shelley described marriage as the world's dreariest and longest journey." His hand grandly sweeps to the side. "Plenty to choose from down there, my friend."

Two young, barely dressed females exit the bar, jigging to music, and descend the stairs in front of us.

"The one in blue's not bad looking," he says.

"And doesn't she know it."

We chuckle.

"The one in yellow shorts at the table with the Cinzano umbrella looks okay."

An ankle biter wearing only a disposable nappy crawls about her feet.

"She looks familiar. You know what that means. I've probably driven her."

"Yes," Fastlove says. "Yes." The second, quieter yes means he's thought of another quote. "William Hogarth said—"

"Poet?"

"Painter and engraver. Early seventeen hundreds. He said there are two things show a woman's age that she cannot disguise."

"I'm betting one of them will be her neck."

"Neck and hands," he says. "Skin wrinkles to heck."

"Plastic surgery these days will stretch it out. Good as new." I sip free beer. "Can you have plastic surgery on hands?"

"Don't know. I suppose one must be able to. One can have it just about everywhere else."

"How did your cousin in Sydney get on with her free plastic surgery?"

"Ah," he says. "It was to be free as long as they could film it for a reality show. Why women felt they needed touching-up once middle age was attained. The production company rang and told her they were going with another woman. Told her there was no drama in her life. She made too much money, owned her own home and didn't have loud kids to scream she's a fool for voluntarily going under the knife."

"So much for reality."

"They want *bad* reality. Can't keep viewers otherwise."

The boy band starts up, butchering a Pointer Sisters number.

"When it's busy like this, "Fastlove says, "I sometimes go down and clear glasses and things. You should hear the vacuous conversations. Boring individuals leading meaningless lives. It's awful. People have nothing of substance to say to each other. They talk on a cell phone while texting on another. I took a train to Brisbane yesterday, sharing a carriage with twenty-five or thirty teens on a trip from a San Diego school. The entire forty minutes were spent discussing hamburgers and takeaway food. Not one of them even bothered to look out a window."

I nod at today's book sitting on the table. *Essays and Selected Letters*, by George Orwell.

"No poetry?"

"It's hard to find. These days it's just prose. Not even good prose."

"As far as I'm concerned," I say, "poetry's only wonderful to its creator. Everyone else thinks it's crap. Even other poets."

He chuckles. "This one in green shorts going up the stairs. She was talking in the bar a few days ago, justifying her drug habit by saying she does it so her diabetic daughter won't feel stigmatized using an insulin needle every day. Ever heard such crap?"

We don't chuckle. We laugh.

"What a cracker," I say.

"I thought of you as soon as I heard it. You can use it in your book."

"Given up on that. Too hard. Maybe I'll look at it in a few years, when I've got a bet of spare time."

He lights a fresh cigarette from the butt of his one dying. "Any stories? I'll understand if you don't want to."

"How about this. Before my trip a chick rang for a job and the receptionist asked when she wanted to come in for an interview. The hooker says, 'I don't do interviews.' So the receptionist says to her, 'But what if you don't like us, or we don't like you?', and the hooker says, 'Oh you'll like me, and it doesn't really matter if I don't like you.' "

"Wonderful." His grin reinforces a love of the insipidly entertaining human condition. "We live a good life."

Dee wanders out for a cigarette break. She sits beside me and lights up.

"Hey Myers. How was your trip?"

"Brilliant."

"You took a partner, didn't you?"

"Yeah."

"Go all right?"

"No."

"Oh? So what now?"

"Same as everyone else. Look for a replacement. But finding someone with a personality is a problem."

"Yeah?" she says. "I think this town is full of personalities."

"That's the problem. It's so good, all the women I meet seem to have two of them."

Fastlove chuckles. Dee smiles.

"I thought you were gay," she says.

"Yeah, well, I am. But I've been experimenting."

Her eyebrows go up.

"No," I say.

"No what?"

"No to your next question."

She stabs her cigarette in a saucer full of butts, then lights another.

"You don't know what I'm going to ask next."

"Yeah, I do. And I won't go out with a smoker."

She points randomly to a bikini clad twenty-year-old bottle blonde walking down the steps holding a vodka mixer in each hand.

"Would you go out with her?"

"No."

"Why not?"

"Sourpuss. Naturally down-turning mouth."

That gets some thought. "Okay, name me someone with a naturally up-turned mouth?"

"Meg Ryan," Fastlove says immediately, like he was ready for the question. "Even when she's mad she can't hide that grin. Cheeky. Lovely."

"There you go," I say. "Meg Ryan."

"Name another one," she says.

31

I get the feeling I'm being sneakily manipulated. For the two weeks that I've hardly left my shack, Grace has been feeding me up on health food. Energy levels are spiking. Even crosswords are easier with a clearer, sharper mind. She cooks and walks about in bright yellow or purple or pink lacy underwear, keeping me perpetually horny. And yellow isn't even my colour. I'm her second lover. Her first, the husband, has been dead six or seven years. I think she's masterfully making up for lost time.

A couple of times I tried ringing for pizza, but the lazy bastards won't come this far out.

Her Merc rolls up the fenceline. Carrying a couple of supermarket bags, Grace gets out dressed in a black sleeveless dress, bends to kiss me, then goes inside. She comes back out wearing light blue lacy underwear and sunglasses. She sits on a deckchair beside me, in tree shade. I hook my pen over a few pages on top of a magazine crossword.

"Stopped by the restaurant," she says. "The manager seems to be coping well."

"And?"

"And I saw Vanessa. She moved in with James. She's still miserable."

"You don't feel . . . odd, sleeping with her old boyfriend?"

"We're only here once, Myers. If you connect with someone, go for it. I'm afraid she'll never find happiness until James is out of her system."

Controlled fire, leaping two storeys or more, noisily crackles and pops its way through a valley cane field. Huge plumes of black smoke rise vertically skyward in the still air. Two-metre blackened stalks that will eventually be turned into sugar remain in its wake. Three abutting burnt fields await the harvester. Like snow, light, black sooty spirals float gently to earth all around us. Good thing wet washing isn't on my line.

"Who was the first person credited with the theory that the Earth revolves around the sun? Copernicus and Galileo won't fit."

"Aristarchus of Samos. Is that right?"

"I wouldn't know. Normal people don't know that shit without looking it up."

She caresses the back of my neck while looking at me with far off eyes. "I've been there. In Greece. It must have stuck in my head."

"You know what the air in the neck of a wine bottle's called?"

"Ullage, I think."

"Marry me," I say.

Her mouth forms a faraway smile. "I'd love to. But you don't really know me."

"You mean Vanessa wouldn't take it well."

"I love my daughter. I had her at sixteen. We virtually grew up together."

"We'll honeymoon in Egypt. Always wanted to see the pyramids."

Grace goes inside and returns with a glass of chardonnay and a cold beer she must have brought from town as a treat.

"Did I ever thank you for picking me up at the funeral home?" I ask. "I was pissed as a newt."

"Didn't know newts drank."

"Wouldn't have a saying otherwise, would we."

"Hmm. I suppose not." She sounds unconvinced. "Remember much?"

It was the eve of Brendan's final showing when I broke in. To share one last beer. I took a dozen, but was half full when I got there. Janet was in the same room. It gave me somewhere to stash empties. My toilet was a dozen plastic pot plants dotted around.

"Should have been fishing now, buddy," I told Brendan's lifeless body.

Before my Hawaii trip we dallied with the idea of a fishing sojourn. Drinking heavily, we came to the conclusion a manly weeklong fishing and shooting excursion could be the go. Shoot some Skippys.

"We can take the camper caravan," he explained. "Camp by the river."

"I'd have nowhere to plug in a computer."

"Got a mini generator," he said. 'Electric lights and everything."

"So much for roughing it. What are we going to eat? I'm not living off what we kill or catch."

"Portable freezer. Plug it into the back of the four-wheel drive and then transfer it to the caravan when we get there. Fill it with meat before we go."

"So that answers the question about keeping beer cold."

"We can rig up set lines on the riverbank a mile or so up and down stream. Check them twice a day, in between catching fish from our campsite."

"Christ," I said, "how much paddling will that be?"

"No paddling. Got a little outboard for the canoe."

"So how are we going to cook this meat and fish?"

"Gas cookers," he said. "You in or what?"

"You're a regular Daniel fucking Boone. Last of the frontiersmen."

His hair was clipped and combed into place by an undertaker who didn't know him. I messed it up, then smoothed it down as best I could. I slipped half a dozen photos into his suit pocket. Hollywood babes he enjoyed watching.

"What the fuck did you do to end up like this?" His hands were down, at attention, under a silk sheet. Maybe they were mangled in the accident. I didn't look.

"Hey buddy, forgot to mention Halle Berry was at the concert, and she mentioned your name. I kissed her for you. Because I'm a gentleman I won't say I slipped the tongue in."

Good thing I didn't forget that. He would have been disappointed not to hear a story. I polished off all but one beer, which I pushed down into the covered half of his coffin. "One for the road."

After two hours I was mulletted. Blurry. I don't recall ringing Grace. I don't recall coming home. Blood spotted my shirtfront from a forehead wound. At some stage I must have fallen.

"Surprised the cops never came round," I say to Grace.

"Why? Nothing was stolen. There wouldn't have been any fingerprints. You were wearing surgical gloves. Purple ones. The same colour James' attackers wore, as it happens."

"Yeah? What are the odds?"

"Hmmm. What *are* the odds?"

Next day, Grace returns with tickets to Greece. Not the musical, the country. If we get on okay while on holiday, she'll marry me when we get back.

"You declined my offer," I remind her. "So the proposal is off the table until asked again."

She's grilling chicken. I had no idea my oven contained a griller. I sip the last of my beer. Wearing only light green lacy underwear, she sips chardonnay and grins, remnants of Vanessa in the curls of her mouth.

"I have money."

"Okay. If you have more than a thousand in your purse, consider the proposal back on the table."

She places grilled chicken on plates beside salads.

"Well," I say. "Do you?"

"You want to look?"

"Your word's good enough."

"Then yes, I do."

32

"Hmmm. A hula doll on a Bentley dashboard. Different. You leaving it here?"

"It's being picked up later."

We park and enter the airport. After checking our bags, I steer her through doors to an airport bar, and order.

"We can drink in the first class lounge," she says. "We're allowed."

"Fuck it — sorry." I'm cutting back my swearing. "We're here now. Might as well have one first."

The cost of two drinks is more diabolical than some Gold Coast clubs. The first class lounge looms after these. I'm assuming booze there is free. If not, it should be. For the price of these plane tickets we could fly economy to Europe a half dozen times.

Every bar seat has a bum on it. After waiting a minute, a couple by the far wall leave, two tables back from the massive windows, and we sit.

A British Airways Airbus and a Japan Airlines Jumbo take off. A large Boeing lands with an odd red bird emblem on its tail.

Grace fills in Customs' cards using a gold pen. Her slender neck and elegant hands I find bewitching. Diamonds sparkle in her ears, on fingers and around her wrist. She suits diamonds. An expensive Gucci handbag sits on the table. She's never had to check a dick for diseases. Never charged a guy's mates to watch her screw him. Never taken it up the blurter as an extra. And probably never had to lie about where she is or whom she's with.

Thank Christ those days are behind me. Long gone. I won't miss them.

Then, from the other side of the crowded bar.

"IT'S BLOODY FUCKIN MYERS! HEY MYERS. WHO'S THE TRADE?"